All the THINGS that could go WRONG

All the

THINGS

that could go

WRONG

STEWART FOSTER

LITTLE, BROWN AND COMPANY
New York Boston

Little, Brown and Company
Hachette Book Group
1290 Avenue of the Americas, New York, NY 10104
Visit us at LBYR.com

Originally published in 2017 by Simon & Schuster UK in Great Britain
First U.S. Edition: September 2018

Little, Brown and Company is a division of Hachette Book Group, Inc.
The Little, Brown name and logo are trademarks of Hachette Book Group, Inc.

Library of Congress Cataloging-in-Publication Data
Names: Foster, Stewart, 1963– author.
Title: All the things that could go wrong / by Stewart Foster.
Description: First U.S. edition. | New York; Boston: Little, Brown and Company, 2018. | "Originally published in 2017 by Simon & Schuster UK in Great Britain." | Summary: Dan and his friends, Sophie and the Georges, are bullies who target obsessive-compulsive Alex, but when Dan is in trouble, Alex is the one who conquers his fears to show up.
Identifiers: LCCN 2017058530 | ISBN 9780316416856 (hardcover) | ISBN 9780316416818 (ebook) | ISBN 9780316416832 (library edition ebook)
Subjects: | CYAC: Bullying—Fiction. | Schools—Fiction. | Friendship—Fiction. | Brothers—Fiction. | Conduct of life—Fiction. | England—Fiction.
Classification: LCC PZ7.1.F675 All 2018 | DDC [Fic]—dc23
LC record available at https://lccn.loc.gov/2017058530

ISBNs: 978-0-316-41685-6 (hardcover), 978-0-316-41681-8 (ebook)

Printed in the United States of America

LSC-C

10 9

393000006004054

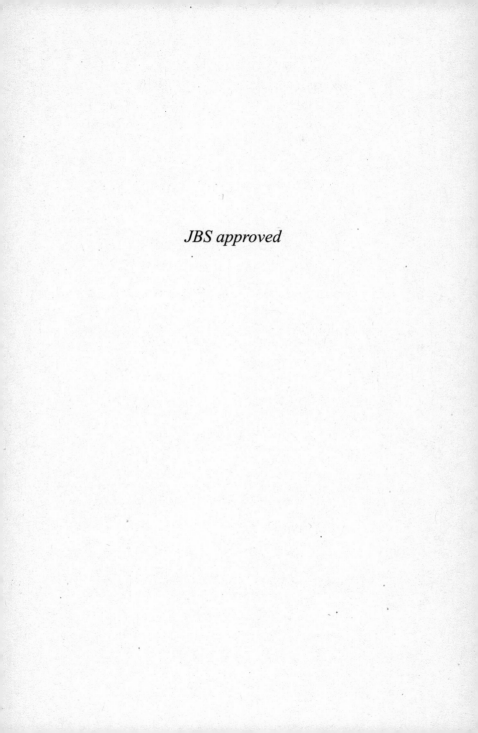

JBS approved

1

Alex: This is me

My Worry List

1. Everybody is going to die.
2. The glass in the aquarium tanks is going to crack on the school trip tomorrow and all the water will pour out and drown everybody in my class and Mr. Francis.
3. It won't happen if I stay home, but if I don't go I'll feel bad for not telling anyone and I'll feel even worse for being the only person in my class who is still alive.
4. All the fish will pour out of the tanks and flap around on the floor with their mouths wide open. But if they flap hard enough maybe they'll make it out the aquarium doors, across the beach, and into the sea.
5. All the fish are going to die. They won't survive in the sea because they're used to being fed in their tanks and all the bigger fish will eat them up.

6. I'm worried about my worries. I could tell Mum and she'd phone the school and warn them what's going to happen. But everyone would laugh and think I've gone crazy.

If I tell Mum my worries, she'll worry too. She hates it when I'm worried and I hate it when she worries about me. I could go on the trip and die with all the others, but then Mum and Lizzie would be left at home on their own when I'm gone.

AAAAAAAAAAAAAAAARGH!

2

Dan: Sharks and dolphins

"There are four hundred and forty different species of shark in the world, and they're split into eight categories, from the really small ones, like the catfish, to the medium-size hammerheads, right up to the huge whale sharks in the Indian and Pacific Oceans."

The aquarium guide holds his arms out as wide as he can reach. "You may have seen whale sharks on TV—they're often mistaken for actual whales—but you can tell them apart by the ridge on their head and the sharpness of their teeth."

The guide points to his own teeth and they light up in the dark. Behind him, fish and tiny turtles are swimming around in a giant tank full of colored lights. There are tanks all around me. It's like I'm in the water with the fish. I could reach out and touch them if they'd keep still. A big yellow fish swims above my head, slows, twitches its tail, and then disappears behind me.

"Dan." I feel a tap on my shoulder, and then Mr. Francis bends down and whispers in my ear. "Are you listening?" He points at the guide, who's now showing my class a picture of a shark. The big yellow fish swims back over my head.

"Dan!"

Mr. Francis turns my head to face the front. The guide starts talking again.

"You can get an idea of how big it is when you compare it with the size of the people on the boat." The guide points at the picture on the wall. The whale shark is big and gray, and loads of people are standing on the deck, pointing cameras at it. It's so big that if it opened its mouth, ten people would fit inside, including me. I wonder if this one ate all the people on the boat after the picture was taken.

"Does it eat them?" I ask.

"Sorry?" The guide shades his eyes with his hand and looks for me in the dark.

"If you want to ask a question, raise your hand." Miss French stands on tiptoe.

"Go on, Dan. Put your hand up," says Mr. Francis.

I wave my hand in the air. The entire class turns around and looks at me.

"Ah, there you are," says the guide. "Yes, young man," he says. "What was your question?"

"Does it eat people? Does it bite people and tear them apart and splat blood everywhere like in *Jaws*?"

The class laughs. I laugh too.

"Boom!" I lift up my arms and pretend to shoot a harpoon into a shark's mouth. The class laughs again.

"Okay, okay," says Mr. Francis. "Settle down."

The guide smiles. "No, not every shark is like the one in *Jaws*. They've got a bad reputation, but they don't all eat people. In fact, very few do."

"Do those?" I point at two sharks circling, chasing each other's tails behind his head.

"No," he says. "They're too small."

"What about when they grow up?" Sophie giggles beside me.

"This is as big as they get. Now I'd just like to show you the silvers—the tiny silver fish that you see floating around in schools. In the ocean, these can be schools of up to a mile long." The guide keeps talking, but I'm not really listening anymore because I'm watching the two sharks as they chase each other around a rock in the middle of the tank.

"Sir!" I put my hand in the air again. "Sir!"

The guide looks at his watch, then at Miss French.

"I think it might be best if we let them ask questions at the end."

"But it's important," I say.

"Okay," says Miss French. "Last one, Dan. What is it?"

"I think those two sharks have a crush on each other."

"Okay, Dan," says Mr. Francis. "I think that's enough of that. Mr. Giles, perhaps you'd like to lead us on to the next tank." The class starts to walk off with Miss French. "Not you, Dan."

"But, sir, I—"

"Come here!"

Sophie and George C. grin as they walk past me.

"You two get a move on, and, Dan, you stand still." Mr. Francis bends down so his head is level with mine. Two puffer fish swim behind him.

"Dan, listen to me: you need to settle down. It's all very well you messing around, but you're..."

I try to listen to what he says, but it's hard not to laugh when the puffer fish make him look like he's got elephant ears. Mr. Francis lifts up his hand and shows me three fingers.

"That's the third time I've told you today."

"But—"

"But nothing. This is a school trip; we're not going to be allowed to visit these places if you misbehave. You're here to learn, not be the joker. Do you understand?"

I look over his shoulder. Sophie and George C. have stayed behind and are standing by a tank like they're waiting for me to act up or do something funny.

"Do you understand?"

"Yes. But I don't want to come again anyway."

"I don't think you mean that."

"I do. That old man is weird, and sharks that don't eat people are boring."

Mr. Francis goes to reply but stops as Miss French walks back around the corner.

"We're moving on to the next tank," she says.

"Okay," says Mr. Francis. "Come on. Let's go and see the crabs."

I follow him into a tunnel where tiny silver fish swim beside us as we walk. I blow out my cheeks and I think I hear Mr. Francis do the same, or it might be the sound of air bubbling in the tanks.

I walk ahead and catch up with Sophie and George C. at the end of the tunnel.

"What did he say?" asks Sophie.

"Nothing much."

"He's an idiot."

"Yeah," I say.

I don't really think he is. For a start, he's better than Mr. Gough, my math teacher, who just sucks on cough drops and stares at the computer all lesson.

We walk into the next room and bump into the back of the others in the dark. The aquarium is like a massive cave: it seems to get darker the farther in you go. I hear the tour guide say something about staying together or we'll get lost.

"We found someone last week who'd been here for two years, and he'd missed taking his GCSEs."

"I imagine some of them would like that," says Mr. Francis.

"I would!"

"Yes, Dan, I think we all know that."

The guide starts to talk about the leatherback sea turtle, how it swims in currents across the ocean and then crawls onto beaches and lays its eggs in the sand. I rest my head against the glass and watch the tiny silver fish shoot off in all directions. I don't need a tour guide to show me around, because I would never get lost in here. I've been here so many times with my big brother that it's like I've got a map of the fish tanks in my head. We used to come down on Sundays and he'd help me sneak under the turnstiles when the security guard wasn't looking. I didn't need to listen to the tour guide then either, or look at the pictures, because Ben would tell me everything.

"If you cut an arm off a starfish, it grows another one like worms grow new heads." ·

"If you put your hand in a tank of piranhas, they'll eat all the flesh and the bones."

I'd tell him I wouldn't dare put my hand in there. Ben said he wouldn't either. The last time we came here he told me how the biggest fish got to be so big.

"See that big fat one?" He pointed at a large yellow fish swimming on its own. "Well, it used to be a little fish, but then it started to eat all the other fish and it got big and strong. That's what you've got to do."

"But I don't like fish," I said.

He laughed, said I knew what he meant. Then we heard footsteps getting close, and Ben searched around on the floor for old tickets that people might have dropped the day before. He found two and gave one to me. The footsteps got louder. Then we saw a shadow and the glow of a flashlight. It was the security guard. I turned to run, but Ben grabbed my arm.

"It's okay," he whispered. "They change the colors of the tickets every day, but he won't be able to tell the difference in the dark."

"What are you two up to?"

"Nothing," said Ben. "Just looking at the fish."

"Mmmm." The security guard shined the flashlight in our faces. My heart was thudding, but Ben just stood still and handed him our tickets. The guard shined his flashlight on them. Ben nudged me. I could see his teeth as he smiled in the dark. The guard gave the tickets back.

"Okay," he said. "Just don't hang around; we're closing in twenty minutes." He walked away.

Ben ruffled my hair. "Told you," he said.

I tap the glass gently. The silver fish gather around my fingertip like they're trying to eat it. I wish Ben were here now. It was more fun with him than with these other kids on a school trip.

"Dan! Dan!" I feel a nudge in my ribs. Sophie's grinning at me. Her teeth and her blonde hair have been turned purple by the lights. "This is boring," she whispers. "Let's go to the souvenir shop."

"Yeah." George C. leans in. "See what we can get." He slides along the glass and Sophie and me follow. Mr. Francis and Miss French are watching the rest of the class as they lean over the tank and touch the turtles and crabs.

A bright light shines through a crack as George C. opens the door. I look back at the teachers and the class. The guide is telling them about the crabs, that they're got exo-blah-blah-blah—a big word for saying crabs' skeletons are on the outside of their bodies.

Sophie nudges me in the back. "Go on," she whispers. "Now!"

I check one more time and we slide out the door. I blink in the bright lights of the souvenir shop.

There are two teachers and some kids in blue uniforms from another school walking around. Sophie and me pass books about fish and the ocean and stop by a shelf full of plastic dolphins and sharks. I stand on tiptoe and look over the top of the shelves. There's a woman behind the cash register ticking off a list and a security guard by the turnstiles that let people out and in.

Sophie opens her eyes wide and nods toward the dolphins and sharks.

"Go on," she says. "It's your turn. I did it when we went to the museum in London." I check that the woman and the security guard aren't looking.

Sophie nudges me again. "Now!"

The security man blows his nose. The woman at the register ticks her list. I reach out, grab a dolphin, and put it into my trouser pocket. Sophie grins at me.

I reach out and grab another. I started doing it at Christmas. I was really scared at first, but Ben said it's like kicking a football: the more you practice, the better you get. He used to do it when we came here together. I wouldn't know he'd taken anything until we got outside and he'd give me a plastic turtle or a rubber octopus and say it was a present.

I pick up more sharks and dolphins and jam them in my pockets. I go to take some more, then stop as the door opens. The guide walks into the shop with the rest of my class behind him. Mr. Francis is at the back, rubbing his beard and nodding like he's counting we're all here. George C. and George W. walk up to me. They look and sound just like each other and have their hair stuck up with gel. I slowly pull back my blazer and show them my trouser pockets.

"Wicked." George W. laughs. "But how are you going to get them out of here?"

"Easy." I start to stroll down the aisle, but my pockets are bulging like I'm a cowboy with guns. I'm going to get caught if I walk out like this.

"Five minutes, everyone!" shouts Mr. Francis.

I stop at the end of the aisle where Elliott Gibbs is standing on his own, looking at a map of the oceans.

"Stay there," I say to him. Elliott flinches.

"It's okay. I'm not going to hit you or anything."

"Not this time anyway," Sophie adds.

"What do you want, then?" Elliott says in a wimpy voice.

"Just stand still. I need your bag," I say.

"But I haven't got anything in there." He squirms as Sophie pulls one of his straps.

"Stay still," she says, "or we'll throw all your stuff on the beach and then we'll get your weirdo friend when we're back at school. Where is the little squirt anyway?"

Elliott shrugs. "I don't know."

"Too scared that we'd get him here?"

Elliott looks at the ground and mumbles something.

"What did you say?" Sophie steps closer to him.

Elliott looks up. "I said, why do you have to pick on Alex?"

"Aww," says Sophie. "He cares more about his little friend than he does about himself." The she pushes her face up close to Elliott like she's looking in a mirror. Compared to Elliott, she's so big and strong she could knock him over against the shelves. "But you're not his friend now...are you?!"

"No," Elliott says. "I don't talk to him anymore."

"Good." Sophie holds Elliott still. I take the dolphins and sharks out of my pockets and slip them into his bag. He tries to turn away as me and Sophie pull the straps tight.

11

"Don't tell anyone," she says.

I push Elliott in front of me and we shuffle forward in the line.

The security guard nods like he's counting sheep going into a pen. I nudge Elliott in the back and he walks through the turnstile.

"Thanks!" I give the security guard the thumbs-up like Ben used to do.

"That's okay, son," he says. "Be sure to come again."

"I will."

My heart beats fast as I push through the turnstile and run out to the seafront. Ben said his heart used to do that too.

3

Alex: A little fish

"Love, how much longer?"

Mum knocks on the door.

"Alex, can you hear me?"

"Yes."

"How much longer? You missed school yesterday and you're making everyone late today."

"I know, Mum. I'm trying."

I squirt the antibacterial soap on my hands and put them under the tap. The water's so hot it stings the cracks and sores on my fingers. I wince, squirt more soap, and rinse them under the tap again. As usual, I'm stuck in the bathroom. The door isn't jammed locked and my bum's not stuck to the toilet seat with superglue. But I'm stuck, stuck and I can't stop washing. My hands are clean, but as soon as I touch the taps to turn them off, my hands are dirty again, and even if I didn't turn the taps off, there are germs on the towel. There are germs everywhere I look. On the taps, on the towels, on the light switch, on the door handle.

Another knock on the door.

"Alex, love." Mum's back again. "Come on! Elliott's dad is outside. You know he has to get to work on time and you're going to make me late for work too."

Water's steaming up into my face. I hear Elliott's dad beeping the car horn outside, and I don't want to make Mum late because last week she got a warning from her supermarket boss.

I'll just have one last wash before I go. I rub my hands together; they sting and they're red-raw like a pomegranate.

But they're clean finally.

Turn the tap off, I think. *Turn the tap off. Use your elbow like doctors do in hospitals.*

I bend over, knock the tap with my elbow. It turns a little. I knock it again, then again until the stream of water is a dribble. Mum will turn it off after I'm done. My hands are throbbing. I hold them in the air. The water drips down my forearms to my elbows.

Knock, knock.

"Mum, I said I'm coming."

"No, Alex, it's me. Hurry up, I need to pee." It's my little sister, Lizzie. "Come on. I'm going to do it. I'm going to do it!"

"No! Don't! I'm coming!" I bend down and push my elbow against the door handle. It flips down and springs back up again.

"Alex! I'm going to go."

"No! Don't!"

I have to get out. I knock the handle again, pull it quickly toward me at the same time, and the door springs open. Lizzie's on the landing with her legs crossed.

"At last!"

14

She rushes past me and sits on the toilet. She smiles with relief as her pee trickles into the toilet.

"That's gross," I say. "You didn't even close the door."

She grins and says something back, but I don't hear because Mum's standing beside me with my school bag in her hands.

"Quick," she says. "You can still catch them." She hangs my bag around my neck like a medal. "Go on," she says. "Your wipes are in there and your gloves are on the kitchen table."

"Okay," I say. "Be safe."

"Alex. We've not got time for that now."

"You have to say it. 'Be safe.' I can't go unless you do."

Mum sighs. "Okay, be safe. Now off you go."

If she didn't say "be safe," lots of bad things could happen: a row of display shelves could fall on her at work, or she could get run over by a delivery truck; Lizzie might fall over in the playground playing netball, or the office that Dad guards could collapse and he'd be trapped under the bricks and glass. Mum, Dad, and Dr. Patrick say these things won't happen, that it's just bad thoughts playing tricks, and I know that's true, but I still can't stop the thoughts jumping into my mind. But at least my class didn't die at the aquarium yesterday, because there was nothing about it on the news last night.

I hurry down the stairs, keeping my hands clear of the banister as I jump the last four and run into the kitchen. My gloves are on the table, just like Mum said. I put them on and then run around the side of the house. Elliott's dad's car isn't there. I run out into the street, but I'm too late; all I can see are the red taillights of the car as it turns onto the main road. I sigh. He did warn me he couldn't wait past eight because he'd be late for work. I'll have to walk to school now, but it takes ages. I'll miss homeroom again and have to walk into history when they're halfway through the lesson. I hate doing that. Everyone turns and looks at me like I've just arrived from Mars.

"Alex! Alex!" Mum's shouting at me from her bedroom window. "Come back in. I'll give you some money for the bus."

"It's okay. I'll walk."

"It's not okay. You can't afford to miss any more lessons."

Mum's right, but I don't want to catch the bus because it's full of people's germs on the windows and on the stop button. I can't touch that button. The last time I was on the bus it went two stops past the school before someone pressed the button. I was lucky because if no one had been on the bus, I'd have ended up at my nan and granddad's in Worthing. I like going there, but I won't learn anything useful. All Nan talks about are her neighbors, and Granddad is always busy washing his car.

I walk back to the house, checking the pavement for bird and dog poop. There are two new white marks since last night and a brown skid mark where someone has spread poop across the pavement. Was it me? Did I step on it as I was rushing out? I check the bottoms of my shoes. The front soles are clean, but there's something brown in the groove on my left heel.

I pass Lizzie's friend, Molly, waiting by the gate with her mum. Her mum says something, but I'm too busy looking at the ground. I walk past them, down the side of our house. Lizzie comes toward me with her school bag on her back. She's in Year Six at the school I used to go to.

"Why are you looking at your shoes?" she says. "Have you got poop on them?"

"I think so."

"Eww!"

I tell her to shush. It's bad enough having poop on me without her going, "Eww!"

"Sorry," she whispers. "Mum says it's Mr. King's fault because he doesn't take his dog to the park. I'll tell him if you want."

"It's okay."

"I will. I don't mind." My sister is very loud and very annoying, but she does care about me lots.

I start to walk on. "I'll see you later."

"Can we play *LittleBigPlanet* later?"

And she's good to play *LittleBigPlanet* with.

"Yeah," I say. "Maybe."

"Great!" Lizzie runs off without even looking where she's going, and I wish I could do the same.

I open the back gate. Mum's standing at the door.

"What's wrong?"

I point at my shoe. "I think I stepped in poop."

"Let me see."

"You're not supposed to help," I say.

"I'll only look."

"But Dr. Patrick said."

"I know what he said, but you'll never make it to school if I don't."

She's right. I won't be able to walk another step if I don't wash my shoe, but she isn't supposed to help. Dr. Patrick says it's like she's

17

making my OCD and my worries okay if she does. But Mum can't help it. She says she hates to see me struggle. She says it makes her feel like a bad mum, but she's not a bad mum: she's the best mum in the world.

I slip my shoes off. She picks one up and lifts it to her—

"Don't sniff—oh, Mum! Gross!"

"It's okay," she says. "I think it's a leaf."

"Are you sure?"

"Yes."

"Are you really?"

"Alex!"

"Sorry." I lean against the worktop. This is the second time I've been late this week and I was late twice last week as well. If only I had been five seconds quicker. If I hadn't washed my hands for one last time, I would have been in the car, swapping Euro cards with Elliott instead of watching Mum clean poop, which she says is a leaf, from my shoe. My shoe! It brushed against my trousers as I walked; now the poop's on my other trouser leg, on my socks, on my skin.

"Alex, where are you going now?"

"Umm." I'm halfway across the kitchen toward the hall. "There's something I've got to do."

"What?"

Dog-poop-trousers-legs-socks-skin. Dog-poop-trousers-legs-socks-skin. My thoughts tumble around and around in my head like my clothes in a washing machine.

"Alex, no. Not the bathroom again."

18

"But—"

"You can't, love. It'll be another hour before you come out."

"Can I just write it down, then?"

"Okay. But promise: not the bathroom."

"I promise."

"Okay. I'll check the other shoe and then call the school."

I climb the stairs and walk past my sister's bedroom. I wish I could just get up like she does, then get dressed, get washed, eat breakfast, and go to school on time. It sounds dead simple. It's only four things, but I can't do any of them without being late.

I sit down on my bed with my pencil and pad. This is my worry pad. I have to write all my worries down when things get really bad. Dr. Patrick told me I had to note down the first things that come into my head because that way I identify the real worries. I rip last night's worry page out. It doesn't count if I just read the old list. My worries don't stay the same; they change all the time.

My Worry List

1. Everyone is going to die.
2. Dan and Sophie will be waiting to pick on me as soon as I walk into homeroom.
3. Mr. Hammond will lean too close to me in math and his breath and spit will go on my face and clothes.
4. I might have to sit at the desk at the front by the window in history. The one with chewing gum underneath.

5. Mum and Lizzie are going to trip over the loose floorboard on the landing, fall down the stairs, and die.
6. Lizzie doesn't wash her hands after going to the bathroom so there are germs everywhere at home.
7. Dan and Sophie will get me at break.
8. The bricks are loose in the wall at school where Mr. Francis parks his car. The wall will topple over and trap him underneath and he'll run out of oxygen and die.
9. Dad never disinfects the steering wheel and he'll try to hug me if he comes around tonight.
10. Everyone is going to die.

I stop writing and read the list again and again, like I'm studying for an exam, but I'm supposed to forget the thoughts, not remember them. I'd get a 100 percent if there were an exam on worries. It's my specialty subject, like people who go on quiz shows on TV. Other contestants have specialties like "Characters in Harry Potter Novels" or "The Life and Times of Shakespeare." I'd sit in a chair and all the lights would go out except for the big bright one shining in my eyes.

"Your name?"

"Alex Jones."

"And your specialty subject is?"

"How to pour big bottles of disinfectant into smaller bottles so I can use them at school."

"Excellent. Your time starts now."

I rip my list into tiny pieces like Dr. Patrick told me. *Out of sight, out of mind.* Sometimes I think of using Mum's shredder just in case she goes through the garbage and puts the pieces back together. I don't want her to see what's in my head.

She's drinking coffee in the kitchen when I go back down.

"You need to get up earlier, love," she says.

"But it's already dark when I get up."

"I know. Maybe you should go to bed at a reasonable time."

"I can't. I keep trying, but every night I get stuck in the bathroom."

She stands up. "Come here," she says. "Give Mum a hug." I walk toward her and she wraps her arms around me. I want a hug, but I can't bear her to touch me because she might have germs on her clothes and hands. I stand stiff like a lump of ice.

"Alex." She tilts her head and looks at me like she can see my worries in my eyes.

"Yes?"

She brushes my hair off my face.

"Do you think you'd like to go and see Dr. Patrick again?"

I nod, but I'm not sure Dr. Patrick can help me. All he does is listen and then tells me to write my Worry List. One time he told me to imagine all my problems were ants. It didn't take my problems away, but it helped for a while until I started to imagine the ants crawling all over me while I was asleep.

"I'll call him during my lunch break," Mum says.

"What about Dad? It costs loads."

21

"I know, but he'll be fine. He'd rather pay for that than have you flooding the kitchen again."

I look up at the brown stain on the ceiling and feel guilty. Last month I stayed in the shower so long it sprayed over the edge of the bath and flooded the floor. I try to forget about it, but the stain seems to be getting darker and bigger every time I look.

Mum hands me my gloves. "Here," she says, giving me my bus money at the same time. "I know you don't like catching it, but it's too late to walk."

I try to smile before I leave.

Outside the sun is shining, making a rainbow on the patch of oil where Dad used to park his car before he and Mum separated. I step around it.

"Oh, Alex! Wait!" Mum shouts, and comes running out with my guitar. "You'd forget your head if it wasn't stuck on," she says.

I wish I could!

Mum smiles as she helps me put my arms through the straps. "Why are you wearing this old hoodie?" She holds on to my sleeve.

"The other one's dirty," I say. "And it's got a hole in the arm."

"What? It was brand-new! How did that happen?" *I can't tell her.*

"Alex, how did you do it?"

"I fell over on the way home."

"And one of the straps is missing on your bag."

"It broke off when I fell."

Mum shakes her head. "Alex, can't you be more careful? I can't do anything about the strap until the weekend, but I'll sew the hoodie. We can't afford to keep buying new clothes all the time."

"Okay." I start to walk toward the gate. I wish I could tell Mum how it really happened, but I can't because the people who did it will do it even more if anyone finds out, and Mum will have to buy me a whole new uniform before long. I open the gate. Mum's still standing at the door.

"What now?" she asks when I turn to look at her.

"Are you cleaning the house this afternoon?"

"Yes, it's my half day at work."

"Can you not move Chewbacca? He doesn't like standing next to Yoda."

"Okay."

"And put Han Solo back on the windowsill."

"Alex!"

"Sorry. I'm going, I'm going." I hitch my guitar up onto my back and wave. "Be safe."

Mum smiles. "Be safe."

As I walk down the path, I try to block out what will happen when I get to school. I think about all the other *Star Wars* characters lined up on my windowsill—six stormtroopers, three of them guarding each end, with Princess Leia, C-3PO, and all the other characters in between. They used to get knocked over when the wind blew my curtains. I asked Dad if I could stick them down with superglue, but he said it would rip off the paint, so I use putty instead. It gets a bit germy, but it's okay because I spray them all with disinfectant, although I think I've been doing it too much because last week Finn's lightsaber fell off.

I reach the bus stop and look at my watch. It's 8:50. I've missed homeroom already. I can't turn back and save all my *Star Wars* characters now. If I had a phone I'd text Mum, but she says we can't afford it, and I wouldn't want the battery in my pocket anyway. The 205 bus comes along the road toward me. I screw my hands into a fist—*germy buttons, germy money, germy breath on the windows, babies with their fingers in their mouths who then wipe them on the seats*—

I start walking.

Dan: The boy from outer space

"Dan?"

"Yes, miss."

"Michael?"

"Yes, miss."

"Sarah?"

"Yes, miss."

"Elliott?"

"Yes, miss."

"Alex?"

No answer.

"No Alex?" Miss Harris looks up from her computer. "No...? Okay, James?"

Sophie leans across me. She must have had fries for dinner last night because her clothes smell of cooking oil.

"The idiot's not coming in," she whispers.

"He's just late, like he always is."

I look out the window as the cars and buses pass the school on their way to town.

"Maybe he's left and gone to another school."

"Sophie, can you please be quiet while I'm doing this," Miss Harris snaps.

"*Sor-ry*, miss," Sophie says in a singsong voice. Then she turns to me and whispers, "Or maybe he's told his mum and dad what we did to him the day before yester—"

"No, he's late. . . . Look." I point out the window. "Told you."

"Ha," Sophie sneers. "Oh yeah, look at him. Weirdo."

I watch as Alex Jones walks across the crosswalk in front of the school, then steps onto the pavement. He walks quickly with his eyes superglued to the ground. Every once in a while, he takes a giant stride and his guitar bounces up and down on his back.

"He looks *sooooo* weird!" says Sophie. "It's like he's jumping over invisible puddles."

"Yeah." I chuckle as Alex turns toward the main school gates.

"Okay, Year Seven, where were we?" Miss Harris claps her hands.

"Brighton," someone says. The class laughs, but I'm too busy watching Alex standing by the front doors, looking up at the building like he's been locked out. Miss Harris says something about the last lesson and the homework she assigned to us. Alex waits by the doors.

"Dan?"

"Yes, miss?"

She sighs. "If you'd stop looking outside, you'd be turning to page forty-three like everyone else."

I open my history book. Miss Harris sits on her desk, and starts to read about the Black Death. Sophie nudges my elbow. Out of the corner of my eye I see her loading an eraser onto a ruler and aiming it at the back of Katie Wright's head. We're sitting near the front, so Miss Harris could easily see her, but Sophie doesn't care.

"Shall I?"

I nod. She lets go of the ruler. The eraser flies past Katie's head. She puts her hand up to her ear like a fly just buzzed in it. Me and Sophie laugh.

Miss Harris glares at us. "Is there a problem?"

"No, miss," we both say at the same time.

"Then look at your books, please."

Sophie puts the ruler down and rests her chin on her hand. "God, this is so boring."

I sort of smile, then start reading my book. I like messing around, but I don't actually think history is boring. Last term we did the Romans and learned how they built straight roads and marched thousands of soldiers along them. How they built big cities and had gladiator fights in the coliseums. I like reading about the Black Death as well, but it's more fun to mess around.

I hear a knock. We all look up from our books. Alex is standing in the doorway with his guitar on his back and his brown gloves on his hands. He never takes them off. I used to imagine it was because his hands had superpowers, like how Cyclops wears dark glasses to protect his eyes.

"Come in, Alex, and sit down," says Miss Harris.

It's not fair. If it were me that was late, I'd be asked why or made to stay behind late. But none of the teachers ever ask Alex. It's like he's got a free pass to come to school when he likes.

He brushes his hair out of his eyes. I reckon he thinks he's Alex

Rider. He does look a bit like him, but he's nowhere near so brave, because as he walks into class he's as jumpy and nervous as Rex, my hamster. His guitar bangs against the door, and a poster falls onto the floor. Some of the kids in the class laugh. Harry Reynolds picks the poster up and sticks it back on the wall. Alex scrunches his face. He does that all the time. It's like he's in pain or has a bad smell up his nose.

"He looks like one of the sharks at the aquarium," whispers Sophie.

"Yeah, with its nose all bashed up against the glass."

Alex starts to walk to his seat. His guitar bangs against a table.

"Alex," Miss Harris says softly. "Have you forgotten that your guitar should be left in the music room?"

"Sorry, I was thinking..."

Miss Harris half smiles at him. "You were thinking, 'Yes, miss, it's a good idea to leave my guitar in the music room.' But it's okay. Just remember next time. Leave it here for now." She points to the corner by the door but accidentally touches Alex's shoulder. He freezes like Miss Harris's hand has turned him to ice (which would be really cool if that could actually happen).

"He's even *weirder* than usual," says Sophie.

Alex puts his guitar down in the corner. Miss Harris steps out of the way as he walks past Elliott Gibbs and sits down in front of me by the window. I see he's got a new patch on his bag to cover the hole Sophie cut in it. And he's wearing a different sweatshirt after we pushed him over in the playground two days ago.

Sophie sniffs. "He smells like a toilet!"

Alex smells like the bleach the janitors use to clean the toilets

28

after school. He spends all of recess in the bathroom, and when he's in lessons he's always wiping his hands and his pens and his books with disinfectant wipes. My mum told me it sounds like he's got OCD. That's when people can't stop cleaning the house or worry that they've left the oven on or forgotten to switch the lights off when they go out. Alex doesn't touch the oven controls in cookery and I've never seen him touch the light switches, but he does lots of other weird stuff. Right now he's wiping the zipper on his pencil case. All the teachers notice, but they don't say anything about it.

Miss Harris starts reading. She tells us how the Black Death came to England from boats that landed in Cornwall and Dorset and ate its way up the country to London, then north to Manchester and on toward Scotland, and how the Scottish people started to fight the English because they didn't want the Black Death there.

Miss Harris looks up from her book. "So," she says. "Does anyone know what the symptoms of the Black Death were?" The class goes quiet. Some of them look at their books, pretend they're reading, and some look around like the answer is floating in the air.

"Miss, miss!" I shout.

"Dan, what have I told you about putting your hand up?"

"Sorry, miss." I raise my hand.

"Yes, Dan."

I start to sing. "First you feel a little poorly, and then you start to swell. Then you start to spit some blood, and then you really smell. Then you know it's time—"

"Okay, Dan, that's enough." Miss Harris holds her hand up. "Let's have another answer, a sensible one."

"I'm *being* sensible! It's a song from *Horrible Histories*—'then you know it's time to ring your funeral bell and along comes Mr. Death and swishes you to hell—'"

"Dan! That's enough." Miss Harris claps her hands. "So, Year Seven, let's have someone else."

I sit back in my chair. It's not fair. Just because I mess around doesn't mean I'm thick. Mr. Francis would have found it funny.

"Anyone?"

The class goes quiet, like they're too scared to answer.

"Alex?"

Alex stares at his ruler.

"Alex? The symptoms of the Black Death?"

He glances sideways, then answers quietly.

"People got a rash and black spots, and the spots grew under their skin and burst and the infection got into their blood." Alex squirms in his seat like the germs from the Black Death are wriggling inside him.

"Yes, Alex. Anything else?"

Alex looks nervously over his shoulder toward me. "Yes, they got delirious . . . and imagined horrible things. . . ." His voice fades away.

"And?" Miss Harris puts her hand up to her ear.

"And then staggered around the street like they were drunk."

"That's exactly what I said!" I shout.

"Dan! Do you want to go to detention?"

I put my elbows on the desk and look out the window. I knew the answer, but she was too busy listening to squeaky-clean Alex. All the teachers like him. I have most of my lessons with him, except for math and gym class, and they're always asking him to answer. He knows everything and smells of disinfectant. It's like he's been decontaminated, then sent from outer space to Earth to learn all about us.

"Shall I?" Sophie's got another eraser loaded on her ruler.

I nod. The ruler springs forward and the eraser flies through the air. Alex puts his hand up to the back of his head like he's just been shot.

"Yes, Alex?" says Miss Harris.

"Nothing, miss."

"I thought you had your hand up."

"No, miss. I—"

"He's got nits, miss." The class starts laughing.

"Good one, Dan," Sophie says.

Alex glances at me, then looks back to the front.

"Okay," Miss Harris huffs. "Read the rest of the section on your own and I'll come around to answer questions." Emma C. puts her hand in the air. Miss Harris walks to the back of the class.

I slouch down in my chair, stretch out my foot, and kick the back of Alex's chair.

"Alex, Alex!" I whisper urgently.

Alex keeps his head down, reading his book.

"Call him Shark Face," Sophie says.

I kick Alex's chair harder this time and it squeaks across the floor. "Shark Face! Turn around!"

Shark Face turns around slowly.

"Ha," says Sophie. "You know your name already."

"That's not my name."

"It is now," says Sophie. She looks around the class. Most of them are reading, James Tadd and Leah are talking, and Miss Harris is helping Emma read. Sophie leans over her desk.

"We saw a shark that looked just like you at the aquarium. With a nose like yours all bashed up like you'd smashed into the glass."

He scrunches his face and turns away. I don't think he really looks like a shark, but I can't say that now.

Sophie scribbles on a piece of paper.

W G T G Y S F

She folds it in half, checks that Miss Harris isn't looking, then taps Katie on the back. Katie looks at the note. Sophie stares at her and holds the note out farther.

"Take it!" she hisses.

Katie takes the note and slides it in front of Alex. He pushes it away without reading it.

Sophie nudges me. I kick his chair again.

"Read it."

Shark Face looks down at the note, then turns around and shrugs. Sophie grabs another piece of paper.

We're Going To Get You Shark Face

She hands the note to Katie. She glances at it, then passes it to Shark Face. As he reads it, his eyes seem to go darker and his eyebrows squeeze closer together like he's in pain.

"Everything all right here?"

Sophie crumples up the note quickly. Miss Harris is only two tables behind us.

"Liam? Hannah?"

"Yes, miss."

"Sophie? Dan? Alex?"

"Yes, miss."

Shark Face turns around to his desk. I wonder if this is the day he'll snitch on us. I feel my heart thud in my chest. Sophie's looking out the window like she's not worried at all.

"Happy with what you're doing, Alex?" Miss Harris stops by his desk. "All good?" I stare at the back of his head, try to force the thoughts out of mine and into his. *Just you dare. Don't say anything.*

Shark Face looks up from his book.

"Yes, miss," he says quietly. "I'm good."

5

Alex: Stomachache and dead presidents

I'm walking along the blue corridor on my way to math. Boys and girls rush toward me, barging into me. "Sorry. Sorry," I say, but no one replies. It's like I'm invisible, being spun around with my guitar on my back.

I look back down the corridor. Dan and Sophie aren't following me. They're not very good at math, so they have Mr. Gough, and then they go to the Rainbow Room, where Mr. Francis helps them catch up with lessons they are behind in. At least for a while I can concentrate on doing my work instead of worrying about getting beaten up.

I put my head down, trying to block out the noise of all the other kids and all the things I don't want to touch, like the walls, their hands, their bags, but they're all zigzagging around me like ants. Miss Keeler is standing in the middle of the hallway, pointing like a traffic officer, telling us not to run.

At the beginning of the first term they gave us a little map of the building. It was like a diagram of a fuse box with big square blocks—music, art, science, math—then the colored lines—red, blue, green—running down the corridors that join them all up. This school is massive, big buildings everywhere. My old school was just one building surrounded by six wooden huts. I know I have to learn things, but I wish I was back there. My OCD wasn't so bad then. I didn't have to take wipes to school and my worries were about normal things, like trying not to forget my sandwiches or avoiding walking on the cracks in the pavement.

The five-minute bell rings just as I reach the math block, and I hurry through the doors to the classroom.

Mr. Hammond is handing out pencils and rulers. He doesn't notice me as I sit down next to Emma. She smiles at me nervously, like being bullied is a disease and she's afraid she'll catch it. Or maybe she's worried because she's not in a girls' friendship group and that's why she has to sit next to me. We're the "no friends" friendship group. Sometimes I imagine that even if you put us all in a room away from the "popular" kids, we still wouldn't talk to each other.

As I pull my math book out of my bag, I can feel Emma looking at the writing on it. I tried to scribble it out with a marker pen, but I can still see *Wimp* and *Weirdo* written underneath from when Dan and Sophie grabbed my bag from me last night. Emma looks down at her book and pretends she hasn't seen it, like everyone does.

I take a deep breath and try to stop thinking about last night, but trying not to think about it makes me think about it more. I can't stop it, and it's even worse when I think that it might happen again tonight. Mr. Hammond walks to the front of the class. He doesn't have to ask us to be quiet, like the other teachers do. All he has to do is put his hand on his head and look at us. It's like he's got a mute switch.

"Okay." He draws a horizontal and a vertical line on the whiteboard. "Copy this," he says. "and label them x and y. Then we'll plot some points."

"Like Battleship, sir?"

"Kind of, Liam, but let's just draw the axis and we'll find out." Mr. Hammond turns back to the board.

Emma looks at me, then back at her book. I wonder if she's noticed the missing strap on my bag too, and the new patch to cover the hole Sophie cut in it. But at least I don't have a hole in this sweatshirt.

Did Mum believe me when I told her I'd fallen over? I hope so because I can't tell her about what's happening. If I tell anyone and Dan and Sophie find out, they'll pick on me even more. They might start throwing mud at me or shoving me off the pavement onto the grass. The pavement is covered in germs, but at least I can see the marks. I can't see them when they're mixed with mud and grass. Or they might rip off my gloves and throw them on the music-room roof like they did last term with Elliott's shoes. It was Elliott's turn last term and now it's mine. His was bad, but it was just Sophie and the Georges. Dan never did anything. He just messed around and made the class laugh, but that was before he decided to be Sophie's friend.

"Alex, is everything okay?" I hadn't noticed that Mr. Hammond had stopped talking to the class and was now standing beside me.

Don't bend down and breathe on me!

I nod and pick up my ruler and pencil, but it's hard to draw a line when the pencil keeps sliding through my gloves.

Mr. Hammond rests his knuckles on the table.

"Alex," he says. "I know you don't like to touch things, but

36

unfortunately that's what hands are for. I think you're going to have to take the gloves off."

I think of telling him about the letter Mum sent to the school at the beginning of the year; he must have read it because it was supposed to be passed to all the teachers. *Alex can't take his gloves off. He doesn't like touching things and his hands are sore and they've got more wrinkles than his nan's.* I made that last bit up. My hands have got more wrinkles than Nan's, but I think Mum just wrote that they were *sensitive*, like they'd shrivel up like fish skin if they were exposed to the sun.

Mr. Hammond is still standing there.

"Just try it, Alex." He sounds like a lunch lady trying to make me eat broccoli. People like Mr. Hammond don't understand. They think that forcing me to do things will cure me, but it won't. It just makes me stress, and stress makes it worse. I've wiped the pencil loads of times, but I still don't want to touch it with my hands because Emma put it in her mouth by mistake last week.

I look up from my desk. The whole class is staring at me, waiting for me to take my gloves off, like I might have a pirate's hook under there. My face begins to burn. I thought this was going to be a good lesson where I could get on with my work and not be bullied by Sophie and Dan, but instead I've got Mr. Hammond and the bad thoughts in my head.

"Come and see me afterward."

I can't tell if he's annoyed or angry, because his face is always straight. He walks away. I think of telling Mum to photocopy the letter and send it again, but I don't think Mr. Hammond would even read it. He knows what's wrong with me; he just doesn't like that my worries control me more than he does. But he's not as bad as Mr. Haynes, my woodwork teacher, who calls me Michael Jackson. I'm nothing like him. He's dead for a start, and even when he was alive he only wore one glove.

The rest of the lesson passes in a blur with Mr. Hammond's voice all muffled like he's talking underwater, but at least he doesn't come and breathe all over me. Eventually I manage to plot the graph points by squeezing my pencil tighter, trapping it between the stitching on my gloves.

My stomach starts to ache when the lunch bell rings, but it's not because I'm hungry; it's because I remember that Sophie and Dan will be waiting for me outside. I wish I could skip lunch and go straight to gym class.

The class pack up their things and I walk toward the dining hall on my own. All the time I'm looking over my shoulder just in case they're behind me. When I get to the line safely, I breathe out. I'll be okay here because, even though there are loads of older kids, there are lots of teachers too. All I have to do is try to stop people brushing against me.

A lunch lady gives me a weird look when I get my food. I think it might be my gloves, or it might be because of the fries and jam doughnut on my plate.

I look around the hall for somewhere to sit. I usually sit at the table at the front by the cash registers so I don't have to pass every-one breathing over my food, but some Year Tens are sitting there and some Year Nines and Eights are behind them. They're all talking in groups, and I don't know any of them. I look around for someone in my year that I do know, but they all seem to be sitting in groups too.

I walk to the end of the front row and along the windows without touching any tables or the glass. I sit down at a table on my own. Outside, the sun is shining and some Year Nines are playing football on the grass. Dan and Sophie are sitting on the benches nearby with the Georges, eating packed lunch. I wish it was raining; then we'd all have to go to the main hall. Dan and Sophie wouldn't risk getting me there.

I pick up a french fry and try to eat, but my stomach is aching so much that I can't even think about swallowing. I rest my head on my hand. A few spaces away from me someone puts a plate on the table and sits down. I look up and see Elliott looking at me. I glance out the window. Dan and Sophie are laughing and shouting. Elliott used to be my best friend at primary school. I think he looks like a scientist because he's got spiky hair and wears tiny round glasses. We used to talk all the time, but now we have to whisper and talk in code like we're spies. We can't even talk properly in the car in case his dad is listening.

He leans toward me. "Are you okay?"

"Yeah."

"Sorry my dad couldn't wait for you."

"It's all right."

Elliott leans a little closer. "What did the note say?"

"That they're going to beat me up."

Elliott puts a french fry in his mouth. "They made me steal sharks yesterday."

"Sharks?"

"Yeah, and dolphins. They said they'd beat you up if I didn't."

"Think they're going to do that anyway. And they're calling me Shark Face."

"Why?"

"Because I look like a shark they saw yesterday."

"No, you don't! You look nothing like it. That's just dumb."

I shrug. I know it's dumb, but the names they make up don't have to make sense. They used to call Elliott Piggy. He doesn't look anything like a pig. It's just that it sort of rhymed with his surname, Higgs. Last term Sophie and the Georges teased and pushed him all the time. They used to mimic his voice because it's squeaky like a mouse's.

We both look around the dining hall and check that no one can see us talking because if they do they might go and tell Dan and Sophie. Elliott picks up another french fry.

"Have you got Joe Hart?"

"What?"

"Footy cards. Have you got Joe Hart?"

"Yes."

"Two of him?"

"Yes."

"Swap for Gareth Bale?"

I nod and make sure no one is watching. I've been trying to get Gareth Bale for ages. If Elliott and me had been allowed to talk properly, I'd have had him ages ago. He reaches into his pocket and I reach into mine, then we slide Gareth Bale and Joe Hart across the table and swap.

"Great! I've got the whole England team now."

I try to smile, but all I can think about is how we used to be best friends and now all we do is whisper because I don't want him to get bullied too. I pick at my lunch. Elliott knocks his foot against mine.

"Alex, did you see that documentary about assassinated American presidents last night? I watched it with my dad. It was brilliant. One of them got shot in the head."

"John F. Kennedy."

"Yeah, the bullet went right through and splatted his brains all over the car, and there was another president who got shot when he was at a theater, and the shooter escaped until the police found him hiding in a barn."

I smile, not because getting shot is a nice thing, but because it's good to listen to Elliott talking to me again.

"Was that Abraham Lincoln?"

"Yeah." Elliott opens his eyes wide. "He was—"

A plate smashes. The noise makes me jump as if Dan and Sophie are standing right behind me.

Everyone has gone quiet and is looking at a girl in Year Eight with her hand over her mouth, staring at her lunch scattered all over the floor.

"Okay." Mrs. Barratt's voice echoes around the hall. "Get on with your lunches—there's nothing to see here." The girl stands still while everyone else picks up their knives and forks and the chatter starts again. I can feel sweat trickling down my back, and my hands are so wet my knife and fork start to slip between my fingers. Elliott looks at me like he knows how I'm feeling. He's the only one who does.

He gently taps his fork on the table.

"Alex," he whispers. "They'll stop...like they did with me."

I try to answer, but now that Dan has joined them it's made it even worse. It feels like they've been doing it forever. It's like I'm trapped in a dark room and I can't find the door.

"At least it's only two weeks until half-term," he whispers. "And then—"

"What's wrong?" I ask.

"They're coming."

I look out the window. The table where Dan and Sophie were sitting is empty. I spin around on the bench. Dan is ambling toward me. His hair is stuck up with gel and his shirttails are poking out under his sweatshirt. He's always getting told off for that, but he doesn't care. He says something to the Georges and Sophie. They start laughing, then Sophie looks in my direction with an evil grin on her face. Elliott picks up his plate even though he hasn't finished. I look at mine. It's full, like I haven't started. Having Dan and Sophie after me is like being followed by shadows wherever I go. I look around for a teacher, but Mr. Matthews is talking to the prefects, and Mrs. Barratt is still talking to the girl who dropped her food on the floor.

Dan barges into Elliott. He's the same size as me and Elliott, but sometimes he seems twice as big.

"What are you talking to him for? Thought you weren't his friend."

"...I wasn't," Elliott says, "and...I'm not." Elliott glances at me, then looks at the ground. I know he doesn't mean it, but it still hurts when he says it.

"Good." Then Dan walks over to me and whispers, "Don't think you can hide in here all day, Shark Face."

"Yeah," says Sophie. "We'll be waiting for you outside the gates."

My stomach cramps as she puts her face up close to mine. I know what she's going to say; she says it to me every day, and it still hurts as much as the first time she said it. She grins at me.

"Alex...Alex."

She won't stop until I answer.

"Yes?"

"Why is your face always screwed up like you've just pooped in your pants?" She laughs in my face.

I take a deep breath.

"Hmmm?" Sophie raises her eyebrows like she's waiting for me to reply, but I can't think of anything to say because what she said makes me feel so angry. Sophie grins and starts to walk away. "Come on, Dan. Smells like he's done it. We'll get him later."

I look to Elliott for help, but he's already gone, and even if he was here he couldn't help. And why should he? I never helped when they were picking on him. I watch them walk out into the corridor, then look down at my plate. My fries have gotten cold, but my stomach aches so much I couldn't eat them anyway. I pick up my plate and look around the room. Everyone else is sitting at their tables, eating and talking, and Mrs. Barratt and Mr. Matthews are talking in a corner like nothing has happened. I really am invisible...except to Sophie and Dan.

6

Dan: The Rainbow Room

"So what can we say we learned from our trip to the aquarium yesterday? Yes, Hannah?"

"That if there was no plankton there wouldn't be any fish."

"Yes, that's true." Mr. Francis points to the back corner of the room. "Harry?"

Harry shifts in his seat. "Turtles swim with the current like Squirt in *Finding Nemo*."

"Mmm." He nods. "Felix?"

"That a dolphin's blowhole is the same as our nose."

I put my hand in the air. *I've got an answer. I've got an answer.*

"Yes, Dan?"

"That sharks fancy each other!"

The class laughs. Mr. Francis holds his hand in the air like he's stopping traffic. "Okay, okay. I love the enthusiasm...but let's not have any more comments about sharks fancying each other."

The class laughs again, then Mr. Francis says something about whales and how they can stay underwater for over half an hour. I hold my breath and try to imagine what it's like. I can't think of anything else to say about sharks, so I pick up my pencil and start drawing another raft on the back of my science book.

"So let's try again," says Mr. Francis. "Yes, Chris?"

"Dolphin babies come out tail first."

"And why's that?"

Sophie puts up her hand. Mr. Francis ignores her like he thinks she's going to mess around as usual.

"Georgia?"

"Because if it came out head first it would drown."

"Well done."

"Oh, I knew that!" says Sophie. Then she looks at me and mumbles, "Doesn't matter. Stupid question anyway."

I don't answer.

"Hey!" Sophie nudges me. "Talk to me." I draw a plank of wood.

"Hey! Why do you keep drawing that raft? Is that all you can draw?"

"No."

"It is." She points at five other rafts that I've drawn.

"No, it's not." I glare at her.

"It is."

"Sophie, Dan! Would you like to share what's so interesting that it stops you listening to your teacher like the rest of the class?"

I put my pencil down.

"That's better. We're talking about yesterday's trip, not doing art."

Sophie flicks my pencil with her finger. It rolls off the table onto the floor.

"Sophie!"

"It was an accident."

Mr. Francis shakes his head, then talks to the rest of the class. Sophie sniggers. "Stupid raft. Hope it sinks."

I slide my book away from her. Sometimes she messes around too much and really gets on my nerves. It's not a stupid raft. It's called *Shooting Star* and it's the *best raft ever*. Ben and me are going to build it together. He got the idea last summer after we watched a film on TV about two men escaping from prison on a raft. They floated down a river, over rocks and rapids, and their raft turned over a lot, but they kept getting back on. It looked really dangerous but like lots of fun.

Ben sketched a raft and we made a list of all the things that we needed, like pieces of wood and floats. The next day we saw some old buoys on the shore, and Ben and me got some planks of wood from a warehouse. We were going to build it over the summer holidays, but then Ben started hanging out with some new friends. I still wanted to build it and kept on at him to help, but he was never around. But that was before he went away. I thought he'd forgotten all about the raft, but then suddenly he sent me a proper drawing and instructions so I could make a start before he comes home.

I reach down, pick up my pencil, and begin drawing again. I add another plank of wood and then a sail. Ben said it would take us ages, but when we'd finished, we'd take it on the sea and paddle between the old and new piers. He said we could take sandwiches and drinks and stay on it all day. I wish I was down at the cave working on *Shooting Star* now. I wish I could work on it all the time.

"Dan...Dan!" I finish shading one of the sails and look up. Mr.

Francis is leaning over with his knuckles on the desk. "I think you and I should have a chat."

I look around the room. The rest of the class have picked up their pens and started writing, except for Sophie, who's smirking because I'm in trouble again.

"What have I done? I was only drawing.... She—"

"It's nothing to do with that," says Mr. Francis.

"What is it, then?"

"Not here. Come with me."

I stand up and look at Sophie. "Don't touch my stuff."

She grins. "Don't want to anyway."

"Dan, now, please... and tuck your shirt in."

I half tuck my shirt in as I follow Mr. Francis across the class-room. He's found out about the sharks. The security guard must have been watching all the time, like on *Caught on Camera*, and now he's phoned the school. But I didn't see any cameras, and even if there were, Ben told me half the security cameras in shops are fake. If it's not the sharks, it must be Alex.

My heart starts to thud and I can feel the blood pumping in my head. I take a deep breath. I can't let Mr. Francis see that I'm worried. He stops in front of me and points to a chair in the *quiet room*. It's not really quiet. It's not even a room. It's just a place in the corner away from the rest of the class with two chairs and a table and two book-cases for walls. Mr. Francis sits down in one chair. I sit in the other.

"So, Dan," says Mr. Francis in a soft voice. "Let's talk about what happened yesterday."

I'm right. It's the sharks.

"At the aquarium."

Elliott's snitched.

I glance through the gap in the books. Sophie's got a nasty smile on her face, like she can't wait to see what's going to happen next.

"Dan. Pay attention to me, not her. Come on." Mr. Francis leans forward and stares at me like he's concerned. I don't know where to look, only that I don't want to look at him. It must be about Ben; something's happened to him. But I don't want to talk about him. I can't talk about him. I need to talk about something else.

"Is it about Rex?"

"What?"

I try to look him in the eye. "Rex, my hamster. Is he dead?"

"No." Mr. Francis looks at me, puzzled. "No, no." He shakes his head. "It's nothing to do with your hamster."

"If it's about my homework, I've done it. I just forgot to bring it in." Mr. Francis holds up his hand. "Dan, stop. It's not your homework."

"Is it—"

"It's your behavior, Dan. The way you acted out yesterday. And Miss Harris says you were disruptive in her class this morning."

I puff the air out of my cheeks. *Phew.* Is that all it's about?

"You never used to act like that. You were doing well at the end of last term; you got to lessons on time, seemed to be happy. Mrs. Edmondson even said you were starting to enjoy French!"

"No one enjoys French."

Mr. Francis smiles. "Well...I thought that was a stretch. But can you hear what I'm saying?"

I shrug. I can't think of any comebacks. I'm just glad it's not about Ben.

"Dan." He sighs. "All I'm saying is that last term you seemed to be happy and this term you don't."

"I'm all right." I smile convincingly. "I'm just tired. Rex kept me awake."

"Dan, seriously now."

"But it's true! He was running around all night."

"Couldn't you move him?"

"Tried that. But it won't happen again."

He looks at me closely, like he doesn't believe me. "Why not?"

"I jammed a peg in his wheel."

Mr. Francis picks up his pen. I think he's given up. I glance through the gap in the books. Sophie has her fingers in her mouth, pulling it wide apart so she looks like a duck. Mr. Francis says something.

"Dan!"

I look back at him. "Yes?"

"Did you hear me? I said we're all here to help."

"I'm fine. I don't need any help."

Mr. Francis looks at me for a long time. I hate it when teachers do that. It's like they're TV detectives who use silence to make the criminal confess. But I'm not going to tell him anything. I'm not going to talk about—

"Dan, is it your—"

The five-minute bell rings. The class starts to chatter. I've just got to keep quiet for five more minutes and then I can get out of here.

Mr. Francis rubs his face like he's tired.

"Maybe we should arrange for some counseling, Dan...with Mrs. Green." He pauses. "What do you think?"

I stare at the ground. I knew it. He wanted to talk about Ben all along.

"What do you think? Dan?"

"I'll put Rex in the shed," I mumble.

"You know that's not what I meant."

Everyone else in my class is packing up and putting their books in their bags. Mr. Francis stands up and turns to the class. "Okay. It's time for you to go...quietly!"

The classroom door jolts open. Some boys from the after-school science club are pushing each other outside the door, trying to get in.

"Science club, can you wait for the room to clear, please?"

I stand up. If I'm quick, I can escape before Mr. Francis turns around. I walk behind him and squeeze in between the gap in the bookcases.

The room is full of boys and girls running around in a whirlwind to see who can get out the door first. I push my way through.

"Yes, Sarah. I said it's very good.... Dan, can you—"

I'm halfway to the door. Sophie hands me my bag and we push our way through the science club.

"Dan!"

I keep pushing toward the door.

"What did he want?" she shouts over the noise.

"Nothing."

"He must've wanted something."

"He said I was doing well."

"Liar. Tell me."

I keep walking. I'm not going to tell her what it was about. She doesn't know anything about Ben. All she knows is that we're building a raft and she thinks it's stupid anyway. She runs to catch up with me. I wait for her to ask me again, but she's grinning like she's thinking about something else. She puts her hand on my shoulder.

"Come on," she says. "Let's go and get Shark Face."

7

Alex: No worries!

I'm in the after-school guitar club. Mrs. Hunter is sitting waiting for me to join the rest of the class. She's looking at my hands. It's like they glow infrared with all the cracks and sores.

"I'm just tuning," I say.

Mrs. Hunter smiles and tells me to join them when I can. Jake, Hannah, and Emma are sitting in a semicircle around her. I turn the keys on the end of my guitar. I tune B straight away, but C is too high and D is too low. It's no good. I try again, but I still can't get either of them. Dad says what do I expect when I spray a liter of disinfectant on the strings every day? My dad exaggerates everything about my OCD. It's not a liter—that's like three cans of Coke. But I do know it's enough to make my strings rust so badly I have to change them every week. The power light flashes on my tuner. I go through lots of disinfectant, and it takes me so long to tune that I go through lots of batteries too.

"Here." Emma's standing beside me with her tuner in her hand. I want to take it. It's not her fault that I can't.

"I'll leave it here," she whispers. She places the tuner on the table, and we both sit down.

"So, Emma," Mrs. Hunter says, "have you prepared your piece and worked on all the things we discussed last week, the rhythm and relaxing your fingers?"

"Yes." Emma leans over her guitar as the sun shines through the window. She places her fingers on the frets and starts to play "Photograph" by Ed Sheeran.

I tune the rest of my strings, then find my pack of disinfectant wipes and wipe my hands, then my guitar for the last time.

Then another last time. Then another last time. Then another.

The room goes dark as the sun goes behind a cloud. I wipe another last time.

I listen as Emma plays the opening bars, watching her fingers move over the strings. It's hard for her to get every chord because her hands are tiny. Her hair falls down over her face as she sings the line about eyes never closing.

Dr. Patrick suggested to Mum that playing guitar might help me with my worries and anxiety. Mum said she'd need to talk to Dad, so he came around before he started the night shift guarding the building and we had one of our family meetings where Dad said he wanted to help but that it was getting really expensive, me seeing Dr. Patrick as well as having guitar lessons. I told him if it worked maybe I wouldn't have to see Dr. Patrick so much. I think they must have had a chat after I went to bed, because I started lessons with Mrs. Hunter the next week.

Emma plays the last chord. Jake tells her she was really good and Mrs. Hunter claps her hands. Emma's face turns red, like it always does.

"You need to get used to applause!" Mrs. Hunter says. Emma turns even redder and she looks at the floor.

"Okay, Alex. Let's see if you've picked up on what we talked about last week. Just remember to smooth it out and think rhythm, rhythm, rhythm."

I wipe my palms on my trousers. I've been practicing loads, so hopefully I've improved since last week. I wipe my palms again.

Rhythm. I need to think about the rhythm—

Wait. What's that white mark on Mrs. Hunter's blouse? Is it bird poop?

It's toothpaste!

"Everything all right, Alex?"

"Umm...yes." I try to block the thought out.

"Okay," Mrs. Hunter says. "Just remind us of what you're going to play."

It's bird poop. It's—

" 'Paint It Black,' by the Rolling Stones," I say.

Mrs. Hunter nods. The white mark is speckled. Splashed. I lean over my guitar. The strings cut into my skin.

It's bird poop. I've seen it at home when Mum hangs clothes on the washing line.

I move the tips of my fingers across the strings and try to find the places where they don't hurt. I scrunch my eyes tight, block out the thoughts, and strum the opening chords. Mrs. Hunter taps time on the table and I start to sing. I've been playing the song all week, remembering the chords and the words because Mrs. Hunter says it looks unprofessional to read the lyrics off our phones.

Jake drops his pick on the floor. The words flow into my head as the tune flows through my fingers. I close my eyes. Slowly I escape into another world where all my worries about germs and bullies and everybody dying have disappeared. Everything is quiet and still. All I can see is darkness and all I can hear is the music and Mrs. Hunter tapping her hand on her knee. I search for the next chord, but my fingers slip off the strings. I open my eyes, find the chord, and the rhythm starts to flow again. Through my hair I see Mrs. Hunter looking at me as I keep playing, concentrating on my fingers and the words while everyone else around me moves in slow motion. Jake picks up his pick.

"Lovely," Mrs. Hunter says.

"You're really good!" Jake puts the pick in his mouth.

Hand-pick-floor-shoes-dirt-outside-pavement-outside-dirt-shoes-floor-pick-hand

I stare at him in horror. He chews on the pick like he doesn't know what's happening. I look at Emma, then Mrs. Harris. I think they're staring at me like I'm an alien.

I look back down at my guitar. *It's in my head, not theirs. It's in my head, not theirs.*

That's what Dr. Patrick would say. *It's my problem. It's nothing to do with them.*

Hand-pick-floor-shoes-dirt-outside-pavement-outside-dirt-shoes-floor-pick-hand-germs on the pick, germs on Jake's hand, germs in Jake's mouth, on his tongue, all the way through his body.

"Okay, now you, Jake—oh, and while it's in my head, remember the lesson is on Wednesday, not Thursday, next week," says Mrs. Hunter.

I look down at my guitar, feel Emma still staring at me. I wish guitar lessons were every day. I wish I was still playing. I wish I was Alex without gloves. I wish I was Alex with no worries.

I go to the bathroom as soon as the lesson finishes, to wash my guitar and my hands over and over again until I think they're clean so I can put on my gloves.

The corridor is empty when I go back out. Everyone seems to have gone home, and the only noise I can hear is the hum of the floor polisher as the janitor cleans the hall. I check left and right just in case Dan and Sophie have waited for me, but even if they stayed behind they'd wait for me outside, like they usually do.

I walk slowly down the corridor. I want to go home, but I don't want to get beaten up on the way. I turn the corner. Emma is standing by the bulletin board. She smiles when she sees me. I smile back and stop beside her.

"You were really good," she says quietly.

"You too."

She chuckles shyly, then we both look at the bulletin board in silence. There are announcements for the Year Elevens for when they take their GCSEs. Things about anxiety and stress and how to study smart. There's a picture of Oscar Wilde with a quote—"Be yourself; everyone else is taken"—and next to it are some new pictures of the Year Ten trip to Japan.

Someone shouts behind me. My heart jumps as voices echo down the corridor.

Two boys from Year Ten run past me, laughing, and disappear around the corner. I let out my breath. I'm glad it's not Dan and Sophie; they must have got tired of waiting after all. Out of the corner of my eye I can see Emma looking at me, concerned. I hear a buzz. Emma reaches into her bag and gets out her phone.

"My mum's here," she says.

I hitch my guitar up on my back, and me and Emma walk out the main doors. It's raining outside. Cars and buses are passing by with their windshield wipers on. Emma waves toward a yellow car pulled in by the bus stop.

"I'll ask if you can have a lift if you want?"

I shake my head. "It's okay." I look into the car. I don't want to get wet or picked on by Dan or Sophie, but I also don't want to sit next to Emma's dog in the back of the car.

"Okay," she says. "See you tomorrow."

"Yes."

Emma runs off. I'll see her tomorrow, but we won't talk. She knows what's happening. All the boys and girls in my class know what's happening. But no one says anything. Especially not me.

I walk over the crosswalk and along the pavement, taking big strides and making sure I don't step on any dog or bird poop. Mum told me once that I should be happy when it rains, because it washes the poop away, but it doesn't: it just makes the germs spread out like an erupting volcano so that they run all across the pavement into the gutter.

I used to walk home with Elliott until the bullying started. We would talk about the war documentaries he watched with his dad, and I'd tell him about my *Star Wars* characters and that when I go to stay with my dad we watch *Battlestar Galactica* DVDs all weekend. Except when Lizzie stays. Then we have to watch things like *101 Dalmatians* and *Spirited Away*.

I stop at the corner of The Drive and Cromwell Road. When I walked with Elliott, it seemed to take five minutes to get home, but now it feels like hours. I wish he was here; he might talk about weird things like dead presidents, but it makes the time go much quicker.

I walk toward the grocery store; some kids from our school are outside. I slow down, check for Sophie and Dan, but as I get closer I see it's older kids from Year Ten. I put my head down and skirt around them. I don't care that the rain is coming down harder. I'm just glad I'm going to get home without being beaten up.

I put my music on, then walk along Church Road. There are more shops here, with wide roads leading off toward the seafront and hotels. I reach an intersection where the red man is lit up bright on the traffic lights. I reach out to touch the Wait button.

Hundreds of people have touched it. Thousands, millions. Zillions. Don't touch it.

I'll be here all day. It's filthy.

It's okay.

I go to press the button.

Wait! Did you ever see anyone clean one?

I've seen the trucks with brushes to clean the gutters and men spraying jet washers to blast chewing gum off the pavement, but—

I take my hand away, look around, and hope that someone else will come along and press the button and turn the red man green.

"Hey, Shark Face!"

My heart jumps. I turn around.

Ah! No! Dan and Sophie are walking along the pavement toward me. Dan's chewing gum and Sophie's got a massive grin on her face. How did they find me? If ever there was a time to press the button, it's now. But I can't.

"What's wrong, think you'll get electrocuted?" shouts Dan.

I look back at the crossing. All I've got to do is reach out and touch the button, then run down the road and I'm home.

Just do it. Just do it.

Someone nudges me in the back.

"What's wrong, waiting for Mummy to hold your hand?"

I stare ahead, pretending I haven't heard, wishing the lights would change to red so I could cross. Dan pushes me in the back again. *Leave me alone. Please leave me alone.* My stomach fills with worms. I need to get away. There's a blue car coming, a red car, a black one. If I go now, I could make it to the halfway island, but they'd catch me there. I wish the red man would change now, but I'm stuck like he is, with nowhere to go. I've got to run—a red car, a white van—I put my foot out onto the road.

8

Dan: Bull's-eye

"Where are you going?" I grab Shark Face's guitar and pull him back onto the pavement. That was close: a white van nearly hit him. He might be really weird, but I don't actually want him to die.

"What do you want?" Shark Face pulls his arm away and blinks at me through the rain.

"Nothing," I say. "Just walking home."

Sophie grabs his bag off his shoulder. "Got any money?" she asks.

"No. Can you please give me my—"

Sophie drops the bag on the ground. "Just a sandwich box," she says. "And the nerd's books." She kicks the bag, and Shark Face's books spill out into a puddle on the pavement. I wait for Shark Face to pick them up, but he just looks at me with his gloved fingers spread out.

"Check his pockets, Dan."

"I haven't got any money," says Shark Face. "I used it to catch the bus."

I go to check, but Shark Face is so used to this that he's already turning his pockets inside out. Two Year Nines walk toward us. Me and Sophie stare at them as they step over Shark Face's books and walk on. Sophie presses her face up close to Shark Face's. He scrunches his face like she's got bad breath.

"No one cares about you," she says. "No one likes you. Not even Elliott."

"He does." Shark Face steps back and wipes the rain out of his eyes.

"Aww, he's crying, Dan."

"I'm not," says Shark Face.

"You will be in a minute," Sophie says. "Shall we tell him, Dan?"

"Yeah," I say. I don't know what Sophie's going to say. She presses her finger against Shark Face's chest.

"Elliott only used to talk to you because he felt sorry for you."

"No, he didn't."

"Are you calling me a liar?" Sophie turns and looks at me. "It's true. You were there, weren't you, Dan?"

"Yeah," I say. "He said he was only your friend because he thought you were pathetic for spending all your time in the bathroom."

"That's not true!" Shark Face stares at Sophie.

"It is," says Sophie, "and then he stopped talking to you because he got fed up waiting all day for you to poop." She laughs.

Shark Face scrunches his face up. For a second, I feel a bit sorry for him, but it's his fault we pick on him because he makes it so easy. Sometimes I wish he'd fight back. It would be more fun if he did that, but he never does. Shark Face looks up and down the road like he's desperate for help, but people are too busy on their phones.

"Come on, Soph, let's leave him," I say. We've picked on him enough today and I'm beginning to get bored.

"Why? Are you going soft?"

"No, I'm getting wet."

Sophie bends down, picks up Shark Face's books, and jams them in his bag. "You dare say anything..." She throws the bag at Shark Face. He doesn't even try to catch it. He doesn't even flinch. It just hits him and falls back onto the ground. He's useless. Sophie chuckles, then stands right in front of him.

"Tell me something," she says.

"What?"

"Why does your face always look like you've pooped your pants?"

Shark Face just stands still like Batman when he's been frozen by Mr. Freeze. Me and Sophie start laughing.

"Why do you always say that?" Shark Face's eyes are bulging like marbles.

"Because it's true," I say.

"It's not."

"It is," Sophie says. "And you're weird, and your sister's weird too. Elliott says she's just like you. He said she stank of disinfectant when he went around to your house."

Shark Face swallows like he's got a golf ball stuck in his throat, then glances across the road. Old Hargreaves, the geography teacher, is walking in our direction. The lights turn red and the crossing starts to beep. Shark Face begins to turn away. Sophie grabs hold of his guitar and he wriggles like a cat trying to get away in a cartoon. Old Hargreaves has stopped by a real estate agent's window.

"It's okay. Hargreaves isn't looking," I say.

Shark Face looks at me like he's going to cry. He's such a wimp. I clench my fist.

"Aren't you going to pick up your bag?" I ask.

"No. I can't."

I pick up his bag. We can't leave it here. Someone will find it, report it to the school, and the teachers will want to know how it got there. "Take it!" I push the bag into Shark Face's stomach. He squirms like it's a knife, then turns away.

"Hit him, Dan," says Sophie. "Where it hurts." She's got a mad look on her face.

But I don't want to hit him. I look at the back of his head, his wet hair plastered to his head. He's so weak it makes me mad. I gather spit in my mouth and take aim. My spit flies through the air. Some of it sprays on Shark Face's guitar, but the big lumpy bit lands on the back of his head.

"Oh my God, Dan!" Sophie puts her hand over her mouth and laughs. "Bull's-eye!" she says.

Alex: I'm not Justin Bieber!

I'm sitting at the dining table. My head is still tingling where Dan's spit landed on it. I know it's not there anymore, but I can still feel it. I was in the shower for an hour, washing and scrubbing until I was happy it was all gone. But now the spot is so sore I can't tell if it's there or not.

Mum's reading a magazine while she drinks a cup of coffee. She was late for work again and the supermarket manager made her do inventory in the storeroom all morning, which she hates because she likes being on the checkouts, where she can look out the window. I can't tell if she's mad with me or not, but she's been reading for ages, and it's so quiet that the only noise is the sound of my knife and fork on the plate and the distant music from Lizzie playing on the PS3.

I scoop my beans onto my fork and swallow, but my throat is aching so much it's like I'm eating bullets.

Mum puts her mug down on the table. I glance up at her.

"I'm sorry I made you late."

"It's okay," she says softly. "Sarah says he would have put me there anyway because I chat to the customers too much. Which is true." I try to smile.

"What about you? Music lesson go okay?"

I look down at my plate.

"Hey, what's wrong?"

I've got spit in my hair and it's burning through my head.

"Alex? Has the OCD been bad today?"

I nod and hope she can't see the tears bulging behind my eyes. I wish I could tell her about Dan and Sophie, but if I did she'd go straight to school tomorrow and everyone would know I snitched. Besides, I've only got to survive one more day and then it's the weekend, but the trouble with the weekend is that it's only two days of peace before the bullying starts all over again.

I scoop up my fork and try to swallow more beans. Mum puts her hand on top of mine.

"Did you want to talk about it?"

Mum gently taps the back of my hand, trying to make me feel better. I don't mind her touching me because she washed her hands before we sat down. "We'll sort this, Alex," she says. "I'll chat to Dad, then we'll make an appointment in the morning. Okay?"

I nod and try to smile. Dr. Patrick might be able to help make my OCD go away, but he can't get rid of Dan and Sophie. Mum picks up her phone. I put my plate in the dishwasher and walk out into the hall.

Lizzie is in the sitting room, kneeling down on the floor, playing *LittleBigPlanet*. The main character, Sackboy, is wearing a poncho and a sombrero. He's supposed to be building a new world on the planet Bunkum, but Lizzie seems to spend all her time jamming the buttons, trying to get him to jump over a skipping rope. I peer out the window. The sun is going down, making long shadows across the garden. I look back at my sister. I wish I could sit down and play *LBP*, solve all the puzzles for Sackboy, and help him build his planet.

The rope gets tangled around Sackboy's feet. Lizzie huffs, then turns to me.

"What are you doing?"

"Nothing."

"Have you been crying?"

"No."

"Then why are your eyes watering?"

"I got soap in them."

Lizzie looks at me like she doesn't believe me, then holds out the controller.

"Can you help me? He's got all tangled up."

I smile. She's only on level 1 and already she's stuck on the rope, but I'm too tired and upset, and my head is tingling so much I think I'm going to have to get in the shower again. Lizzie holds the controller out farther, like she's got an extendable arm.

"Pleeeeease." She does the annoying "please" face that she puts on when she wants something—*pleeeeease* can I stay up? *Pleeeease* can my friend come for a sleepover? *Pleeeease* can I have an ice cream? It's even more annoying when she flutters her eyelids and says, *"Pretty* pleeeease, Alex."

Argh! She just did it again and won't stop until I help.

I take the controller, wipe it, and press X. Sackboy starts jumping over the skipping rope. It turns faster and faster and I keep pressing the X until the skipping rope blurs and my thumb starts to hurt. Lizzie laughs.

"He's going to do it, Alex!"

The rope stops turning and Sackboy jumps up and down, celebrating with his hands in the air. I hand the controller back to Lizzie.

"No, you do it," she says. "As soon as you go, I'll get stuck again."

"I can't," I say. "I've got homework."

She starts to blink her eyes. My head starts to tingle again.

"Ple—"

"No! I said I can't! I've got to go."

"Where?"

"Doesn't matter."

I throw the controller on the floor. Lizzie gives me a weird look, like she knows there's something wrong. All I want to do is go to my room. I stand up and walk into the hall.

"Alex, what's going on?" Mum takes her ear away from the phone.

I don't answer, but I can hear Lizzie saying something about me being grumpy as I rush up the stairs. I feel bad about shouting at Lizzie. It's not her fault my head is tingling where the spit landed. She doesn't know what Dan and Sophie did. I go into the bathroom, take off my shirt, and lean over the bathtub. I turn on the shower and wash my hair again, and then again. My head is sore, my hands are stinging, and I feel worn out. It's like the water washes away all the germs but takes all my energy with them down the drain.

After I dry my hair on a towel, I sit down on my bed and pull the books out of my bag. Dan and Sophie's footprints are all over the covers. It's as if they've followed me like a herd of elephants all the way back to my house. I clean the covers with my wipes, then flip the lid of the laptop. It's so dark now that the screen lights my room like a lamp.

I've got stacks of history homework to do. I google *the Great Plague of London* and read about how 15 percent of the population died in the heat of one summer, but nothing goes into my brain because all I can think about is Dan's spit on my hair. I want to wash it again, but I read somewhere that if you wash hair too much it starts to fall out. It's bad having spit on my head, but it would be even worse if I was bald.

I'm going to go bald. I'm not.

I'm going to go bald and everyone will think I'm really ill.

I put my hand on my hair to try and stop it disappearing.

"Alex!"

Mum's standing in the doorway with the phone in her hand.

"I'm going bald!"

"What?"

"Nothing."

Mum gives me a sideways look and holds out the phone. "It's Dad," she says. "He wants a word."

I take the phone. Mum walks out of the room, shaking her head like she's trying to work out what I just said. I wipe the phone and put it to my ear.

"Hi, Dad."

"Hello, mate, what are you up to?"

"Doing homework."

"Mum says you've had a bad day."

"Yeah." I sigh.

"What's up?"

Got called Shark Face all day. Got my books trampled on. Got spat at on my way home.

"Alex?"

"Nothing much. Just stuff."

"You sure?"

"Yeah, I'm fine."

"Well, you don't sound it, but I've got something that'll cheer you up."

Great! Dad's built a rocket, and me and him are going to fly to Mars, away from Dan and Sophie.

"How would you like to see *The Force Awakens*?"

We're not going to Mars but to the cinema!

"Yes!" I clench my fist. I've wanted to see *The Force Awakens* for ages. "Have you got the DVD?"

"No," Dad says. "It's not out yet."

"But they stopped showing it at the cinema after Christmas."

"They did, but there's a special showing tomorrow evening. I know you don't like surprises, but this way you have less time to worry, and it won't be so crowded as it was before."

I pick up Han Solo from the windowsill. Dad tried to take me to the cinema over the Christmas holidays, but I took ages in the bathroom and then I couldn't get in the car because I'd dreamed someone had stolen it the night before and cut the brakes. Dad got really annoyed with me, but not as annoyed as I was with myself. I've seen every *Star Wars* film except that one, and it was even worse when I got back to school because everyone was talking about it.

Dad tells me I need to be ready by seven o'clock and I can't be late, because he's buying the tickets tonight. It means I'll have to start getting ready as soon as I get home from school in case my OCD goes crazy, but I'm so happy I'm going I don't want to think about that now.

I put Han Solo back on the windowsill next to Chewbacca.

"Alex, are you still there?"

I smile even though Dad can't see me. I lean Han Solo over. "Chewie, we're home!"

"What?"

"It's what Han Solo says."

Dad laughs. "I've never heard you say that."

"Me and Elliott used to do it."

"He could come too if you like."

I think of Elliott at school after Christmas running around, then curling up and balancing a ball on his head, pretending to be BB-8. I only knew what it was because I'd seen the film trailers on the laptop.

"No, it's okay," I say.

"Why not? You two really got along."

"I know. But I just want to go with you." Dad goes quiet like he knows I'm lying. I would really like Elliott to come too because he loves *Star Wars* nearly as much as I do, but we might get seen by other kids from school and he'd get picked on again.

"Okay," Dad says. "Maybe another time. I'll get off now, leave you to your homework."

"Okay. Be safe."

Dad doesn't reply, but he has to say it. His phone could

self-destruct, or a burglar might break into his building and beat Dad up in the dark. My chest begins to ache. I wish he was coming home tonight; that way I could make sure nothing bad happens to him. The house is quieter since he and Mum split up. Mum said they still love each other but are happier when they're apart, which is how I feel about Lizzie sometimes, but right now I want Dad to say "Be safe" so the phone won't blow up in his hand.

"Dad, are you still there?"

"Yeah, I'll see you soon."

"No, Dad. Please say it. Be safe."

"I've got to go and check the alarms."

"Dad! *Pleeeease*," I say, like Lizzie.

"Okay," he says. "Be safe, mate. . . . But, Alex?"

"Yes."

"We need to stop this soon."

"I will, Dad. Promise."

"Good night, mate."

The phone goes quiet. I take a deep breath and lie back on my bed. I can't wait to go to the cinema, but I wish Elliott could come too. My head starts to tingle again.

I've got to wash my hair. I've done it ten times. Then do it again. No. No!

I get up, take my guitar out of its case, and sit down on my bed. I need to do my homework, but I can't do anything until the thoughts go away. I wipe the strings, then pinch the fingers of my left hand on the frets. As I play, the strings vibrate through the guitar against my chest and make the ache ease. I play a tune. I don't know what it is, but it sounds okay, and then some lyrics come into my head so I sing them too. My worries start to float away, higher and higher, like clouds drifting across the sky. I watch them drift away from me, over the tops of tall buildings and hilltops, until they're tiny soap bubbles on the horizon, and then they disappear, and the sky is clear blue and I can feel the warmth of the sun shining brightly on my face as I float on the sea.

I hear someone giggling and open my eyes.

"Ha-ha! You're singing Justin Bieber!"

Lizzie's standing in the doorway, pointing and laughing at me.

"I wasn't."

"You were! You were singing 'Over the mountains, across the sky.' I heard you. You think you're Justin Bieber!"

"I don't....I wasn't." I feel my face burning. "I was just singing. Mum!"

"You were singing 'Be Alright.'"

"I wasn't!"

"You were. You were singing about the oceans and the sea."

"Go away," I say. "Mum!"

I stand up. Lizzie runs out. I push my door closed and lean my back against it to stop her coming back in, but I can still hear her giggling on the other side. I take a deep breath and bump the back of my head against the door. I can't wait to see *The Force Awakens*, but this day is getting worse the longer it goes on. I've been spat on and I'm going bald, and now I can't even escape from all my worries and Dan and Sophie without getting Justin Bieber songs stuck in my head.

Dan: There's a dragon in my brother's bedroom

My mum's on the phone in the kitchen.

Hello, love, she mouths, and then points at the phone.

Who is it? I mouth back.

Mr. Francis.

What? Mr. Francis! Why's he calling? Mr. Hargreaves must have seen us get Shark Face. We should have waited until he'd turned off the main road. I reach for the cookie tin and try not to look worried. Mum puts her hand over the mouthpiece.

"Where have you been?" she whispers.

"Down the seafront, checking on *Shooting Star.*"

"I said only on weekends. You've got school during the week." I grab three cookies and shrug.

My mum shakes her head, then takes her hand away from the phone. "Yes... yes, I understand. He's just come in now."

I feel guilty for lying to her, but she'd be so mad if she found out what I've just done to Shark Face.

I go up the stairs to my room. Mum's still on the phone—something about how she'll talk to me and to Dad. I shut my bedroom

73

door loud enough so she thinks I've gone in, but really I'm crouched down on the landing. I do it all the time when I'm in trouble. Ben used to do it too. Sometimes we'd sit together and try to guess which one of us our mum was talking about. It used to be Ben who was in trouble for walking out of school or stealing drinks from shops, but now that he's gone away, the only person Mum talks about is me.

I crawl to the edge of the stairs.

"I know," I hear her murmur. "It's hard to know what to do. Yes, I'm sorry.... Wednesday will be fine."

I imagine Mr. Francis on the other end of the line, writing my name down in his datebook. I'll say it was a mistake. I was just spitting my chewing gum out, and Shark Face's head got in the way.

Mum's voice grows louder as she walks out into the hall.

"No, I don't know. Like I said, he's only just got in."

I poke my head around the banister. My mum's at the bottom of the stairs, going through my bag!

"Red, you say? Yes, I've found it. I'll make sure that he does." Math homework? Is that all this is about?

"Okay, we'll see you Wednesday."

No! I don't want Mum and Dad coming down to the school again.

The phone beeps as she presses the End Call button. I see her shadow at the bottom of the stairs. I crawl across the landing, open the door, and creep into my bedroom.

"Dan?" She's halfway up the stairs. I pick up my sketch pad quickly.

"Dan?" She knocks on the door.

"Yes."

She leans into my room. "What are you doing?"

"Just drawing. Ben wants me to design a sail for *Shooting Star*." I show her the drawing that I actually drew last night. Mum looks at it like it's blank.

"So...that was Mr. Francis."

I start to draw.

"He said he'd been trying to get me at work. He said he tried to talk to you today, but you just walked off."

I shade the sail.

"Dan? Are you listening?"

"Yes....It was boring," I mumble.

"What was?"

"The lesson. Him."

"He was just concerned."

I shrug.

"Do you want to talk about it?"

"Not really."

Mum sits down at the end of my bed.

"Are you sure? That's the third time he's called this term."

"It's nothing." I sigh. "He's just picking on me."

"I don't think Mr. Francis is like that. Is it that Sophie girl?"

"No." I look her in the eyes. She waits for me to say something else, but I stay silent. I know she doesn't like Sophie. She thinks she's a bad influence on me, that my behavior has changed since we became friends. I don't think it's true, but I suppose I do get into more trouble when Sophie's around.

I pick up my Xbox controller. Mum's still looking at me.

"We should do something together." She claps her hands like she's had a great idea. "I'm going to your gran's for dinner tomorrow. Want to come?" she asks.

"No." I can't think of anything worse.

"Why not? You've not seen her in ages."

I shrug. "All she does is knit and watch *Pointless* all the time."

"Dan, that's not true."

"Yes, it is."

"Well, I'll think of something we can do."

I get up and walk over to Rex's cage.

"Dan, are you listening?"

"Yeah." I flick my fingers across the cage bars so Rex will come out of his red house. Mum sighs, then pauses for a bit. "Dan, this is getting tiring. You're not interested in anything or anyone. Mr. Francis is concerned about your attitude and your progress, and so are your dad and I. Dan." She stands next to me. "I know this is hard for you, but Mr. Francis thinks your behavior is linked to what's happened to Ben."

"It's nothing to do with Ben!" I shout.

Mum jumps back, startled. "Okay," she says. "We just thought—"

"Well, you thought wrong! I'm all right. You're all keeping on at me, but there's nothing the matter with me."

"Okay," she says softly, trying to calm me down.

I look back at the cage. Rex has come out of his house and is sleepily nibbling the end of my finger.

Mum sighs. "Come down and eat something with me and your dad when he gets in."

I squeak at Rex through my teeth.

"Dan, did you hear?"

"Yes," I mumble.

Mum walks toward the door. "And don't forget to feed Horace."

"I won't."

Mum walks out of my room and down the stairs. I put my pad down and go next door into Ben's room. The bed is made and there are pictures of all the Brighton & Hove Albion players on his wall. His Xbox controllers are on his beanbag, and *The River Wild* DVD case is open and empty on the floor. It's like Ben's just got up to go to the bathroom and will be back any second. The room has been exactly like this for three months. When Mum cleans it, she puts everything back like it was.

I used to love coming in here, but it's horrible when Ben's bed is empty and his TV is blank. I pick up the DVD case. Me and Ben watched the film again the night before he went. We used to sit and watch it and pretend his bed was the raft and we'd dig our paddles over the side as we went down the rapids. But the night before he went we didn't do that. Ben just sat really quiet. His room has been quiet ever since. Last week I overheard Dad tell Mum the room was like a morgue.

I hear a click. I turn around and see Horace, Ben's bearded dragon, lying on a branch in his glass tank. His eyes are wide open and the skin is flapping on his neck every time he breathes. I check the temperature chart Ben has stuck to the wall. If Horace is dark, he's too cold; if he's bright green, he's too hot. Tonight his body is green like an army uniform. The chart says that's okay. Now all I've got to do is feed him.

I take the top off a plastic container and pick out a cricket. It's Horace's favorite; he licks his lips when he sees one. I drop the cricket in front of him. The cricket lands, tries to scuttle under the branch, but then *zap!* Horace's tongue shoots out and the cricket is gone.

I wish I could text Ben and tell him Horace is okay. I wish I could talk to him, but he's not allowed to have a phone. He's not even allowed to send emails. But he is allowed to send letters, because he's not dead. It's just this house and my mum and dad that make it feel like he is.

I give Horace two more crickets, put the lid on his tank, and go back into my room. I pull open my bedside drawer, lift up my comics, and find the last letter Ben sent.

Dear Danny,

Hope you're good. I am. I've made a new friend. He came in last week. His name's xxxxx and he comes from xxxxxx but he supports xxxxxxx. He's great but he gets a bit fed up because this place is a long way from his home. We play Call of Duty and FIFA on the Xbox all the time. He's better than you but not as good as me. Ha! I've got to go to bed early tonight because they still make us get up really early in the mornings. We've got lessons all day tomorrow. History in the morning. It's so boring.

How are you getting on with Shooting Star? You can take the drawing to the cave if you want. But don't leave it there because it'll get damp.

And how's the Observation Tower going? It must be nearly finished. Can't wait to go up it when I get home. Tell Dad I miss going to see the Albion, but I get to see the goals on television.

I've got to go now. I want to get in the shower before the other kids use up all the hot water. Hope you have a good week at school and remember what I said, you've got to be a big fish and eat all the others up or they will eat you.

Ha!
I'll send another letter next week
                    Ben
PS Come on, you Gulls!

I glance over the letter again. I wish the detention center people hadn't crossed out Ben's new friend's name and who he supports. Ben doesn't send many letters, so it's horrible when bits are crossed out. Mum said they do it deliberately to protect the young person's identity, but I wish they didn't, because I'd like to poke fun at Five X when his team loses. It's got seven letters so it could be Chelsea, Arsenal, Everton, or Watford, but it might not even be a team in the Premier League. I've tried to work his name out too, but there are so many names with five letters—Aaron, Billy, Chris, David—and it might even be a nickname. I gave up trying to work it out, so I just call him Five X instead.

A car engine rumbles outside. I leave the letter on my bed and walk over to the window. Dad gets out with his briefcase in his hand and waves when he sees me. I wave back and he smiles, but he won't be smiling after Mum's told him they've got to go down to my school again.

The front door opens and I hear Dad talking to Mum in the kitchen. He's saying something about sales of a new TV being slow and that two sales assistants are out sick. My dad owns a TV shop in town, which is great because we get the biggest TVs at home, but it also means he's really busy when people are out sick. He tells Mum that Maurice should be back tomorrow. Then Mum says she's tired too, from answering the phone at the NHS call center all day.

Then it goes quiet and I hear Mum say something about Mr. Francis and I don't want to hear them talk about me being in trouble again and that I don't care about anything. I do care about some things. I care about Ben and *Shooting Star.*

I reach under my bed and get the cardboard tube that Ben sent his drawing in. I slide the paper out and flatten it on the floor with my hands. It's huge and has lots of details, like the one the architect did for the back extension, except it's more interesting than that.

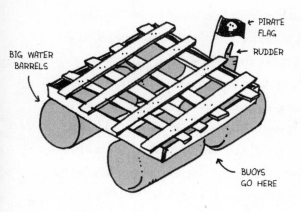

PIRATE
FLAG

RUDDER

BIG WATER
BARRELS

BUOYS
GO HERE

OTHER THINGS WE NEED:

* BIG WATER BARRELS (ASK DAD IF WE CAN HAVE THE ONES IN THE GARDEN)
* BUOYS (IF DAD WON'T LET US)
* EMPTY BOTTLES (WE ALREADY GOT SOME BUT NEED LOADS)
* SAIL (ASK MUM FOR A SHEET)
* RUDDER
* ANCHOR
* PIRATE FLAG

I smile when I read *pirate flag*. I wish it was Saturday tomorrow so I could work on her, but most of all I wish the next six weeks pass quickly so Ben can come home. I'll tell him that.

I reach up onto my bed and grab my notebook and pencil. Then I read Ben's letter again so I can answer all the things he wrote. But when I read it again it sounds like he's having a brilliant time and not missing me like I miss him. Sometimes I wonder if he feels bad about what he's done. But he never writes anything about what happened. It's like he's on holiday. I wish I was with him. Maybe he's just trying to be brave. He wouldn't have sent me the drawing of *Shooting Star* if he didn't miss me.

Ben doesn't write very often, but I write to him nearly every day.

Dear Ben,
  I'm okay. I went down the cave last weekend and worked on Shooting Star. I've put all the bottles we collected in a corner

81

and I've tried to nail the base plank to the frame but it's really hard without having you to help. I'll try again this weekend.

We went to the aquarium yesterday. It wasn't as good as when we go but I got a boy to steal some dolphins and sharks. I'll ask Mum if I can send you one. I miss you but I've made some new friends. One of them is a girl!! Sophie's got really short hair and swears a lot and sometimes she gets me into trouble. I think I'm in trouble at school now, but I'll be all right. The other kids in the class are scared of her but I'm not. I let her do what she wants.

I'm a big fish, but sometimes I don't feel like being a big fish, especially without you around.

Love, Dan

PS I'll check on the Observation Tower when I go to work on Shooting Star on Saturday.

"Dan!" Mum shouts up the stairs. "Dinner!"
I roll Ben's drawing up and slide it back under my bed.

Alex: *The Force Awakens* me

The cinema foyer is crowded with people. Parents are in line for tickets while kids run around, pretending they've got lightsabers and fighting cardboard cutouts of Darth Vader. I can't wait to see the film, but I can't wait for it to be over too, because then I can go home and be safe for the weekend. I managed to avoid Dan and Sophie at school most of the day, but I could hear them sniggering behind me in English and history and I know they told the Georges what they did to me, because George W. bumped into me in PE and asked if spit was better to wash my hair with than shampoo.

"Watch out for ground fire!"

I dodge out of the way of a boy running toward the ticket counter. He was way too close to me. Everyone is too close to me. I wish I'd brought my lightsaber with me so I could swish it around and keep them all away.

"Here you go, mate." Dad hands me my ticket, then checks his watch. "I'm just going to the bathroom. Do you need—" He remembers I won't use the toilets. "I'll just be a moment," he says to Mum.

"May the Force be with you," Mum says.

Dad rolls his eyes, then walks off and leaves me standing with Mum and Lizzie. They're not going to watch *The Force Awakens* with us, but Mum thought it would be good for us all to have some "family time." I like it when we're all together, because it feels like we're a proper family again, but I'm also glad Lizzie isn't coming with me and Dad, because she makes slurping noises with her Coke and fidgets in her seat. The time we went to see *Ice Age* she pretended she was Scratch and munched on popcorn all the way through. I know Mum really wants us all to be together, but there's no way I'm going to watch *Kung Fu Panda 3* with them.

Mum asks me if I'm sure I don't want to go to the bathroom, because Dad loves *Star Wars* films too and will get annoyed if I have to get up halfway through. I tell her I'm okay, that I went five times before we left so I wouldn't have to go here. Then she asks me if I want a drink or any sweets, and Lizzie's telling her all the sweets she wants, but I'm not really listening. The worms in my stomach are wriggling even more because now all I can think about are the germy people coming out of the bathrooms. I try to block it out. I don't want the day to be ruined by my worries, because I've been looking forward to seeing this film for ages. I've watched all the rest on DVD. Dad told me that Darth Vader is even more frightening when he's on a big screen.

"Oh, Alex!" Mum makes me jump.

"What?"

"Isn't that—" She turns me around and points through the crowd, but there are so many people I can't tell who she's pointing at. "There. Isn't that Dan's mum?"

84

What!

My heart jumps. People are walking straight at me, swerving around me, nearly nudging my elbows.

"I don't think—"

Mum points again. *It can't be!*

"It is." She waves.

"Mum, can I get some sweets?" I pull Lizzie toward the sweets containers stacked against the wall.

"I want Mum to come."

She doesn't do anything when I want her to.

"Hi!" Mum smiles and waves again.

It's okay. So what if it is Dan's mum? Dan wouldn't go to the cinema with his—

"Oh, look, Alex. Dan's with her too."

Oh no! He would be.

"Mum, please—"

"Hi! Fiona!"

Dan's mum walks toward us. All I can see of Dan are his arms swinging as he follows behind her. I look around for Sophie—she's always with him—but the foyer is as busy as a Tube station and she could be hiding anywhere in the crowd. I look toward the bathroom and wish that Dad would come out right now and take me into the film. Dan wouldn't dare do anything if he was here.

Dad, hurry up.

"Hi!"

"Hi!"

Ah! Too late.

Our mums smile at each other. Dan's standing right in front of me, wearing a *Star Wars* T-shirt. He glares at me like he's mad that I'm here. I look at the ground and wish it would open up.

What's he doing here?

"Just the two of you?" Mum says.

"Yes, Dave's working, so I get to watch *Star Wars*! Lucky me!" Dan's mum pulls a silly face.

"Well, it could be worse. I've got *Kung Fu Panda 3*!"

They both laugh and look at Dan and me. I try to smile, but Dan's just staring at me. We're standing like dogs with our owners in the park. We're probably supposed to say hello to each other and then go running after a ball, but all I want to do is get away from him. I look around the cinema, anywhere but at Dan. If only Darth Vader wasn't a cardboard cutout, I'd run over to him and ask to borrow his lightsaber.

Mum gives me a ten-pound note. She's so happy bumping into her friend that she hasn't noticed the worried look on my face.

"Go and get some pick-and-mix," she says.

"What?"

"Pick-and-mix."

"But I don't want any."

"I know, but get some for Lizzie."

I don't want to leave Mum, but I've got no choice. I might be okay if Dan stays with his mum.

"And you, love." Dan's mum gives him a tenner too.

I'm in trouble now.

"And get me some chocolate Brazils.... How funny." She turns to my mum. "I was only saying to Dave last night how, until parents' evening, we'd never bumped into each other before, and then seeing you..." They keep talking, but their words turn to a buzz in my panic.

Dad, where are you? He's been gone so long in the bathroom that it's like he's getting back at me because I always take so long in there. Dan walks off in front of me.

"Come on, *Alex*," he says creepily, then smiles like all of a sudden he's my friend. Mum pushes me gently in the back. She doesn't know what Dan does to me at school, and there's no way she can tell, because he looks like any other kid in his T-shirt and jeans. He looks like *me*. We walk toward the sweets containers stacked high against the wall. Lizzie flips the lid of the white chocolate mice. I tell her to use the tongs, not her hands, because of the germs. Out of the corner of my eye I see Dan grab a handful of red snakes and put them in a bag. He checks that Lizzie isn't looking, then stands by my side. I wait for him to call me a name or elbow me in the ribs. He puts his head close to my ear. He wouldn't spit on me here, would he?

He grabs my arm, then whispers. "Don't you dare snitch, Sharky. And just because our mums are talking doesn't mean we're friends."

I pull my arm away. "I won't," I say. "And I know we're not friends." We look at each other for a long time. Lizzie taps my arm.

"Alex, can you hold the bag open?"

I hold the bag open with my gloves on while Lizzie gets the scoop. Dan looks over his shoulder and checks that his mum isn't watching.

"Creeps like you only pretend to like *Star Wars*," he whispers. "Bet you don't even know who Admiral Ackbar is."

"I do."

"Okay, then, who is he?"

"He's the commander of the Rebel Alliance who led operations against the Galactic Empire."

Dan looks surprised. "Who told you that? Your dad?"

"No," I say. "I've seen all the films."

I wait for him to say something else, but he just reaches out for more sweets. I didn't know he liked *Star Wars* too. I wish he didn't.

People barge past me to get to the pick-and-mix. Lizzie grabs more mice and drops them into the bag.

"Are you one of Alex's friends from school?" she asks.

"Yeah," Dan says, smiling.

"Are you watching the film with Alex?"

"No."

"Why not? He knows *everything* about *Star Wars*." Lizzie looks at me like she's proud of me, but I just want her to be quiet. "He's got lots of pictures of C-3PO and BB-8 on his bedroom wall and he can do loads of the voices too."

"Can he?" Dan looks at me like he's trying to work out if it's true.

"Yes," says Lizzie. "Do C-3PO, Alex."

"No. I can't."

"Oh, go on!"

"No."

I push Lizzie aside and look up at the film times on the big screen. *The Force Awakens* starts in ten minutes and I need to get away from Dan because Lizzie is telling him everything. If I don't shut her up soon, she'll tell him I go to sleep with Chewbacca on my bed.

"Lizzie," I say. "We need to go and pay."

We walk toward the cashiers, but Lizzie won't stop talking. "Have you got any posters on your wall?"

"Yeah, of course. Loads."

"So you love *Star Wars* as much as Alex?"

"Yeah..." He turns away from Lizzie like he's as annoyed with her as I am. "I need to pay for these," he says.

"So do we. Come on, Alex." Lizzie trails after Dan. I look at the clock again. Seven minutes. I've just got to survive seven more minutes and I'll be free of Dan.

The assistant weighs the sweets, then presses lots of buttons like he doesn't know what he's doing.

Hurry up! Hurry!

He presses more buttons and Lizzie's still yapping.

"My brother doesn't eat sweets," she says. "Because they're full of germs. But he's going on *The X Factor*!"

No! Shut up!

"Shush!" I grab hold of Lizzie and try to put my hand over her mouth to stop her words coming out.

Dan laughs.

"I'm not," I say.

Lizzie wrestles away from me. It's like she's doing this on purpose. "He is. He plays his guitar all the time and thinks he's Justin Bieber."

"Lizzie," I say. "Shut up." She runs back toward Mum. Dan is grinning at me. My chest is thudding and my face feels like it's burning red. Why did Lizzie have to go and say that? Things are bad enough without everyone at school thinking I'm going on *The X Factor*.

I pay for the sweets and leave Dan to pay for his. I just want to get to the film now, but Mum's still talking to his mum. At least Dad has finally come out of the bathroom.

"All done?" asks Mum. I give her the change.

"And you, love?" Dan nods to his mum. "I was just telling Alex's mum about your boat. How you were working on it on your own yesterday, and we thought maybe Alex could help?"

What?

"What?" Dan's eyes are wide open like he can't believe it either.

"What do you think? I thought it would be more fun if you had help." Dan's mum puts her hand on his arm.

"No way!" shouts Dan. "I'm not having *him* there." He's suddenly flipped like he does at school.

"Dan!"

"Get off me!" He wrestles his arm away. "No! He's not going near it. It's mine and Ben's." His voice cracks like he's going to cry.

"It's okay," Dad says. "He doesn't have to do it if he doesn't want to."

"No," Dan's mum says. "He should. He spent all last weekend at the cave on his own. It would be good for him, and Francesca says Alex doesn't go out much." Then she looks down at me and smiles. "You'd like to help, wouldn't you, Alex?"

Dan's staring right at me.

"Erm..." I open my mouth, but no words come out. I try to think of an excuse, but my mind is blank. I look at Mum and Dad for help, but they're already nodding their heads. It's like it's a conspiracy to get me out of the house. They can't be serious. Going outside, meeting Dan. He'll call me Shark Face all the time and hit me with pieces of wood. We'll be in a dirty, dark cavern full of rats and germs and he'll block the door so there's no escape. It can't happen! It's like all my nightmares rolled into one.

"Dan's mum says it's down by the pier, so you don't have to go far," Dad says. Then he looks at Dan. "I know it's your raft," he says. "But I'm sure you could do with some help, and I've got some spare tools I could lend you if you like."

"That'd be nice, Dan," his mum says. "You're always saying it's hard to lift things on your own."

Dan opens his eyes wide like he's saying *Get us out of this or I'll smash your face* to me. I don't want to do it either. I just want to get away from here. The foyer is beginning to empty—the film must be starting—but Dad's just standing there, smiling at Dan like he's made a friend.

"When are you down there next, Dan?"

"Don't know." Dan shrugs. "Go when I feel like it."

"And when will that be?"

"Like, never." He glares at me.

"Dan!"

Dan squirms as his mum rubs his hair. "He's terrible," she says. "He's joking all the time. He goes down on the weekends, so he'll be there tomorrow morning. He's the only boy I know who gets up earlier on the days he doesn't go to school."

"Ah! That's a shame," says Dad. "I'm going to struggle to get there because I'm working the night shift tonight."

Phew.

"I'd bring him down, but Alex is busy in the morning," says Mum.

Double phew.

I remember I'm going to see Dr. Patrick. I won't have to help Dan after—

"I'll tell you what." Dad jumps in. "It's a shame for Alex to miss out."

It's really not.

"How about I drop him down for a couple of hours in the afternoon?"

"Is that okay?" says Mum. "It means I can get on and make cakes with Lizzie." Dad nods.

"Great," says Dan's mum. "It's all working out, love." She puts her hand on Dan's shoulder. I wait for him to go off again, but it's like a storm has blown over and he's given in. I haven't, though.

"But it's our afternoon together, Dad."

"That's okay," he says. "We've got this evening, and it's half-term soon. Me and your mum can juggle things around." Dad can't wait to get rid of me; it's like he's already opened our front door and is pushing me down Grand Avenue toward the seafront.

Dan gives me a look that says *We're doomed.* Dad checks his watch. "Oops!"

At last!

"We'd better get in or we're going to miss the start. . . . But listen," he says to Dan's mum, "I'll get those tools from the garage, nothing too dangerous. Don't want them sticking each other to the walls with staple guns!"

Dan probably would.

"Oops," Mum says. "Come on, Lizzie, or we'll miss *Kung Fu*

Panda." She rolls her eyes. "Lovely to see you, Fiona. Meet for coffee sometime?"

"Yes," Dan's mum says. Then she looks at Dad.

No, don't even think it.

"Maybe we could all sit together."

No!

"We can't," blurts Dan. "We got booked seats."

Phew.

He starts to walk off and we all follow. Dan's mum says how nice it was to have met up, then whispers something about Dan's brother. I didn't know he had a brother. She says something about four months, but I don't hear anything else because Dan has pushed open the doors and music is playing loud and there's a picture of a man running around with a phone on the giant cinema screen.

"We're right at the back, Dan, row W," his mum whispers.

"We're in row E, Alex," Dad says. "Twenty-three and twenty-four."

Good, at least he's nearly the whole alphabet behind us.

We sit down in our seats and I blow out my cheeks. There are germs all over the place in here and it feels more horrible to think of them creeping around in the dark, but, worse than that, I know that Dan is sitting somewhere behind me and I'll feel his eyes burning into the back of my head.

I think about tomorrow. There must be some way out of it. Maybe I should say I'd rather spend time with Lizzie. I could offer to help her on *LittleBigPlanet* because she's been stuck on Pluto for ages. Or I could pretend to have a cold, but Mum won't fall for that. She'll just say I should get out in the fresh air.

Ah! This was supposed to be the best night, but it's turned into the worst.

I sniff. Then sniff again. There's a horrible smell coming up from the floor.

It's dog poop. It can't be. It's dog poop.

I lean forward, turn my foot, but I can't see my shoe in the dark. I sniff again.

It's definitely dog poop.

It's not. Dogs don't go to the cinema. I stepped in it in the parking lot. They don't go there either.

I shuffle in my seat. Cold sweat drips down my neck.

Dad leans forward and whispers, "Alex, what's up?"

"Nothing."

"Then why are you rocking the seats?"

"Sorry." I look down into the dark. "I can smell dog poop."

Dad sniffs. "Alex, there's nothing there. Maybe it's someone's hot dog... or that guy's popcorn." He points to a man eating at the end of our row. The smell doesn't smell like popcorn, but maybe Dad's right, because things always smell weird at the cinema.

I take a deep breath and let it out slowly.

The room goes even darker and I read the writing on the screen—

A long time ago in a galaxy far, far away...

Dad leans over. "You okay?"

I nod, but I don't really mean it. There's a weird smell coming from my feet, and somewhere behind me Dan is sitting in the dark, thinking bad things about me and aiming sweets and spit at the back of my head. I glance over my shoulder, but all I can see are silhouettes of heads. I turn and face the front—***Star Wars, The Force Awakens*** lights up in massive writing on the screen.

It's dog poop.

It's not. It's not.

Dan's going to spit at me.

He's miles back. He can't reach from there. Deep breaths. Deep breaths.

The words roll away from me on the screen—**Luke Skywalker has vanished. In his absence, the sinister FIRST ORDER has risen from the ashes of the Empire—**

Dad nudges my arm and I see him smile in the dark. I make myself smile back. I've waited for ages to see *The Force Awakens*, but now that Dan is here I wish I'd gone to see *Kung Fu Panda 3* instead.

12

Dan: What Mum just did!

I'm in my bedroom playing *Call of Duty* on my Xbox. Mum and Dad are downstairs watching TV. I can't believe what Mum just did at the cinema. She kept on about it in the car all the way home. *Alex looks like a nice boy. Alex has got such pale skin; it'll be lovely for him to get out. Alex this, Alex that.* I just sat in the back, getting really mad. The only place Shark Face should go is in the sea.

I put the controller down. I need to tell Ben. I pick up my pen.

Friday

Dear Ben,

Mum is so embarrassing. I just went to see The Force Awakens with her this evening. It was great but not as good as when I saw it with you before Christmas. I kept thinking about when you poured Coke down the boy's neck who was sitting in front of us.

96

This time I had to drink the Coke because Mum was right next to me. We got popcorn too and sat right at the back. She was really embarrassing because she kept going AWWWWWWWWWWWWWWWWWWWWWW! every time BB-8 rolled across the screen.

But this is the bad bit. We bumped into a weird kid from school and Mum invited him to the cave to help with Shooting Star. He's totally weird. He wears gloves all the time and washes his hands lots. I tried to get out of it. I don't need help. Especially not HIS!

He's a weirdo!

But don't worry. I won't let him touch anything. He probably won't turn up anyway.

Hope not.

I stop writing. I'm still mad, but I feel better for telling Ben. I reach up onto my bedside table and reread his last letter. I pick up my pen again. I've forgotten to tell him about the Observation Tower. The workmen have been building it for months on the seafront. They've blocked the site off with fencing and boards, but when I look through the gap there's a huge crane and cement mixers and trucks inside. They'd just finished building the concrete column when Ben last saw it. I try to tell him what it looks like now, but it's easier to draw.

The Observation Tower looks like this.

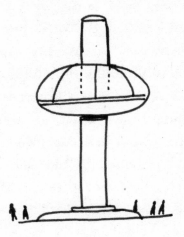

My drawing isn't very good. It looks like
a spaceship. It's going to be ready next week
during the holidays. I'm going on it with
Sophie and the Georges, but I'll go on it again
when you come home.

Love, Dan

13

Alex: What's wrong with me?

"Alex!...Alex!"

Mum walks up the stairs and knocks on my bedroom door. We've just got back from the cinema and I'm in my bedroom, curled up on my bed. *The Force Awakens* was brilliant, but when Finn was fighting Kylo Ren at the end, I kept thinking that will be Dan and me tomorrow. The only difference is I won't have a lightsaber to fight him off with.

"Alex." Mum knocks again.

I have to do something to get out of building the raft. I lean forward and wrap my arms around my belly.

Mum pushes the door open. "Didn't you hear...Hey, what's wrong?"

"My stomach hurts," I say in a fake ill voice.

"Maybe you had too many sweets at the cinema."

"I didn't have any," I say.

"Then maybe you're hungry. Did you want to make yourself some toast?"

"No, I'm not hungry."

Mum looks at me with a concerned expression on her face, like she does when I'm ill for real. I feel guilty for making her worry, but I can't go tomorrow.

"What do you think it is, then?"

"I don't know, but it's getting worse."

Mum sits on my bed. "Show me where it hurts."

"Just there." I point to my left side, just below my belt.

Mum reaches out. I wrap my arms around myself again.

"I just want to look, Alex. It could be appendicitis."

Appendicitis. Appendicitis!

"Sonia at work said her son had it. It can be serious."

"How serious? Mum, how serious?"

"Don't panic, it probably isn't. Just show me again. You said on your left side."

"Well, it was, but it...it moves around."

"I'll check on the Internet." She stands up and goes toward the door. "Just stay there."

"Will you do C-3PO now?"

I lift my head and see Lizzie standing outside my room with a PlayStation controller in one hand and a model of C-3PO in the other. I look at my windowsill.

"Give it back."

"Only if you do it."

"No."

"Then I won't let you have it," she says.

She's so irritating, but if I don't do it she won't leave.

"Just once."

"Okay."

I make my body stiff and put on my C-3PO voice. "'Don't blame me. I'm an interpreter. I'm not supposed to know a power socket from a computer terminal.'"

Lizzie laughs. "Do it again."

"No. Just let me have it back." I hold out my hand.

"Pig." Lizzie throws C-3PO onto my bed. "What's wrong with you anyway?"

I've got appendicitis! I was faking, but what if it has turned into appendicitis?

"I don't know. Mum's just going to look."

Lizzie slowly walks into my bedroom like she thinks whatever I've got is contagious. She points at the end of my bed.

"Can I sit here?"

She's had a shower and Mum has just got her clean pajamas out of the laundry.

I nod. She sits down and fiddles with the PlayStation controller like she's hinting for me to help her.

"I can't do it now," I say. "But maybe I can after tomorrow."

"Is that why you're ill? Because you've got to meet that boy tomorrow."

"What? No! I'm just not feeling very well."

"Because I think he's nice."

"It's not that."

"It's okay. I felt like you do when I went to Jessica Burns's party. . . . But it went away when I had a poop."

I scrunch my face. "I don't think this is the same."

Mum comes back in. "I think it's okay," she says. "Your appendix is on the other side."

Phew!

"Maybe just lie down and read for a while—you've a busy afternoon tomorrow—and don't forget you're seeing Dr. Patrick first thing. I'm sure he'll help you feel better."

Mum walks out of the room and I lie back on my bed. A pain shoots through my stomach for real. Mum doesn't understand. Dr. Patrick doesn't take bullies away or stomachaches. He just tries to work out what's in my head, and right now my worry is that I don't want to see Dan tomorrow. If he's horrible at school when there are loads of people around, he'll be even worse when we're on our own. What was Dad thinking? He knows I hate going outside. After the film finished, I told him I'd rather spend the afternoon with him and so would Lizzie, and that he could take us to Pizza Hut. But he said we could do that another time and then shot off to work.

I can't go and build the raft. It'll be horrible. I close my eyes, and my head sinks into my pillow. This was supposed to have been the best day, but it's turned into the worst.

Dan: Blue lights

I'm riding my bike along the seafront. The cave is only a mile from my house, so Mum says I can ride as long as I keep to the cycle path and text her when I leave to come home. But I don't, because she's always texting me anyway. As I ride, the wind blows across the sea so hard it's almost knocking me sideways.

I stop by the Observation Tower construction site and peer through the gap in the boarding. Inside are yellow dump trucks and the massive crane and the hut where the workmen go to eat and look at the plans. There are no workmen here today, just two security guards wearing white hats, walking across concrete and dust. They look in my direction like they think I'm going to break in. I put my feet on the pedals and cycle on, past the old pier. It caught fire years ago, and now all that's left is the metal sticking out of the water like burned fingers.

I can't wait to get to the cave and start work on *Shooting Star*, but I wish Shark Face wasn't coming. All he'll do is get in the way. At least he's not coming until this afternoon, so I've got all morning by myself.

I pass Al's Pizza, then the new pier with the slot machines and roller coaster at the end, where me and Ben used to go. Then I ride past the big wheel, then down a slope toward the beach where the caves begin. They're deep, dark holes cut into the rock, and a road runs above them like a railway line over caverns. Some people use the caves as cafés and art galleries, but the ones past the pier are used to store things like fishing nets and buoys and motors for boats. The cave I use belongs to Mr. Kendall. He owns an ice-cream stand and uses the cave to store the deck chairs and umbrellas he rents out in the summer.

Ben used to work for Mr. Kendall. He had a key to the cave so he could set the deck chairs out on the beach early in the morning, and then during the day we were allowed to work on the raft. But that was before Ben started to hang out with his new friends.

I get the padlock key out of my pocket. I undo the lock and pull the doors open. The cave is dark and smells fishy like the sea. I search for a switch on the rock wall, and the bulb hanging in the middle of the cave flickers on. *Shooting Star* is underneath it. She's raised off the ground on tires and covered in a tarp to keep her dry.

I step over the empty plastic bottles I collected from the bins last week. Everything is just like I left it. Old fishing nets and buoys are piled up in a corner, and there's an old blackboard where I pin Ben's drawing of *Shooting Star* so I can keep track of what I'm doing. I get the tube out of my bag, unroll the drawing, and pin it on the board.

I reach out and trace my finger over the lines. Ben said I need to make the frame first. It's made of twelve pieces of wood, six underneath and six on top, crisscrossing one another like a potato waffle. I pick up a piece of chalk and draw it on the blackboard. Then I draw two stick men on top for me and Ben.

I stand back and look at the pictures. There's no way I'm going to let Shark Face help. This is mine and Ben's. I don't care if his mum did text my mum last night. She said Shark Face was looking forward to coming down this afternoon. But there's no way I'm going to have that twerp hanging around.

The light flickers as a bus rumbles along the road above my head. I pull the tarp off *Shooting Star* and take a deep breath. She looks nothing like Ben's diagram. All there is are four planks of wood resting on the tires that me and Ben tied together in a square frame. The rest is just a pile of wood and bottles on the floor. I was here all last weekend, but it looks like I've not started. I need to go a lot faster if it's going to be ready for when Ben comes home in six weeks. I look at the diagram again. I've got to tie four more planks across and then I've finished the row. I bend down, pick up a plank of wood, then slide it across the frame. It slips off and bangs on the floor.

I pick up the plank and try again. This is what happened all last weekend. It's useless without Ben to help me. I drop the plank of wood and aim a kick at it.

"Stupid raft!" The plank knocks some bottles that roll across the floor like bowling pins

"Hey, everything okay?"

I jump and look up. Mr. Kendall is standing at the cave entrance, with a cigarette in his hand.

"Yes." I bend down and pick up the plank again.

"Doesn't look like it. Here, let me help." He puts his cigarette in his mouth and grabs the other end.

"No, you can't. I want to do it on my own."

Mr. Kendall puts the plank down and blows smoke out of his mouth. "Well, you're not doing much of a job of it."

"I'm okay."

"You're just like your brother. He always wanted to do things on his own."

"Good," I say. I pick up the plank to show him I can do it by myself.

Mr. Kendall makes an *mmm* sound. "Well, that's all very well, but watch you don't make the same mistake as he did. Silly lad."

"It wasn't his fault. And don't call him silly." Anger bubbles inside me, makes my hands ball into fists.

Mr. Kendall chuckles. "Hey, calm down!" He takes another puff of his cigarette. "I see you've got his temper too. Anyway, I only came in here for a new pole for an umbrella." He walks toward the back of the cave.

I sit down and try to untangle an old fishing net to make rope. Mr. Kendall is just like my granddad. Old and grumpy and always saying bad things about Ben: Ben's silly. Ben's gone off the rails. Ben should be made to join the army to give him some discipline. But my brother isn't silly, and he hasn't gone off the rails. He's just somewhere else. He's somewhere else and I wish he was here.

Mr. Kendall walks past me with the umbrella pole tucked under his arm. I focus on unpicking the fishing net and pretend he's not there. He stops at the cave entrance, turns around, and looks at me like he knows he's upset me.

"Listen." He sighs. "Don't get me wrong, he's a lovely lad and all, but he should know the difference between right and wrong. We make our own fortunes."

I untie a knot. I don't know what he means. Ben knows the difference between right and wrong. He didn't do anything *really* bad, not on purpose; he was just unlucky, like I am when I get caught messing around. I want to tell Mr. Kendall all of this, but I don't want to annoy him, because when Ben comes back I want him to still have a job.

"So are we okay?"

I nod. "Suppose."

Mr. Kendall smiles. "Just tell him to hurry back," he says. "I'm getting too old for all this. Oh, and remember, if ever you forget your key, there's one under the—" He stops talking. Above us a police siren blares along the road. Mr. Kendall looks up like he can see the police car through the rock. "Someone's in trouble," he says.

The siren gets louder as the car gets closer. I imagine the cars and buses stopping to let it pass and the blue lights flashing along the seafront. *Flash, flash. Flash, flash*, then silence. Just like the night the police came for Ben. I was in my bedroom and I could see the lights flashing in the windows of the houses across the street. Then I heard the doorbell and the deep voices of policemen talking in our hall. I thought maybe Dad had had an accident or there'd been a burglary in our road. But then the policemen went into the lounge with Mum, Dad, and Ben, and they closed the door.

107

I look out of the cave as Mr. Kendall shuffles away. I don't want to think about the night the police took Ben away. I want to think about the day he comes back in six weeks' time. I stand up and pick up a plank. I don't care how hard building *Shooting Star* is. I just need to get it done.

Alex: The man inside my head

It's Saturday morning at the clinic and I'm so tired I'm falling asleep in the waiting-room chair. I pretended I had a stomachache, but then my worries took over and tumbled around and around in my head all night: *Everybody is going to die. I've got to meet Dan. I'm turning into Justin Bieber. The spit is still in my hair, germs on my hands. I'm going bald. I've got to meet Dan. I've got to meet Dan. I've got—*

"Alex!"

I jump awake.

"Come in." Dr. Patrick holds his hand out like he's showing me where to go, but I've been here so many times I could find my way in the dark. I walk past him and sit down in a red chair by a big window. Dr. Patrick sits opposite me.

"So." He smiles. "Your mum says you've been having a few problems."

Just a few.

"Anything in particular?"

I shrug. "It's everything, really."

"And it's making you panic, clean, wash a lot?" He looks at my hands. I go to take off my gloves to show him how sore my fingers are, but Dr. Patrick lifts his hand and says he doesn't need to see. He's not the sort of doctor who looks at sore hands. He's a psychotherapist, which means he treats people like me, who have got problems in their head.

"Can you think of any changes that might have made things worse, something different that's affected your routine?"

I wish I could tell him what's happening, but he can't do anything about my being bullied. All he would do is call the school. If I wanted to, I could do that myself. I can't tell him about Dan, but there's lots of other stuff that I can talk to him about. I tell him about my bad thoughts about germs on the guitar pick and the button on the crossing, and that when I go to sleep I think everyone is going to die and then when I wake up and they haven't I think that they're going to die today instead.

"Okay, that's a lot of things."

I've got a lot of worries.

"Are you writing them down, like I asked?"

"Yes."

Dr. Patrick looks at me for a long time. It's like he doesn't believe me or is waiting for me to say something else. Dad says I should try to tell Dr. Patrick everything or he won't be able to help, but some of the things are too embarrassing and he might not understand.

"Okay," says Dr. Patrick. "I'd like you to try something for me. Have you heard of the Arabian Knights, where one of them has the ability to morph into any animal he likes?"

"No." I sit back and wonder what's coming next. I want help, but it usually means I have to do things I don't like, such as touching the toilet seat with my bare hands or walking on the grass with no shoes. It's supposed to make me confront my fears, but most of the time it makes me feel worse.

Dr. Patrick leans forward. "Alex, it's nothing to worry about. Think of it as a game, like Transformers, except I'm asking you to imagine you can change into an animal, not a machine."

Dr. Patrick sees the worried look on my face.

"It's fine. Just try it for me.... Close your eyes, only for a few moments."

I close my eyes. Everything is quiet except for the rumble of traffic going by outside. Dr. Patrick talks in a whisper, but I can hear him so clearly it's like his mouth is right by my ear. He tells me to imagine that I'm a mouse, really tiny, and I'm at the bottom of the stairs and I'm so small that each stair looks like a huge building and they're stacked on top of one another to become a mountain.

"Alex, are you a mouse?"

I find it silly to pretend to be a mouse, but I'd do anything to make my worries go away. I nod.

"Good. Now I want you to put all your worries in little boxes, boxes you can pick up and move. Put labels on them if you like, and line them up at the bottom of the stairs."

I screw my eyes tight and put my worries into boxes. In my mind, I label them and arrange them in a line.

"Right," says Dr. Patrick. "It's very simple. I want you to imagine that you are as tiny as a mouse, but that you can climb the stairs, the

111

buildings. Maybe imagine you have a ladder and you're leaning it against the steps and you can scurry up them."

This feels even sillier, but I told Mum and Dad I'd try anything, and Dad said seeing Dr. Patrick is expensive, so I screw my eyes tight and imagine I'm a mouse. It's like I'm a rat in *Ratatouille* and I'm climbing from the floor up onto the shelves.

"Okay," says Dr. Patrick. "Now as you climb I want you to imagine that you're growing too. With each step, you're getting bigger. You turn from a mouse into a cat...from a cat into...a horse...or anything you want...as long as it's bigger...and then, when you reach the top stair, I want you to feel as big as an elephant."

I start to climb slowly and imagine my skin stretching and my bones getting bigger, and with each step I slowly change from a mouse to a cat to a horse...and then...an elephant.

"Okay," whispers Dr. Patrick. "Now I want you to turn around and look back down the stairs. At the bottom are all your worries. Can you see them?"

I nod.

"Well, see how small they are now, now that you're at the top of the stairs, now that you're an elephant?"

I want to tell Dr. Patrick the worries are small, and some of them are, just for a while. But they haven't all shrunk. One box is still there. And something's jumping around in it, bashing the sides, knocking the top open.

A cheetah springs out of it. I open my eyes quickly. The cheetah looked just like Dan.

16

Dan: The alien lands

I'm outside the cave, taking the tops off the bottles and emptying the dregs of Coke and lemonade onto the floor. I gave up on the planks because they kept falling off the frame every time I tried to bang in a nail. I couldn't even tie the bottles together to make a big float because whenever I tried to pull the string tight, a bottle jumped out and went flying across the cave. It's useless.

I screw the top on a bottle and rest against the cave door. I watch an empty roller coaster climb the track into the sky. On the beach some people are watching a man unloading crab nets from a small boat, and a flock of seagulls are swooping above it. I look along the promenade to see if Shark Face is coming, but the only people I see are Mr. Kendall drinking a cup of coffee outside his ice-cream stand and some boys and girls skateboarding by the pier. I knew the wimp wouldn't come. He's probably sitting at home with his mum and sister, watching TV. Or maybe he tried to come but did something really stupid, like losing his gloves.

I check that the bottle top is tight, then walk back into the cave. I can't do the planks or the bottles, but there must be something I can do on my own. I walk over to the back of the cave and Ben's instructions.

Unpick fishing nets.

Yes! I can do that. I walk to the back of the cave and pick up a fishing net from a pile that me and Ben found washed up on the shore. I get a penknife from the shelf and sit down on an upturned bucket. This is easy and I don't need anyone to help me. Especially not Shark Face, but it's so late he's not going to turn up to—

"Hello?" A deep voice echoes around the cave. I don't reply.

Between the stacks of tires I can see a pair of men's shoes and pant legs. The shoes scuff across the floor.

"Hello?...Ah, there you are, Dan."

I can't see the person's face because the sun is shining behind him, but it sounded just like Shark Face's dad.

"How's it going?"

"Fine, thanks," I mumble.

"So I see. I brought the tools." He holds up a blue bag.

Ha! Great. He's brought some tools but left Shark Face at home. I stand up.

"Oh, and I brought this little guy to help." He looks beside him like he thinks Shark Face is there, but there's just an empty space.

Ha! He's run off. I bet just seeing the dark has scared him.

"Alex, come on."

Shark Face drags his feet as he walks slowly across the opening and stands next to his dad. The sun comes out behind them. It's so bright that all I can see is the shapes of their bodies, like aliens getting off a spaceship. They walk toward me. Shark Face's dad taps his hand on the corner of the frame.

"So this is it," he says. "The raft. It looks good. Hard work, though."

"No, it's dead easy. I did that on my own this morning," I lie.

"Well, I hope you leave something for Alex to do. I used to love building rafts. It's great. What do you think, Alex?"

Shark Face shrugs. "It's okay," he mumbles.

Okay? Just okay! It's better than anything he could do. He couldn't glue matchsticks together, wearing those gloves.

"... Well, I think it's grand." His dad smiles. "Once you've finished, you'll be able to sail all the way to France!"

I fake a smile. He's trying to be cool, like he wants to be my friend. Or maybe my mum has told them about Ben and he feels sorry for me. I hope not. I don't want anyone to know, especially not Shark Face. I just want to be left alone to get on with *Shooting Star*.

Shark Face's dad opens the bag. "I'm not sure how much of this you'll need... just a few wrenches, and a hammer, and I've got some rope in the shed that Alex can bring tomorrow."

"Tomorrow?!" me and Shark Face say at the same time.

His face is white like he's seen a ghost, and mine probably looks the same.

Shark Face's dad points at Ben's diagram on the blackboard. "Well, looking at the detail on that, I'm pretty sure you two won't be finishing anytime soon."

I glance at Shark Face. He's standing with his gloved hands stuck out by his sides. He has to get us out of this. It's his dad. I don't want him coming back. He's not going to be much help; he'll be terrible at untying the nets with gloves on.

His dad rests the bag on top of *Shooting Star.*

"Anyway, I need to press on. Alex's mum has packed some sandwiches, and there's money if you kids want to get drinks." He smiles at Shark Face. I think he smiles back, but I can't tell, because his face is screwed up like he can smell the fishy water in here.

Shark Face's dad turns away "Catch you in a couple of hours, mate," he says as he walks off. I wait for Shark Face to run after him, but he just stands there, staring into space like his feet are glued to the floor.

I walk around the side of *Shooting Star.* It's so quiet I can hear my shoes scuff on the floor. I stop and stare at Shark Face. He stares back. We're like two boxers in the ring getting ready to fight. I can't tell if he's mad at his dad for just leaving him, or if he's scared because he's here with me. If I were him, it'd be both.

A truck rumbles across the road above us. Shark Face looks up at the ceiling like he thinks it's going to fall in. Another one trundles over. Shark Face opens his eyes wide. He really is scared. That's how I can get rid of him.

"It gets really bad later," I say. "We get a load of buses, and when two go across at the same time it feels like it's tanks bashing through the ceiling." I grin nastily.

He looks back up at the ceiling like he thinks a tank is falling through *now.* I wait for him to run, but he starts to look around the cave as the rumbling fades away.

116

I sit back down on the bucket and pick at the net. If I ignore him for long enough, he'll go for real. Out of the corner of my eye I see Shark Face walk down the side of *Shooting Star*. He stops by the blackboard and looks at Ben's drawing. A bubble of anger grows inside me. I don't even want him to look at the drawing.

He turns away and puts his hand on the plank I couldn't hammer in.

"Don't touch it!" I stand up.

He looks at me, startled. "But it's loose," he says.

"I don't care. I don't need your help."

"I was just—"

"You were just going to get lost!"

Shark Face takes his hand away and looks out at the sea. I stare at him and hope he'll walk.

"I didn't want to come here." He looks back at me.

"And I don't want you here, so that's good. Just go home."

"I can't," he says.

"Why not? Worried you might get stuck at the crossing again?"

He gives me a hurt look, then takes a step toward the cave entrance.

"That's right," I say. "Go, Shark Face. This place has nothing to do with you."

A seagull squawks outside. Shark Face stops like a car at a red light. He turns around.

"I told you, I can't go home."

"And I said why not?" I walk toward him.

"Because if I go back, my mum will know something's wrong."

"There *is* something wrong: you're a weirdo and I don't like you."

He swallows. "That's not what I meant. She'll keep on asking me what's wrong until I tell her."

My mouth opens, but no words come out. Shark Face is right. He can't go home. If his mum tells my mum he went back early, then my mum will know something is up. I can't risk getting in any more trouble, especially as Mum's already got to go down to the school next week.

This is the worst. How can I get rid of him without Mum finding out what I've done? I glance up and see Shark Face looking at me.

"Stop staring at me," I say. "Just go and swim in the sea with the rest of your friends."

17

Alex: Everybody is going to die

"So how did it go?"

"All right."

"Just all right?"

I nod.

Dad puts the car in gear and we pull off along the seafront. I rest my head against the window as we pass the old pier. It's like a big black sea monster sleeping on its back with its tentacles sticking up out of the water, waiting for people passing by in dinghies and on windsurfers. Suddenly it's going to wake up and grab the people and drag them back under the sea.

It's the second monster I've seen today.

"You okay, buddy?"

I nod.

"Dan seems like a good lad. Quite funny."

"Yeah." *If calling people names is funny. If spitting on people is funny.*

Dad looks across at me. "Look, I know you didn't want to go, but

119

it's good that you get out and have some fresh air. Which bits of the raft did you do?"

I don't answer. There's nothing to say, because I didn't do anything. Nothing. Dan wouldn't let me touch the raft, and even if he said I could, I wouldn't have been able to because all the wood and the bottles were covered in germs. He just sat on a bucket, unpicking a net, pretending I wasn't there. I wanted to leave because I thought the buses were going to come through the roof and crush us, but I couldn't go because there was a seagull swooping down outside and Mum would have known something was up if I'd gone back too soon.

"Alex? Which bits did you do?"

"I untied a few knots," I lie.

"Well, that's a start. Maybe you'll get to do more tomorrow."

"What? No, Dad. I can't. I've got—"

"It'll be good for you, Alex. Mum and I have been worried about you. You've been stuck in the house too much these past few months. You've stopped hanging out with Elliott and you know your OCD has been getting worse."

I press my head hard against the window. This isn't happening. I screw my eyes tight shut. *I'm dreaming. I'm dreaming.* It's one massive horrible dream.

I open my eyes slowly. It's not a dream, because Dad is still talking about the raft, saying Mum is going to make me and Dan more sandwiches for tomorrow. But I'm not listening; because thoughts of crashing buses and seagulls dropping poop are rushing through my head. I roll my head against the window and try to make them go away. I don't think Dad has even noticed because now he's talking

120

about how he wished it was him building the raft because he used to love building things when he was my age. I wish it was him building it too. Maybe he'd like to work with Dan. Maybe he thinks I'm so useless that he wishes Dan was his son.

"I'd love it," he says. "Remember what I told you about when Uncle Tony and I built a go-kart? We made it out of wooden pallets, and Uncle Tony got on it and forgot to put his feet down to brake and crashed into a wall."

Dad laughs and I force a smile. He's trying to cheer me up, but it will take more than Uncle Tony and his broken leg to do that. I wish I could tell Dad why I hated it at the cave, and what was happening at school, but every time I think about it I get a horrible feeling in my chest like an elephant has sat on it. He wants me to be like Dan, to play and build things like he did when he was a boy.

I used to be able to. When I was eight, before my worries started, we built an obstacle course in the yard with poles I had to climb over and a net I had to crawl under. At the end we had a rope and I'd swing from it and land in the sandpit. Dad said it was like an army assault course, and every time I went on it he timed me with a stopwatch and gradually I got faster. It took me two minutes when I first had a go. It took me one minute and five seconds at the end. If I tried now, I wouldn't even get started. I would just be standing on the patio, too scared to even go on the grass.

"Alex... you're miles away."

I wish I was.

"I guess you really are tired." Dad smiles and reaches across to rub my head.

Germs on the steering wheel. Germs on his hands. Germs on my head.

I pull away before he can touch me.

Dad sighs. "I don't know, Alex," he says. "I can't even rub your head."

"I'm sorry."

Dad stares at the road and doesn't answer.

I wish I could let him do it. I wish I could let him hug me, but every time he comes near me all I can think of is germs. I heard him talking to Mum once. He told her I made him feel dirty, but he washes and showers like everyone else. I can hug Mum and Lizzie, but not him, and I don't know why. Mum said it's just a phase I'm going through. I hope it is, because I'd love to be able to hug Dad right now.

On the seafront a boy's red kite is flying high in the sky. A man is paddling a canoe through the waves, a lady is serving fries from a food truck, and a little airplane is dragging a sign across the sky that says:

BRIGHTON OBSERVATION TOWER. GRAND OPENING TUESDAY 21ST APRIL

I can feel Dad looking at me.

"Do you want to go to that?" he asks. "I know Mum wants to take you to see your nan and granddad sometime in the holidays, but we can work around that."

I nod. I'm thinking of going with Elliott, but I'm worried about all the people who will be there, and I'm worried that if I do go on it, then the observation deck will spin to the top of the tower and fly off through the air. I do want to go, but I've got to get through tomorrow and another week of school before I can even think about it any more.

Dad smiles at me kindly. "It's okay, mate," he says. "We'll get this OCD sorted."

"Hope so," I mumble.

Dad looks across at me. "We will." He smiles at me like he means it.

I know Dad wants to help, but he's so busy at work and I'm not sure he really understands what's in my head. Even I don't sometimes.

I look back out the window.

The boy with the kite is going to get pulled up into the sky. The man in the canoe is going to be swept away.

The lady in the food truck is going to catch fire. The plane is going to crash into the pier.

If only those things were all I had to worry about.

18

Dan: The great escape

I wheel my bike around the side of the house and go into the kitchen.

"Is that you, Dan?" shouts Mum from the sitting room.

"Yeah." I check the worktop to see if there's a letter from Ben, but all that's there is an electricity bill. I sigh and open the fridge.

"Dan, no more Coke, love. Your teeth are going to fall out."

I grab a can of Coke and walk back into the hall and toward the stairs.

"Hey!" my dad shouts out. "Don't go hiding in your bedroom."

"I'm tired," I say as I trudge into the sitting room.

Dad points at the TV. "Spurs are getting hammered," he says. "It's a good game. Almost as good as the Albion. We won three nil. You should have come."

"I thought I said—" Mum begins as I take a swig from my can.

"Oh, that's great, Dad. Who scored?" my dad says sarcastically, pretending to be me.

I don't know why Dad keeps doing that. He's knows I hate going to football without Ben. I sit down on the arm of the sofa next to Mum.

"Dave, leave him alone. He's had a long day."

"Was there anything in the post for me?" I ask, hoping Mum might have put the letter in my bedroom.

"No, love, I'm sorry." She puts her hand on my knee and smiles. "But, hey, how did it go with *Twinkling Star*?"

"It's *Shooting Star*."

Harry Kane misses an open goal.

"Oh, how did he miss that?" shouts my dad.

Mum shakes her head. "Yes, sorry, love. I meant *Shooting Star*. How did it go? Have a nice time with Alex?"

I take another swig from my can. "Was okay."

"Oh, I'm glad," says Mum. "He's seems like a nice boy. What did you talk about?"

"Not much. Just did stuff on *Shooting Star*."

"That's nice. I'll text Francesca in a bit. I know she worries because he doesn't have many friends. Maybe he could come back for a snack after you've finished tomorrow."

"Tomorrow?!"

"Yes."

"Mum, tell me you're joking. I'm not working with that idiot again."

Mum gives me a sharp look. "Dan! That's not nice. You said you enjoyed it today."

"I said it was okay!" I stand up. "How can you do this to me?"

"I just thought it would be nice for you to have some company."

"I don't want company. Well, not his."

"Dan, don't storm off. Let's—"

"I need to feed Horace."

125

"Penalty!" shouts Dad.

"Dan!"

I walk into the hall. No way am I going to work with Shark Face again, and he's definitely not coming over. I don't want him on my road, let alone in my house.

"Do me a favor, Dan—do some homework instead of going on your Xbox!" shouts Mum. Then she says something to Dad, but he doesn't answer.

"Dave!" she snaps.

"What!"

"Turn the bloody TV down.... I said he's not right."

"Well, I'm bloody trying! But he's not interested in seeing the Albion anymore."

"I know, but..." Mum's voice fades away as she closes the sitting room door. I think of staying to hear what they're talking about, but I'm too mad about Shark Face. They'll only be saying the same stuff about me and Ben, and then it'll turn into a row. They never used to do that.

I walk upstairs and into Ben's room. Horace is light green all over. This means his temperature is okay, but mine is boiling. How can Mum even think that I want Shark Face here? Who cares if he's got no friends? That's his problem, not mine.

I feed Horace three crickets and put the lid back on his tank. I'll write and tell Ben how big he's growing. He used to be the size of a mouse, but now he's almost as big as a cat.

I wish Mum and Dad would just stop arguing about me and Ben

and take me to see him. Then I wouldn't have to write letters or get fed up waiting for him to reply. I could sit down next to him and he could tell me everything himself. I asked Dad to take me last weekend, and the weekend before that. But Dad always looks at Mum and says it's not a good idea. He says it's because it's a long way to travel. But I don't think it's that. It's because the place where Ben is at is full of bad kids and I'll get scared. But from what Ben says in his letters, he's having a nice time and it's doesn't sound scary at all.

I walk into my bedroom and take his last letter from my drawer. He's been in that place for three months, but it feels like a year. I read the last bit again.

> I've got to go now. I want to get in the shower before the other kids use up all the hot water. Hope you have a good week at school and remember what I said, you've got to be a big fish and eat all the others up or they will eat you.

> Ha!

I sit down on my bed and read that last line over and over. *You've got to be a big fish and eat all the others up or they will eat you.*

I open my laptop. I don't know where Ben is exactly, but I know it's somewhere near Milton Keynes. I search maps and type in *Brighton to Milton Keynes*. It's 115 miles away and takes over two hours to drive. I can't drive, but I could stand at the roundabout with my thumb in the air and hitchhike like people do in films. But Mum would be mad if I got a ride from strangers. I click on the train icon. It's nearly the same distance, but the train has to go to London. Then I'd have to get off and go on the Tube and then get on another train. I'd get lost in the Underground on my own and I don't have any money anyway.

I zoom out until I can see southeast England and the English Channel on the map. I trace the coastline with my finger. If *Shooting Star* was ready, I could sail her up the coast to Margate and then cut in and sail down the Thames until it joins the river Colne. I zoom back in again. The river doesn't look very wide, but then *Shooting Star* is a raft, not a ship. I could sail her up the river Colne and then into a stream that seems to disappear near St. Albans. And then I could walk the rest of the way from there. I could do it. I'll ask Mr. Kendall if there's a life jacket in the cave and I'll take sandwiches and a drink and a flashlight so I don't bump into the rocks if it gets dark.

I trace my finger around the route again. It's simple. I don't have to look for road signs or platform numbers. I just have to get to the seafront and turn left at the pier. There's a bit of land sticking out by Dover, but I could get around that okay.

Dover.

It's really busy. I saw loads of boats and massive ferries there when we went on holiday to France. I'll never be able to navigate *Shooting Star* between them.

I close my laptop. It's a stupid idea. How could I think it was possible? Even if I could squeeze *Shooting Star* between the ferries, their waves would be so big that she'd sink.

I lie down on my side, facing the wall. Sometimes, late at night, I'd knock on his wall to see if he was awake. I'd knock twice and he'd knock back twice if he was. Then he'd add some extra knocks, like he was drumming a beat. I had to repeat them and add another beat of my own. The highest number we ever got to was thirty. Then dad would shout out for us to stop.

I raise my hand and think of knocking now. But there's no point when I won't get a reply.

19

Alex: Things I could do to get out of going to the cave tomorrow

I'm in bed and I'm tossing and turning. I can't sleep. I can't sleep because there's a list going around and around in my head. One thing chasing another, spinning and spinning, around and around like a dog chasing its tail.

I turn onto my side. The red numbers on my alarm clock are flashing 3:06 a.m. It's no good: I'm going to have to write a list or I'll be awake all night.

I turn on the lamp. My posters light up on the walls. Han Solo is fighting Darth Vader, and the stormtroopers are surrounding him, and there are so many of them it's like they're surrounding me too and trapping me in my bed. But I'd rather be surrounded by the evil First Order than go to that cave again tomorrow.

I pick up my pen and paper.

Things I could do to get out of going to the cave

1. ~~Tell Mum that everyone is going to die.~~

You do that every day. I scribble through it.

1. ~~Tell Mum I've got stomachache.~~

Did that. I scribble that out as well.

1. ~~Paint red blobs on myself and pretend I've got chicken pox.~~

But you've already had chicken pox.

1. ~~Go to Lizzie's room and paint red marks on her.~~

But Lizzie will freak out and scream the house down.

1. ~~Sneak around to Dad's flat and disconnect a wire from his car so he can't take me.~~

But what if I disconnect the brakes by mistake and Dad goes down the hill to the seafront and the brakes don't work and he smashes through the railings and disappears into the sea and then he dies? Oh God, how could I even think that? I'm a terrible person.

I scribble that out too.

1. Tell Mum I've got too much homework.

But you told her you finished yesterday.

Argh! It's useless. I'm going to have to go. No one cares that the roof of the cave could collapse because of the weight of the buses and the trucks carrying concrete to the Observation Tower. They'll fall into a giant hole, and all the people on them will either get injured or die. And then the ambulance and the police cars will arrive and they'll fall into the hole too.

I stop writing. I think it's making it worse. I put my pen and book down and lie back on my bed. I try to think of what Dr. Patrick said. Imagine your worries are tiny, like a mouse, like an ant. Imagine you're as big as an elephant. Imagine you've climbed the stairs and left all your worries behind. I try and try and try....I close my eyes. Slowly, slowly, one step at a time, without looking back. After ten, I stop, take a deep breath, and look back. But I don't feel safe. I feel like I'm falling all the way back down toward the monsters at the bottom of the stairs.

I turn on my side and pull my duvet up to my chin. The clock says 3:26 a.m. I close my eyes. Only seven hours until I'm back at the cave.

Dan: This *Shooting Star* is mine

I'm down at the cave, unknotting a net. I've been here two hours. I've made two balls of string from the nets, and I've managed to empty some bottles that Mr. Kendall saved for me, and I went down onto the beach and found a piece of driftwood that I might be able to use for an oar. But I still haven't actually been able to do anything to *Shooting Star*. I really wish I could, because the quicker I get her done, the quicker I get rid of Shark Face.

He's standing by the side of *Shooting Star* now. Every time I glance up, I can see his white sneakers and the bottoms of his jeans. I bet he thinks he's cool, but he looked like a real geek in his red hoodie at the cinema. I was hoping he wasn't going to turn up, but he walked in just as I started on the net. I pretended I didn't see him. He hasn't spoken and neither have I.

I pick up my penknife, put the tip against the net, and pick at a knot. It's boring, but if I keep working and ignoring him, maybe he'll go away. Why did he have to turn up? I know he can't go home, but if I was him I'd walk over to the shops or go to McDonald's and then go on the beach and swim in the sea. But that's what normal people do, not weirdos like him.

I glance up as Shark Face shuffles his feet, then walks down the side of *Shooting Star* and stops by the blackboard in the opposite corner to me. He's looking at Ben's diagram. I don't even want him to do that. I yank at the net. My penknife falls out of my hand and onto the floor. Not only is unpicking nets boring, it's also hard work.

I sigh and pick up the knife.

Shark Face turns around. "It would be quicker if I help."

"What?" I glower at him. "I told you yesterday. I don't want your help."

He shrugs. "Then we're going to be stuck together for ages."

I can feel the bubbles rising. "What do you mean?"

"My dad said I've got to help you finish it."

"When did he say that?" I stand up and walk toward Shark Face. He scratches his neck nervously with those stupid gloves. "What does he know anyway?"

"Your mum texted my mum, and then my mum told him when he picked me up. She said your mum was really pleased I was here."

"Well, I'm not!"

Shark Face shrugs and looks back at the board.

"And stop looking at the drawing. It's *my* raft, not yours."

He looks out at the sea. He's making it up, but why would he? Maybe Mum did say it. She's been so worried about me that she's getting off work early to see Mr. Francis on Wednesday. And her and Dad are arguing about me all the time. Maybe they think Shark Face will be a good influence on me. I bet teachers would think that too, that *squeaky-clean Alex* will make me behave better. I don't want to be a squeaky-clean geek like Shark Face.

But what if Shark Face is right? What if he really has to keep coming here until I've finished? He'll be here next weekend, and if I still haven't finished, he'll be here for half-term too.

I crawl under the frame and drag out a plank of wood that I need to make the base.

"Come here, Shark Face," I say.

"Why?"

"Just come here."

He edges toward me like he thinks I'm going to spit on him again.

"Pick up the other end."

"You want me to help?"

"We've got no choice. We're stuck with each other."

"That's what I said."

I nod at the plank. "Are you going to help or not?"

Shark Face looks at the plank like he's checking for dirt. Then he looks at his gloves.

"Come on," I say. "The quicker you do it, the quicker you get out of here."

Shark Face grimaces. It's like he thinks the plank is electrified and he's scared of getting a shock.

"What are you waiting for?" I ask.

Shark Face scrunches up his face and picks up the plank.

"Now put your end on the frame and I'll do the same with mine."

"I know," he says. "I saw the diagram."

We rest the plank on the frame. I walk over to the corner where me and Ben put the jar of nails that we took from Dad's shed. The light doesn't reach here very well, but I soon find the jar, then look for the hammer. I lift the nets and move some bottles, but I can't find it anywhere.

"Here."

Shark Face is standing beside me with a hammer in his hand. "My dad put one in his bag."

"Oh. Erm..."

Shark Face pushes the hammer toward me. I take it.

"Thanks," I mumble. I don't want to use anything that's his, but I don't want to waste time fumbling around in the dark. I unscrew the jar and take out a long nail. "You hold the plank still and I'll bang the nail in."

Shark Face puts his hands on the plank, then looks at me suspiciously. It's like he thinks I'm going to miss the nail on purpose and hit his hand. I don't like him, but I would never do that. He moves his hands farther apart so the plank is steady, and blinks as I carefully hammer the nail in. Then I bang another nail right next to the first. Now we have to do the same to the other side of the frame. I go to tell Shark Face, but he's already picked up another plank and is waiting for me. I bang two nails in that side, then put my hand on the plank and test it. It doesn't budge, not sideways or up or down.

I get another plank. Shark Face takes his end and we rest it on the frame. Ben's instructions say the planks have to be thirty centimeters apart. I look at the frame and try to guess, then my phone suddenly buzzes in my pocket. It'll be Mum checking on me again. I look at my phone. It's not Mum; it's Sophie.

136

Hey, Dan, we're all going to McDonald's. Wanna come?

I think of what to reply. I can't tell her that I'm at the cave, building a raft with Shark Face. She'd try to get me out of our group and she'd spread it around school tomorrow. I think of saying I'll meet her in half an hour, but I really need to get *Shooting Star* done and Mum would go crazy if she found out. Wait, what if they decide to come down to the seafront? It'd only take them twenty minutes to walk down the hill. It's bad enough being stuck in the cave with Shark Face. But being seen with him? That would be even worse. Worse than when Sophie saw me in Sainsbury's with my mum.

I put my phone back in my pocket and pretend I never saw the message.

Shark Face holds out a tape measure. "My dad put it in the bag," he says. "We have to follow the instructions."

"I know that! It's my raft, remember." Sophie's message is still in my head. Everything will go wrong if she finds out. I walk over to the doors and pull them together just in case she walks by.

Shark Face doesn't seem to notice I'm worried. He's too busy looking at the light flickering as another bus rumbles overhead.

I walk back to *Shooting Star*. Shark Face measures out thirty centimeters and marks the wood with a pencil; then he does the same on my side. Then he holds on to the plank and I bang the nails in again.

We do four more planks in exactly the same way until the first layer of the base is done.

I stand back to look at *Shooting Star*. All the planks are straight and neat, just like in Ben's drawing, and not one of them moves. I can't believe we've done it so quickly. I feel myself smiling, but I don't want Shark Face to see that I'm happy. But he's not even looking at me. He's too busy looking at the ends of his gloves like he thinks he wore them through.

I walk over to the blackboard to check the drawing. Now we have to tie the planks to the frame just to make sure they're secure. I go back to the corner and pick up one of the balls of string. I wrap it around the part where the base plank joins the frame. Shark Face puts his finger on the string and then whips it away quickly as I make a knot and pull it tight. Then we move on to the other planks.

Whenever I've been with Dad at the TV repair workshop, he always chats and puts the radio on, but me and Shark Face work in silence. I don't want to talk to him and he doesn't want to talk to me. We're machines on a car-production line, working side by side without looking at each other or talking. The only time Shark Face stops is when the light flickers each time a bus rumbles over the road above us. But he only stops for a second and then starts to work even quicker. It's like someone has flipped a switch to make him go into overdrive.

Once we've tied all the knots, we go back to the planks and lay them across the top like the potato waffle in Ben's drawing. Shark Face does the measuring and I hammer the nails in. I start to get hot and out of breath. I can hardly keep up with him. He's going so fast that I wish I had his gloves, because my fingers are getting sore.

We tie the last plank. Where the wood was piled up in the middle there is now an empty space. I walk down the side of *Shooting Star*, looking at her like my dad does when he buys a car. We've done the base in only two hours. I tap the wood. *Shooting Star* is beginning to look like the raft in the film, but she's going to be even better by the time I've finished. I check the strings again and hope I don't look as happy as I feel. Shark Face is smiling like he's happy too. But *Shooting Star* isn't his.

"Just because you helped doesn't mean you get to go on it," I say. The smile drops from his face. "And Ben will check everything anyway."

"Who's Ben?"

"It doesn't matter," I snap.

"Is he the one who drew the diagram?" Shark Face points at the blackboard. "Because I think he's made a mistake. He—"

"No, he hasn't!"

"He has." Shark Face walks toward Ben's drawing.

"He hasn't made a mistake!" I run around the back of *Shooting Star* and block his way. "My brother has *not* made a mistake. It's his drawing, and it's got nothing to do with you anyway. It's our raft, not yours."

"I know. I was just—"

"You were just going to shut up!" I kick a bottle across the floor. Shark Face steps away from me. What does he know about building a raft? Ben took ages to draw it and work it out. He didn't just make it up. He looked it up on the Internet and we calculated the weight of the planks and weighed ourselves on the bathroom scale. He said we had to surf over the top of the waves, not get sunk by them. Everything had to be as light as possible, even us, so he said we'd both have to stop eating crisps and drinking so much Coke. Then he worked out how many bottles and buoys we needed to make

Shooting Star float. He didn't make a mistake. He spent ages on his computer working it out.

I walk toward the cave entrance. Shark Face is looking at me like he doesn't know what to say or do. I keep walking. I just want to get away from him.

"Where are you going?" he mumbles.

"Looking for bottles," I lie.

"Shall I come?"

"No!" I turn and look at him. "I don't want anyone to see you with me. And don't you dare say anything about this at school tomorrow. You even say my name and you're dead!"

21

Alex: *I* made a mistake

Mum's in the kitchen cooking dinner as I walk in the back door.

"Hey," she says. "Did you have a good time?"

"It was okay," I say quietly. Mum looks at Dad.

"I'm sure he did, but he just doesn't want to admit it." Dad goes to rub my head. I duck out of the way.

"Sorry, I forgot." Dad shakes his head.

Mum puts her hand on his arm like she's trying to calm him down. "Thanks for picking him up." She pauses, then smiles. "Would you like to stay and have something to eat?"

"No, that's okay," says Dad. "I'll grab something at work." I kick off my shoes, run through the hall and up the stairs.

"Alex! Come here!" Lizzie shouts out from the sitting room.

"I need to go to the bathroom!" I shout.

"Just come here."

"I—"

"*Pleeease!* Just come—"

She won't stop asking until I do. I crouch down and peer through the banister into the sitting room. Lizzie's kneeling on the floor, playing on the PlayStation with a friend.

"We're playing *Minecraft*," she says. "And this is Chloe." She points at a girl with blonde hair and glasses.

She's got my controller in her hands.

I nod.

"We've built a castle and a moat," says Lizzie. "And we're going to collect sheep and put them inside."

"That's good." I take a step.

"Yeah. Do you want to help?"

No, I want to wash my controller.

"That's okay."

"Why are you so grumpy?"

"I'm not. I just need to go to the bathroom."

"You are."

I am grumpy, but I'm also desperate for the bathroom. I put my hand on the banister and continue up the stairs.

"That's my brother," Lizzie says. "He's weird, but he plays guitar—"

Don't you dare say it!

"—and thinks he's Justin—"

"I don't!" I shout.

"Bieber!"

Lizzie and Chloe giggle as I reach the landing. I go into the bathroom, lock it, and then wash my hands ten times so I can finally pee. Then I go to my bedroom.

I lie on my bed. My hands start to tingle. *Germs on the planks.*

Germs on the bottles. They got through my gloves, through a gap in the stitching. *Germs on the planks. Germs on the bottles. A gap in the stitching. Don't put them on my bed. Don't touch anything. Germs on my bed. They'll grow overnight and be all over me.*

Aaargh!

I jump up and go back to the bathroom and start washing again.

Two hours. *Two hours.* I was in the cave for two hours on my own after Dan left. It was so quiet that every time a wave crashed on the beach it echoed off the cave walls like I was inside a shell. And then the light flickered as the buses rumbled, and the whole time I thought the ceiling was going to crack and crumble all over me. I thought of going outside, but I could hear the seagulls screeching and I couldn't risk it in case they dropped poop on me.

I turn off the tap. My fingers are still tingling, and then I spot a speck of dirt under one nail. I turn on the tap and start washing again. This is what happens when I go out. This is why it's safer to stay in. I quite liked working on *Shooting Star*, though. At least when me and Dan were nailing the planks of wood, I was concentrating on that and not my worries. I blocked out the dirty floor. I blocked out the germy bottles. For a while, I even blocked out that everybody is going to die. But I did think one time that Dan was going to nail my hand to the wood and I wouldn't be able to get it off and I'd have to get in an ambulance with a plank of wood stuck to my hand.

The morning went really quickly and everything was going all right until I said his brother had made a mistake on *Shooting Star*. Then Dan lost it like he sometimes does at school.

I wish I hadn't said anything or even looked at the drawing. But I

143

couldn't help spotting the mistake. If they fit the buoys underneath it, *Shooting Star* will flip upside down. It's the same as when I used to be able to go to the swimming pool. If you try to sit on a float, it flips you over or shoots up out of the water. The buoys need to go at the sides, not in the middle. I was going to keep quiet, but even though Dan is horrible, I can't let him drown.

I wash my hands. This is going to be the *last* time. Then I catch myself in the mirror. My face is white and my eyes are red, like an albino rabbit's. I'm tired from being out all day and I bet I'll be tired tomorrow too; I won't sleep tonight because I'll be worried I'll blurt it out at school that I've been working at the cave, and Dan really did look like he meant it when he told me I'd be dead if I said anything. If only it was half-term this week and not next.

I dry my hands and go back into my bedroom. The smell of sausages and onions is drifting up the stairs. I pick Chewie up off my pillow and lie down on my bed.

"What am I going to do at school tomorrow, Chewie?"

I can't think of anything for Chewie to say back. He just stares at me through the fur around his eyes. The tune from *Minecraft* is coming through my floorboards and I can hear Mum and Dad laughing in the kitchen. My fingers start to tingle.

No! The germs are gone now. You can't!

I force my eyes closed and take deep breaths. I was in the cave for so long I can still hear the waves sloshing around in my head. I like that my room is safe and doesn't have germs, but for a while I liked being outside, even if I had only swapped my room for a dirty cave.

But even that got better when Dan closed the door and blocked out the seagulls.

I've only worked on her for two days, but I'd really like it if *Shooting Star* was mine. I'd only have to get through this week and then I could work on her every day on my own over half-term. When she was ready, I'd drag her out of the cave, across the pebbles and down to the sea. I wouldn't care about the germs. I'd push her out until the waves reached my chest, and then I'd grab a rope and clamber on. The waves would lap around me, and *Shooting Star* would bob on them, but I'd pick up a paddle and dig it into the water and I'd go past the pier where the water gets darker and deeper. Then I'd stop paddling and look around. The beach would be gone, the people would disappear, and the sea would be calm and clean and there wouldn't be a single seagull in the sky. All my worries would be gone—no Dan, no Sophie, no Georges, no need to go to school at all. I'd be like a normal person.

I open my eyes. "Chewie. What was I thinking? That will never happen."

I was stupid to even think I could ever go on *Shooting Star*. Dan only wants my help because his brother isn't around. I wonder where he is. Maybe they don't live together. Perhaps his mum and dad have split up, like mine, and Dan chose to live with his mum, and his brother chose to live with his dad. I thought of living with my dad, but I couldn't because Dad would have had to change his job or I'd have to sleep on my own every night. And I didn't want to leave Mum and Lizzie by themselves either.

I roll onto my side. For a moment, I was dreaming of floating on *Shooting Star*, but now all I can think of is Dan's face and what will happen at school tomorrow. Nothing will have changed.

I hear a knock on my door.

"Alex."

"What?"

"Can we play—"

"No!"

22

Dan: My brother is too busy to write to me

Sunday

Dear Ben,

I hoped that I would have a letter from you when I got back from the cave, but I forgot the postman doesn't deliver on Sundays. Maybe I'll get one tomorrow. I've been working on Shooting Star again today. She's looking great. I've nailed all the base planks together and I've tied them too.

This is what she looks like now.

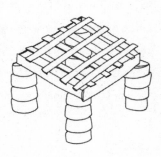

I had to stop because the weird kid I told you about started getting on my nerves. He said there's something wrong with your drawing of Shooting Star. I told him to shut up because he didn't know anything about making a raft! He made me really mad, so I left him and went to the pier on my own. I found some money that people left behind in the slot machines. I'll save it so we can go on the roller coaster when you come home.

I've got some questions about Shooting Star.

Some of your writing has got smudged and I can't tell if I need 300 or 500 bottles.

Am I supposed to use two tires for seats or will they be too heavy? Do I need to make paddles or will we just use our hands?

Do I need to get us life jackets? I think that's all I need to know. Hope I get to see you soon.

Love, Dan

PS Dad said Albion were great on Saturday. We'll be top of the league when you get back. I haven't been on the Xbox because I've been busy but I hope you are still beating XXXXX at FIFA. Write soooooooooooooooooon!

23

Alex: I hate Mondays

When the doorbell rings at three in the morning, it's never good news.

It's Monday morning and I'm sitting in English, trying to read *Stormbreaker*. Mrs. Shepherd is telling the boys and girls who got to the lesson late to sit down and do ten minutes' reading time, like the rest of us. I start to read again, but I've tried five times and the words still haven't gone into my head, because Emma gave me a message from Sophie.

> Hey, Shark Face. We're going to dunk you in the toilet.

I try to block it out, but it feels like the whole class is staring at me. Especially Dan. He was glaring at me as soon as I walked in, like he was sending me messages, daring me to tell anyone I'd been at the cave with him over the weekend. For a moment, on the way to school, I thought he might not be such a bully. But I was stupid to think that, even just a little bit. He hasn't changed at all. From the horrible way

149

he looked at me when I sat down, I think he really meant what he said about me being dead if I even say his name. He's sitting four rows behind me, but as I read I can feel his eyes burning like Cyclops's into the back of my head.

I look at the page and try to read again.

Alex Rider was woken by the first chime.

We're going to dunk you in the toilet. We're going to dunk you in the toilet. *His eyes flickered open, but for a moment he stayed completely still in his bed—***We're going to dunk you in the toilet. We're going to dunk you in the toilet.**

I stare at the page. I want to get out of here. I want to go home and sit in my room, but I'm trapped like a rat. I can't tell other kids I was with Dan and I can't tell the teachers about Dan.

When the doorbell rings—

Say my name and you're dead! Say my name and you're dead!

I screw my eyes tight. A line of cold sweat trickles down my back. I need to write a Worry List, but Emma is sitting right next to me and I can't let her see. Out of the corner of my eye I see Harry leaning across his desk, talking to Elliott. I think they've become friends, because they partner up in drama. Elliott sees me looking at him. I wonder if he can tell I'm upset, the same way I always knew when he was. I thought of telling him about Dan in the car this morning, but his dad had the radio on low and he would have heard.

Elliott nods at me, then looks down at his book. He knows something's wrong, but not how bad it is.

When the doorbell rings—

We're going to dunk you in the toilet. Say my name and you're dead!

Dan and Sophie will be waiting for me in the corridor at break time. I could pretend I need to see a teacher and stand outside the staff room and say I'm waiting for a new book. They'd never pick on me there. But I did that last week and Mr. Hargreaves told me to move because I was blocking the corridor. It's useless. They always find me; it's like they track me with GPS.

When the doorbell rings at three in the morning, it's never good news. Alex Rider was woken by the first chime.

They've never threatened me with head flushing before.

I rest my head on my hand. I wish I was Alex Rider. Sometimes I think I was named after him and that my dad is really a spy and not a security guard. And my mum is a secretary for all the MI5 agents and she gets me all the gadgets that the spies use—pens that are scanners, shirt buttons that are cameras, and watches that spin around on the wrist and turn into guns. I run through the streets, chasing after bad guys, and when I catch them I handcuff them to car-door handles or lampposts and sit on the wall while I wait for the police to arrive.

But I'm nothing like Alex Rider. Mum gets my pens from Tesco, and all my watch does is remind me how long I've got until they get me at break time. I'm nothing like Alex Rider, because Alex Rider wouldn't spend two hours a day washing his hands. The only thing we share is our name. He runs around the streets, saving the world, while I walk along them, trying to avoid dog poop.

Alex Rider was woken by the first chime....

Emma nudges me again. She's got another message in her hand.

Shark Face. Don't forget your handwash and shampoo.

I push the note away and flip to the blank pages at the back of my book. Emma glances over. I make a barrier with my arm so she can't see what I'm writing.

My Worry List

1. Everybody is going to die.
2. The toilet is filthy and poop will go in my hair.
3. I wish Dan would die.
4. I wish Sophie would get run over by a bus.
5. I'm a terrible person. I deserve to die for thinking that.
6. There's white stuff on the desk.
7. I <u>really</u> don't wish Sophie would die.
8. But I think the old man on the crossing is going to die.
9. Everybody is going to die.

Everybody is going to die.

My collar feels tight, like a snake is wrapped around my neck, and my hands are sweating inside my gloves.

Everybody is going to die. Everybody—

"Everybody is going to die!" I shout. "Everybody is going to—" I stop and look around. I'm standing up behind my desk, but

152

I don't remember standing up. Everyone in the class is staring at me; some of them have their hands over their mouths, trying not to laugh.

"Alex, is there something wrong?" asks Mrs. Shepherd with a concerned expression on her face.

"Everybody—is—going—to—die."

Mrs. Shepherd walks toward me. "Well, I hope not," she says. "Or we'll never find out what happens to Private Peaceful." She's trying to be kind and funny at the same time, but it doesn't stop the rest of the class from laughing. Mrs. Shepherd tells them to shush. I sit back down in my chair and try to loosen my tie. There's cold sweat running down my back and I can feel my heart thudding against my ribs. Emma is looking at me. Mrs. Shepherd is looking at me. The whole class is looking at me, just like that dream you have where you go to school with no clothes on.

"Okay, okay, that's enough, Year Seven.... George, I said enough!... Now just get back to some quiet reading."

Some in the class are sniggering as they look down at their books. Mrs. Shepherd kneels by my side.

"Alex, are you okay?" she whispers.

Everybody is going to die. Dan and Sophie are going to put my head down the toilet.

"Did you want to go outside in the corridor?"

"No," I whisper.

Mrs. Shepherd looks at me for a long time. I stare at my book and try and read the first line again, but the words still won't go into my head.

"Maybe come and talk to me after," she says.

I nod, but I know talking to a teacher will only make things worse, but I need to tell somebody soon because my heart feels like it's going to explode.

Mrs. Shepherd stands up and tells the class to stop reading. Then she hands out copies of *Private Peaceful* for us to read in pairs. Emma turns the pages, but I think she knows I'm not reading, because she's looking at me more than she's reading the words. My mind is going crazy and I can feel my pulse beating through my hands onto the desk.

"So," Mrs. Shepherd says. "Who can tell me what Private Peaceful is thinking as he walks toward the..." Her words start to fade.

I can't think about Private Peaceful; all I can think about is Dan and Sophie getting me at break time. There must be a new place to hide—around the back of the sixth-form block, in the closet in the gym where all the basketballs are kept, maybe the janitor's closet, or the room by the side of the printing office. I'll try to get out of the classroom first. I should have gone outside when Mrs. Shepherd asked me to. I wish I could see the nurse and she could wrap a bandage around my head and make the thoughts go away.

24

Dan: When the bell rings, it's time to look for Shark Face

"Dan, Sophie ... stop pushing in."

"We're not," says Sophie.

Mr. Henderson points at the line for lunch. "Then make it one line, not two." Sophie nudges a girl from Year Eight in the back. "Budge up!"

The girl steps forward and me and Sophie barge into the line. George C. and George W. are behind us, talking about what they did in the town center over the weekend. Something about playing football with some older boys in front of the Grand Pavilion. But I'm not listening. I still haven't had a letter from Ben. The mail came when I was eating breakfast, but Mum said there was only a letter from the council and a voucher for Pizza Hut.

The Georges and Sophie burst out laughing and make me jump.

"You should have come, Dan," sniggers George C. "The old guy from the pavilion came out and chased us across the grass. He didn't stand a chance."

"Yeah, I texted you," says Sophie. "We went in the pool down by the front, then to McDonald's."

"Okay, keep the line moving!" Mr. Henderson barks at us. "And make sure you clear your tables when you leave."

I inch forward in the line. I can't tell Sophie where I was. If I play dumb, she won't ask—

"Dan, where were you? Working on your stupid raft?"

"It's not stupid!"

"Ha-ha. Look, he's getting all touchy."

"I am not! It's just that it's not stupid.... Anyway, that wasn't where I was."

"So what did you do? Go shopping with your mum?" The Georges laugh.

"No!"

I can't tell them where I was, but I have to say something. "I was...I was working with my dad.... The delivery driver at work was sick, so I went with Dad and helped him deliver TVs."

"What, all day?" asks Sophie.

"Yeah. Lots of people are getting TVs.... My dad says people are getting ready for the Olympics."

"So what did you do Sunday?"

"Umm." I feel my face burning as I think of what to tell her. It's like she knows something. Like she saw me walking to the cave, or when I went looking for bottles.

"Come on, my love," says a lunch lady. "Others are waiting." I hold out my tray and she drops a lump of lasagna on my plate, and at the next counter I grab a carton of orange juice. As I join the line to pay, I try to think of what I can tell Sophie, but luckily she's moved on to someone else.

"There he is." She nudges me and nearly makes me drop my lunch. "Over there, by the window." She laughs. "Sharks have to eat sometime."

I look over toward the window and see Shark Face staring at me. Elliott is sitting a few places away, but Shark Face isn't talking. I stare back at him. *You dare tell anyone you were at the cave with me. You dare tell that our mums are friends.*

"Go on." Sophie nudges me in the back. "Let's go and sit at his table and tell him what we're going to do to him."

I stop and look around the hall. Mr. Henderson is standing by the main doors. Miss Harris and Mr. Gough are talking by the wall at the back.

Shark Face is still staring at me, like he's scared. But what if he suddenly got up and blurted something out like he just did in English?

I walk toward him, but three boys in Year Eight have overtaken us and they've put their trays down on Shark Face's table.

Sophie stands behind them. "We're sitting here."

The boys look at her. If they knew what she was like, they'd move.

"You four!" Mr. Henderson shouts and points at us. "Find somewhere else to sit. There's plenty of space at other tables."

Sophie makes an *urgh!* noise and elbows one of the boys in the back of his head.

"Ow!"

"Shouldn't have got in the way, then," she says. Then she looks at Shark Face. "Everybody's going to die! Everybody's going to die!"

157

she says in a squeaky voice. "The only one who's going to die is you, Shark Face, when we dunk your head down the toilet later."

The Georges laugh.

Shark Face darts his eyes at me, like he's trying to send me a message.

My mum and Dan's mum are friends and I helped him build a raft over the weekend.

What if he said that out loud?! I can't show him I'm scared. I have to be a big fish, like Ben said.

"Yeah," I say. "And bring your mop and gloves so you can clean it."

Sophie laughs, then pretends to accidentally knock another boy's head. We sit down at a table two rows back. The Georges start talking about *Dirt Rally*. George C. says that he's getting fed up with it because he can't win even if he's driving the Subaru Impreza. George W. says it's easy, but I'm not really listening, because Sophie is trying to talk to me with her mouth full of tuna casserole.

"You were too slow." She nods toward Shark Face. "We could have sat next to him if you were quicker," she says. "What's wrong with you?"

"Nothing." I stab a piece of carrot with my fork. "I've just got to be careful."

"Why?"

"I can't get in any more trouble. Mr. Francis phoned my mum and she's coming in on Wednesday."

The corners of Sophie's mouth turn up.

"It's not funny."

"What's it about?"

I shrug and act like I don't care. "Don't know. Think it's because I keep getting in trouble in class."

She shovels a forkful of tuna casserole into her mouth. "Just tell your mum it's the teachers' fault and the teachers it's your mum's fault, like I do." She elbows George C. "Isn't that right?"

The Georges suddenly stop talking about cars.

"Yeah."

"Yeah."

Then Sophie points her fork at Shark Face. "If we can't dunk his head today, we'll get his sneakers in the gym."

"Tie the laces together...." says George W.

"Yeah, and throw them over a telephone wire on the way home!" adds George C. We all laugh.

Shark Face looks over his shoulder at me like he knows we're laughing about him. He's not going to tell anyone. He wouldn't dare.

25

Alex: Looking for answers

I'm sitting at the dining-room table doing my English homework on the laptop. Mum's in the kitchen baking more cakes for Lizzie to take to the school cake sale tomorrow. I turn the page of my book and look at the questions Mrs. Shepherd assigned us.

In *Private Peaceful*, the book begins in an unusual way. It is designed to grab the readers' attention, but also to make them ask questions.

1. What do you notice about the title?
2. What tense is Section One written in?
3. Write down three questions you might have about the grammar and use of description.

The mixer whirs in the kitchen.

What do I notice about the title?

I don't notice anything. It's just two words on a page. *Private Peaceful*. It's just two words that begin with *P*. I put my elbow on

160

the table and slump my head on my hand. I can't think of anything else about the title. I used to love English, but now I can't even think about it. All I can think of is Dan, Sophie, and the Georges trying to stuff my head down the toilet. It's the worst thing they could do to me. They got together and thought up the cruelest thing they could. I wish I'd let them do it because at least now it would be over and done with and I would be upstairs cleaning myself. But I got out of school before they could catch me, and now they won't stop until they do.

I stare at the questions for so long that the words start to blur. How much longer will they go on bullying me? How much longer do I have to keep looking for places to hide?

The mixer stops. I hear Lizzie complain that the batter is still lumpy. Then I hear a click, and the whir starts again.

My chest is aching and I just want to cry. I want to tell someone. I wish I could go out into the kitchen and tell Mum and she'd say everything is going to be okay.

I imagine myself in the kitchen with Mum giving me a hug and Lizzie offering to let me lick cake batter off the spoon. I'd feel safe and warm, standing by the oven. But then Mum would tell Dad and he'd go down to the school and make everything worse.

I'm aching inside, but I don't know what to do.

I look at the laptop. The Internet has the answers to everything. I get up and push the door closed. Mum will think I'm just blocking out the noise. I wipe the keyboard clean and then start typing.

What do I do if I'm being bullied at school?

My finger hovers over the Enter key.

Wait, I can't. Dad says computers have memories and they

remember all the things people look up and all the Internet sites they go on. A security guard at his work went on one of the office computers. I don't know what he was looking for, but he got sacked afterward.

What if Mum goes on the laptop after I've gone to bed? She's only got to type in *What* and my question will come up. And I can't do it on the computers at school. Someone will notice.

I delete my question and type in *How to delete history*.

But what if Mum sees I've typed that? She'll wonder what I'm hiding. Aargh!

I look back at my homework like the words are going to jump into my head, but *Private Peaceful* still isn't making any sense. It's fighting with everything else. If only I'd gone out of class when Mrs. Shepherd asked. I felt so bad I might have told her then. I look back at the screen. What if it's not me who's being bullied? What if it's somebody else?

I type, *My friend is being bullied. What should I do?*

I take a deep breath and hover my finger over the Enter key again. I've got to find out. I need help.

I press Enter.

How to help a friend who is being bullied in school: 13 steps, wikiHow

What to do if you know someone is being bullied? Don't suffer in silence.

My best friend is being bullied. What should I do? Yahoo Answers

What to do if you are being bullied: how to deal with bullies.

162

Cyberbullying. Text bullying. What to do if…

I'm not being cyberbullied and I'm glad I haven't got a phone, or Sophie and Dan would be sending me messages all the time.

I scroll down. The list goes on and on. There are millions of answers.

The fourth one is the one I should pick, but I can't risk it. I click on the first one. A picture of a girl talking to another girl comes up on the screen.

The mixer stops whirring in the kitchen, then I hear the sound of a spoon scraping a bowl. The cake is nearly done. They'll be putting it in the oven, but they've still got to wash up. I think I've got enough time before they come into the room.

I scroll down the page. **Tell the bully to stop.**

I can't.

Avoid bullying back. Once you've told the bully to stop, walk away. Don't bully back; the bully may target you or make things worse for your friend.

Make things worse for your friend?! That friend is me!

Report the bullying. People you can tell include your parents, teachers, or a religious leader.

I can't, I can't. I don't know any religious leaders. But maybe I could go to church and talk to a priest in a confessional. I could pull the curtain and be anonymous and the priest will talk to me like I've seen in gangster movies.

The door creeps open and Lizzie peers around the corner. I click off the screen. She's standing in the doorway with a spoon in her hand.

"Mum says to come out if you want to scrape the bowl."

"It's okay."

"Yes!" She jumps up excitedly. "Means I get it all." Then she shouts, "Mum, Alex says I can have it all!" as she goes back into the kitchen.

I shut the laptop down.

Tell a parent, tell a teacher, tell a religious leader.

I can't tell Mum and Dad. Mum will be upset and Dad will think I'm weak for not standing up for myself. He already wishes I was like Dan. I can't tell any religious person, so that leaves a teacher, but it never worked for Elliott. He told Mr. Henderson, but Mr. Henderson didn't even ask who was picking on Elliott; he just said to ignore the bully and maybe they'd go away. I can't tell him, and even when I was really upset, I didn't tell Mrs. Shepherd. I think of other teachers I could tell, but I hardly know any of them and they always look too busy. My Head of Year, Mr. Francis, seems to listen. He helped Emma when she got upset because her mum was ill for a long time. But, no, I can't, I can't! Mr. Francis knows Dan better than he does me. They have a lesson in the Rainbow Room and I've seen them talking in the corridors. But that means he must know what Dan is like, because Dan was sent to see him last week when he threw a pen at the whiteboard. Mr. Francis might be the best person after all. I could go and see him after my guitar lesson on Wednesday when everyone else has gone home. That way I won't have to worry about it all of half-term.

The door opens again.

"I said I didn't want any," I say. Lizzie sucks on the spoon.

"Mum says where are your sneakers because they're not in your bag?"

"I think I left them at school."

"Then make sure you go and get them first thing!" shouts Mum.

"Okay." I sigh. I don't know how to tell Mum that Sophie and Dan took my sneakers and now they're hanging from a telephone wire two miles down the road.

26

Dan: Uh-oh, it's Wednesday

"Thanks for coming," says Mr. Francis.

"Sorry I'm late." My mum blows out her cheeks. "There was a problem at the office, and then there was traffic."

"It's fine, really. Take a seat. Dan and I were just chatting."

"That's nice." My mum smiles at me and sits down. I don't think she minds being here, really, because she thinks that Mr. Francis looks like George Clooney. But George Clooney wouldn't have been blah-blah-blah-ing about me going to see Mrs. Green, the school counselor, for the last ten minutes.

"So." Mr. Francis sits down opposite us with a notebook on his lap. "As I said on the phone, this is just a little chat to see how things—"

"Everything's fine," I say.

"Dan, let Mr. Francis speak," says my mum.

I sit back in my chair. Outside, some Year Nines are waiting with their bags to get on the minibus, and the custodian is walking around the parking lot, picking up garbage. I glance at the clock. It's just four. Mum doesn't have to be here. I kept out of trouble all of Monday and yesterday and I haven't done anything wrong today.

The minute hand clicks on the clock.

I could be in my bedroom, writing a letter to Ben or planning what to do next on *Shooting Star*. I could be sitting on my bed, playing *FIFA*. I could be messing with Rex. I could be doing loads of things that are better than sitting in the Head of Year's office, listening to Mr. Francis talk to my mum.

"What do you think, Dan?"

"What?"

"Mr. Francis thinks it might be a good idea for you to see Mrs. Green."

"I know, you already said, and I said I don't want to."

"But we think it might help."

"I don't want help," I say. "I'm just bored. Everything is boring. *This* is boring."

"Dan!"

"It's okay." Mr. Francis looks at me for a long time. I look down at my shoes and scuff them on the carpet.

"It's just that we can't go on like this, Dan. It's not good for you. I've noticed you've become more distracted in class these past couple of months, and you've been having angry outbursts."

"I haven't!"

"See, just like that. It's not good for you and it's affecting the rest of the class. I know things have been difficult. Mum says you're missing your brother."

"I'm not! It's nothing to do with him."

"It's okay. I'd miss my brother if—"

"I said it's not that!"

I look up and stare at Mr. Francis. He stares at me.

"I'm sorry," says Mum, looking embarrassed.

Mr. Francis wins the staring competition this time. I look out the window and watch the Year Nines get on the bus. I don't know where they're going, but I wish I was going with them so I could get out of this room. Mr. Francis is like a detective asking questions, and he'll find out what we did to Shark Face on Monday. Worst thing is I feel a bit bad about it. It was the Georges' idea, but it was me who threw his sneakers over the telephone wire.

"So we'll do that, Dan. Okay?"

Do what? They've made a decision without even asking me.

Mr. Francis makes a note on his pad. "You go to lessons as usual, but then come and see me at the end of each day . . . for the rest of this week."

The minibus goes out the gates. I don't even know why I'm here. Mum and Mr. Francis don't understand. No one understands. Except Ben, and he's not here.

I walk toward the door and wait for my mum, but she's still standing with Mr. Francis.

"We'll be with you in a minute, Dan," says Mr. Francis. "Just wait outside."

I sit on a chair. I hear voices echoing, something banging, and the hoot of the floor polisher coming down the corridor. I put my hands in my pockets and bump the back of my head gently against the wall.

168

The school is more like a church when everyone's gone home. I try to listen to what my mum is saying to Mr. Francis, but all I can hear is mumbling, and then I can't even hear that as the floor polisher gets closer. I hope it's nothing embarrassing, like I cried when Ben left or that I used to sleep with a toy monkey.

27

Alex: All I've got to do is say three words

"When you're ready, Alex. Just remember: rhythm, rhythm, rhythm." Mrs. Hunter puts her hand on her knee, like tapping out the rhythm will help me get started.

I put my fingers on the frets, then take my hand away and wipe my palms on my trousers. Mrs. Hunter has stopped tapping her hand. Emma and Jake are looking at me like they're willing me to play. I wipe my hands again and put my left hand back on the neck of my guitar. I want to play, but my fingers are so sore that the strings are cutting into them like knives. I pull my hands away again.

"I'm sorry."

"It's okay." Mrs. Hunter looks at my hands and winces like she can feel the pain too. "Jake, let's hear what you've been up to and we'll try Alex again after." Jake leans over his guitar. "Tempo, tempo, tempo, and don't worry about the words. We're here to learn guitar, not audition for *The X Factor.*"

Emma and Jake smile and I try to. None of us want to go on *The X Factor*, even if my annoying sister thinks I do.

Jake starts to play "Thinking Out Loud" by Ed Sheeran. I look at my hands. The threat of having my head flushed in the toilet has made me wash twice as much this week. It still hasn't happened, but just the thought of it and having Dan staring at me all the time is making me stress even more. The school used to feel huge, but now it's so small that I've run out of places to hide. I've only got to last two more days until the holidays, but even then I have to see Dan on the weekend. There's no escape. I went to see Mr. Francis at lunchtime. As I walked down the corridor, I practiced the three words in my head—*I'm being bullied. I'm being bullied*—but when I got there his office door was locked. I'm going to try again after this lesson.

Jake plays the last chord. Mrs. Hunter tells him that he's improving but he needs to try to work on moving his fingers clear of the strings a bit quicker. Then she looks at me.

"Would you like to try again, Alex, or leave it until the next lesson after half-term?"

"I'll try," I say. I lean over my guitar and put my fingers on the frets. Dr. Patrick said I can't let my worries stop me from doing things that I enjoy.

I pinch the strings and they cut into my fingers and I start to play "Sorry" by Justin Bieber. I don't care what Lizzie says. I like the song and she isn't here anyway. I nod my head, count the bars, and then try to sing. But I can't remember any of the words.

"It's okay," whispers Mrs. Hunter. "Keep playing."

My fingers move over the strings and the frets, but it's like they don't belong to me. Music is supposed to help me escape, but now all I can think about is what I'm going to say to Mr. Francis after we've finished. *I'm being bullied. I'm being bullied. I'm being bullied by Dan and Sophie and I can't make it stop.*

I finish playing. Mrs. Hunter says I did well, then tells us what we have to work on over the holidays. I pack my guitar into its case, but my hands are shaking so much I can hardly close the clasps. Jake opens the door and walks out. I can sense Emma looking at me, like she's waiting for me to walk out with her, like I did last week. But she can't see me walking to Mr. Francis's office. No one can. I turn away from her, wipe my guitar case down. Mrs. Hunter picks up her bag. I keep wiping. I hear footsteps behind me. When I look back over my shoulder, everyone has gone. I put my guitar on my back and walk out.

I'm being bullied. I'm being bullied, I repeat as I go down the corridor. All I've got to do is say it once, and then it could all be over.

As I turn the corner into the blue corridor, my chest pulls tight and my heart is thumping so hard it's like it's beating against the walls.

Dan: Snap!

Mum has been chatting to Mr. Francis for ages. I'm getting really bored and just want to go home. I get my phone out of my bag. We're not supposed to use them during the day, but lessons finished half an hour ago. I text Sophie.

Where did you go?

She messages back straightaway. Met Leanne and went to the park. Did you give Shark Face a hair wash?

No. We waited for you.

Get him tomorrow.

Yeah.

The polisher suddenly stops. I stop texting. Mr. Jevons isn't a teacher, but he's still able to take our phones away. I hear footsteps. It sounds like Mr. Jevons is heading toward the storeroom to get more polish, or maybe he's gone to take the plug out of the socket. I put my phone in my bag and lean forward with my elbows on my knees. Mr. Jevons's footsteps get louder. I wait for the sound of the storeroom door opening, but the footsteps keep going, then stop level with me.

"Oh!" someone says. I lift my head.

Shark Face is looking straight at me with his mouth open like he's been struck by lightning.

"What are you doing here?" I hiss.

"I was just..."

"You were just going!" I say.

Mr. Francis's door opens.

"Thanks so much," says my mum. "I'll chat to Dave tonight and see if he agrees."

I stare at Shark Face. *You dare!*

"Oh, hello, Alex," says Mum, like she's happy to see him. "How are you getting on?"

"I'm...I'm...okay," Shark Face stutters.

"Just keep in touch," says Mr. Francis. He puts his hand on my shoulder and guides me out into the main corridor. Then he looks at Shark Face and smiles. "Yes, Alex, what can I do for you?"

Shark Face darts his eyes in my direction. *He's been bullying me.* That's what he's going to say, and he's going to say it now, right here in front of Mr. Francis and my mum.

Shark Face opens his mouth.

You dare. You dare.

"Alex?"

"Nothing," he says. "I was just getting my guitar and then going home." He turns and walks down the corridor.

Don't say it, Mum.

"Alex, would you like a lift home?"

Shark Face starts walking so quick he almost runs.

29

Alex:

Aaaaaaaaaaaaaaaaaaargh!

Dan: Shark Face goes for a swim

"Hold him still, Dan. Hold him—" Sophie starts to giggle. "Come on. Just grab his legs."

"No. Don't. Please." Shark Face is trapped against the bathroom door. We've been looking for him all lunch hour and finally found him in the bathroom.

"Please, *pleeeease*." Sophie giggles again. "Come on, Dan, and you, George. What are you waiting for?"

George W. bends down and tries to grab one of Shark Face's legs. Shark Face kicks his hand away.

"No. Don't. Don't!"

"We just want to wash your hair. Dan! Come on!"

I reach down for Shark Face's leg. His knee whacks against my chin. He looks so scared that I'm beginning to think this is a bad idea.

"Why don't we just put his head under the taps?" I ask.

"What?! No way! You said he'd been to see Mr. Francis! Just grab him."

"Is anyone coming?" I say to George C., who's by the door, on lookout. He steps out into the corridor, then comes back in.

"It's okay," he says. "Just hurry."

I kick Shark Face's bag out of the way and it slides across the floor to the sink. George W. nods at me, then we try to grab Shark Face's legs at the same time, but they're flailing away like a trapped spider's. He kicks me on my arm and one of his knees knocks George W. in the face.

"Ow!" George W. shouts, and holds his hand up to his nose.

"I didn't see him. I didn't tell him anything."

"We don't care," says Sophie. "We're going to do it anyway."

Shark Face kicks again.

"Come on, George," says Sophie. "You're useless." She wraps her arms around Shark Face's chest. "Just grab his legs anywhere and then we'll tip him up."

Shark Face scrunches his face up. It's the same face he pulled when he was picking up the bottles. I get a weird feeling in my stomach. Almost like I feel sorry for him. But I can't feel sorry for him. Sophie will think I've gone soft.

"Dan! Come on!"

"No, don't, Dan." Shark Face stares at me like he's going to cry any second.

"Don't, Dan," says George W. in a reedy voice. "Don't, Dan."

No! Shark Face called me Dan in front of them. He's going to tell them he was at the cave with me next. They can't know that. I bend down and wrap my arms around his knees.

"Come on!" I shout at George W. He grabs Shark Face's ankles, and the three of us lift him and tilt his head toward the toilet. I wait for him to shout again, but his body has gone stiff, like he's too frightened to shout anymore.

"Closer," says Sophie.

Me and George lift his legs higher. Coins fall out of Shark Face's pockets. Some of them go into the toilet; others rattle as they hit the edge and roll across the bathroom floor.

Shark Face reaches out and puts his gloved hands on the toilet seat. Sophie knocks them away and reaches for the flush.

"Someone's coming! Someone's coming!" says George C. urgently. We drop Shark Face on the ground.

Sophie bends down. "Don't talk to a teacher," she says. "Or we'll put your head right in there next time."

"I haven't talked to anyone. I didn't get to see Mr. Francis," says Shark Face.

"We don't care. Just promise you won't."

"Okay." Shark Face looks up. "Okay."

But he's not looking at Sophie. He's looking at me.

31

Alex: The worst thing anyone could do

My gloves are covered with wee and poop.

I can take my left one off, but I'll have to take the right one off with my bare hands. I need a pair of gloves to take off my gloves.

I'll use toilet paper instead.

The toilet paper is full of germs. I'll use my disinfectant.

The disinfectant is in my bag and I'll have to touch my bag to get it out and then I'll have to wipe that too.

I'll take the disinfectant out, then wipe my bag, then wipe my gloves, then take my gloves off, then wipe the disinfectant packet, then wipe my hands.

Don't panic. Don't feel sorry for yourself. I'm in charge. You're not.

I am. I've just got to get this done.

I sniff.

There's poop in my hair.

It didn't actually go in the toilet.

It did. I need to wash it, but I need to touch the taps with my gloves.

There's poop on my arm too.

It's everywhere. On my sleeve, up my nose. Every time I breathe, I can feel it traveling down my throat and into my lungs.

Calm down.

I need to calm down. I rest my head against the bathroom wall. If only I'd spoken to Mr. Francis yesterday.

If only Dan wasn't there.

If only I wasn't such a wimp.

If. If. If.

Put your worries into boxes.

Dan, Sophie, George W., George C.

Make the boxes smaller.

It's not working. I'm bashing the boxes down, but the worries are jumping back out.

It's got to work. I've got to get home.

I reach into my bag.

My Worry List

1. Everybody is going to die.
2. My hands are covered in poop. It's under my fingernails, growing up my fingers, spreading across all the veins on the back of my hand. It's creeping up my arms, across my chest, and into my heart. I hope Dan touched it. I hope he dies.
3. No, I don't hope that. I hope he gets ill. I hope when he drinks his Coke in the cave that he picks up a can of rat poison by mistake.

4. I'm a bad person for thinking that. I don't want him to die. But if he did, at least he wouldn't be at school to pick on me.

5. But he'll be waiting at the cave on Saturday. I hope Dad's car breaks down so we can't get there.

6. The brakes will fail and we'll crash through the railings on the seafront, flip over like the car Elliott saw on Police Interceptors and we won't stop rolling until we reach the sea.

7. Dad's going to drown and all the people and dogs on the beach will get flattened. I don't want Dad's brakes to fail. I just want him to run out of gas so we don't even get there.

8. The car will run out of gas right in the middle of an intersection and a bus will smash into us and me and Dad will die and Mum and Lizzie will be left at home all on their own. I've got to go to the cave to stop Dan drinking the poison and I'll walk so nothing can happen to Dad's car.

9. I can't walk. It'll take me ages because of the dog and bird poop. By the time I get there, Dan will have drunk the poison.

10. Dan's going to die.

11. Everybody is going to die.

32

Dan: I feel a bit bad

It's nearly time for dinner and I'm lying on my bed playing *Call of Duty*. But I can't concentrate. Major Ingram keeps getting blown up before I have time to fire. It's because I feel a bit bad about what I did to Shark Face yesterday. When I was walking home today with Sophie and the Georges, they were talking about the things they were going to do over half-term. I kept quiet about working with Shark Face, but they kept pretending they were him and were shouting. "Please, Dan! Please stop them, Dan!" as we walked down the road. Then they started laughing and I pretended I found it funny, but I kept thinking of the way he stared at me as I walked out. It was like he was blaming me for everything, like I should have stopped it. But I couldn't, even if I'd wanted to.

My phone buzzes. It's a message from Sophie.

Are you coming to McDonald's with us tomorrow, or not?

Don't think so.

Loser! But you're going to OBS Tower on Tuesday. Yes?

Yes.

I'd rather be working on *Shooting Star*. But I am looking forward to the tower opening. George C.'s dad has got him two VIP tickets and he might be able to get some more. Everyone at school wants to go up the tower.

The front door clicks open and slams shut. Dad's just got home. It's Friday night, so he'll have brought Indian takeout home for dinner. He shouts up at me to come and get it.

"In a minute!" I shout back. I guide Major Ingram between some oil drums and tanks and press Pause. I go to run downstairs but stop when I hear Dad raising his voice.

"Really!" he shouts. "You want to do this now, when I've just got in?"

"Well, when else?" says Mum. "You're either working or watching football."

"Well, not in the middle of dinner." I hear him slam the food down on the kitchen table. "I already said what I think," says my dad. "Definitely not. I don't see how it helps either of them."

I wish they wouldn't argue. Every time one of them shouts, it makes me go hot inside. Dad walks into the sitting room. My mum follows behind. "Just think about it, Dave. Mr. Francis—"

"Mr. Francis, what does he know? He's a teacher, not their father. I think it's a bad idea."

The sitting room door closes. This is going to turn into another fight about me and Ben. I creep halfway down the stairs, but all I can hear are mumbles. What does my mum want to do? And why doesn't my dad want to do it? I think of going down and putting my head

183

against the door, but they caught me doing that the night the police came for Ben.

I couldn't hear much, just odd words, like *drink*, *liquor store*, and *cigarettes*. Then I heard something about a girl. That's when the door suddenly opened and I saw Ben standing between two policemen in the middle of our sitting room and Mum was on the sofa with a policewoman. I thought Mum was crying, but then she took her hand away and told me to go upstairs. I went into Mum and Dad's room and looked out the window. There were two police cars parked outside with their lights flashing. Then I saw Ben being walked down the path and put into the back of one of them.

A cupboard door slams in the kitchen. The argument is getting so angry I don't want to hear any more. I put my headphones on to block it out. Major Ingram gets blown up right away. I can't concentrate, but I have to do something. I keep the headphones on but unplug them so I can walk around in silence. I unhook Rex's water bottle and refill it in the bathroom. Then I put some nuts in his bowl and put his bottle back.

I look around my room for something else to do. I don't feel like drawing and I've watched all my DVDs. I go into Ben's bedroom and check on Horace. He's light green, so he's feeling okay. I give him three crickets and he snaps them up like I've not fed him for a week.

Through my headphones I hear a door slam, then footsteps thudding up the stairs. I walk out onto the landing. Mum slams her bedroom door shut. I take my headphones off and hear her crying in the bedroom. I hate listening to them argue. I hate it when Mum cries. My heart beats like a drum. I put my headphones back on, but in my head I can still hear the noise. I have to do something to block it out, something I can concentrate on.

I go into my bedroom and write a letter to Ben.

Friday

Dear Ben,

It's the holidays so I'm going to work on Shooting Star all week except for Tuesday when I am going to the Observation Tower. I think I'm going to work on Shooting Star on my own until you get back because something happened yesterday to the weird boy I told you about.

I've got some more questions for you.

I can't find any of those big drums so is it okay just to use bottles?

I think Shooting Star is going to be heavy when she's finished.

Shall I get a boat trailer thing from that man you spoke to so I can take her from the cave to the sea?

Do I need that stuff that Dad used to paint the back fence, to stop Shooting Star's wood from getting soggy?

Shall I get the mascot now or shall I wait for you to come home?

Oh, and this isn't a question about Shooting Star, but I just wondered if you ever feel bad about what you've done? ~~Because I~~ Never mind. I think that's all I need to know.

Hope you're still beating Five X.

Love, Dan

PS I didn't send a picture because she looks the same as last week. I'll draw another one tomorrow.

33

Alex: Everybody is going to die, for real this time

"Are you sure you don't want me to come with you?"

"I'm sure." I look out the car window.

"I could help you carry the bottles?"

"No, Dad. I said I'm fine!"

"Okay. Sorry I asked," he says sarcastically, then he starts tapping his hands on the steering wheel in time to a song on the radio.

We're driving to the cave, and so far none of the things have happened that I put on my last Worry List. Everybody is still alive: people are taking the buses and walking along the pavement, and Dad's car hasn't run out of gas because the gauge is still showing half full, and the brakes haven't failed, because he just pressed them and now we've stopped at the traffic lights. That just leaves worrying about whether Dan has drunk rat poison. But I took so long getting out of the house that I could be too late already. It's nearly eleven o'clock and he'd have stopped for a drink by now. He'll be crawling around the cave with foam dripping out of his mouth like a zombie. He'll chase me out onto the seafront and we'll crash through the ice-cream stand and burger stands and ketchup will spread like blood all along the beach and the promenade.

Dad turns on his left blinker and we pull out onto the seafront. I shake myself out of my daydream.

Oh no! Dad's singing and doing a dad dance in his seat beside me.

What do you mean, ooh. When you nod your head yes
But you wanna say no.

Dad smiles at me.
Arrgh! That's all I need.

What do you mean, hey.

"Dad! Can we turn it off?" I pick at my gloves.
"What do you mean?" Dad sings and laughs at the same time.
"Dad!"
"What?" He reaches for the radio. "I thought you liked Justin Bieber. Lizzie said—"
"No, Dad. I really don't."
He shakes his head as he turns the radio down. "I don't know, Alex. Things are hard enough without you being so difficult. You've been like this since Christmas. Mum says it's your age, but I hope not, or we've got years of this."

Grumpy. He thinks I'm grumpy. I wish that's all it was. If only he knew. After I got flushed, I stayed in the bathroom at home, scrubbing my hands and hair all last evening. And when I woke up, I started scrubbing so much that my hands feel like I've got needles stuck in them, and my head feels like it's on fire. But Dad doesn't really understand my OCD, so why would he understand if I told him I was being bullied? All the stories he tells me about his school and building stuff with my uncle—it's obvious he had a great time growing up. He never got spat at or had his head almost stuck down the toilet.

We drive along the seafront in silence until we pass the pier and pull over by the aquarium.

"I'll catch you later." Dad doesn't look at me. It's like he's upset with me or I've upset him. But I don't want him to be either of those things. Me being bullied isn't his fault, and the worries are in my head, not his.

I slowly reach for the door handle. My head feels so mixed up. I like working on *Shooting Star*, but I don't want to see Dan. Most of all, though, I don't want to leave Dad when he's gone quiet like this. I turn and look at him.

"I'm sorry, Dad. It's not your fault."

Dad sighs, and then a smile creeps across his face.

"I know, mate." He goes to rub my head, then stops.

Steering wheel, germs, hand. I wish you could, Dad. I wish you could.

Dad drops his hand down onto a button by the handbrake and pops the trunk. "Don't forget the bottles."

"Okay. But don't drive off yet."

I get out of the car and lift the trunk with the tips of my gloves. I wouldn't normally be able to pick up the bottles, but Dad has put them in big clothes bags from Dr. Barnardo's, and I think they might be clean, but I don't know why my OCD thinks that. I pick them up and close the trunk.

"Got them?" Dad leans across the passenger seat.

"Yes. Thanks."

"Tell Dan I'll see if I can get some more this week."

"Okay."

He nods for me to close the door, but I can't let him drive off. Not yet. *Drive safe.* I have to say it, but he's not going to like it.

"Dad?"

"Yes, mate?"

"Drive safe."

"What?...No, Alex. I'm only going to be gone a couple of hours."

"Please, Dad. Just once."

Our car will get flattened by a bus and trap Dad inside it and the gas will leak from the tank and set all the huts along the seafront on fire and all the people in them will run down the beach and jump into the sea to escape the flames.

"Dad. Please."

Dad shakes his head and looks out through the car windshield. All he has to do is say it once and everything will be okay.

"Dad?"

"Okay. Okay. Drive safe." He sighs. "But this has got to stop, Alex."

"I know, Dad. It will. I promise."

"Now can you close the door? I need to get some sleep after working the night shift. And don't forget to tell Dan you're going with Mum to see Nan and Granddad tomorrow."

"I won't." I nudge the door closed with my elbow. Dad pulls away.

190

Maybe he's tired—that's why he's being quiet. But somehow I think it's my OCD that tires him out.

I dodge the traffic as I cross the road. A car beeps at me and someone shouts, "Use the crossing, you idiot!" but I'm too busy looking for dog poop and seagulls to reply.

I think of turning back, but Mum will be mad with me for not getting fresh air, and I don't want to go back, because I did quite like working on *Shooting Star* last weekend.

Dan's legs are poking out from underneath *Shooting Star* like a mechanic's when I get to the cave.

I wish it would fall down on top of him.

No, I don't.

There are bottles scattered all over the floor and two dirty yellow buoys in the middle of them. Dan still hasn't moved. He's drunk the poison and he's dead. My heart beats fast and my hands are sweaty.

I drop the bags on the floor; one of them falls over. I hear Dan grunt as he pulls a piece of string tight under *Shooting Star*. He's not dead; he's just ignoring me like he did on the first day. A warm flood of relief washes over me. He's a bully, but I don't want him to die.

I walk to the back of the cave and look at the drawing of *Shooting Star*. I don't want to be here with Dan, but just seeing what the raft will look like when she's finished makes me want to work on her again.

"Didn't think you were coming, Shark Face."

I sigh. For a few hours at home, I was Alex, but now I'm Shark Face again.

Dan wipes his hands on his hoodie, then nods at the bags I left on the ground. "You got some bottles," he says without looking at me.

191

I nod. "My dad did."

"That's what I meant."

He picks up a bag and looks inside. He's acting like nothing bad has happened. Like dunking somebody's head down the toilet is something he does every day. I want to tell him how bad it felt, that it was the absolute worst thing he could do to me, but if I tell him that, he'll know I'm weak and he'll get Sophie and the Georges to do it again.

He puts the bags at the back of the cave with the rest of the bottles. "We don't need them yet. We're doing this today." He nods at a can of creosote and two brushes on the cave floor. "She'll rot if we don't make her waterproof."

All the time he's talking he's not even looking at me. It's like he's talking to the air, the floor, the cave walls. It's like he hates me so much he can't bear to see my face. I hang my bag on the hook. Dan flips the can open with an old spoon, then picks up a brush. He glances at me quickly.

"Come on, Shark Face. Are you going to help or not?"

I walk toward him slowly. I feel so mixed up. Part of me wants to help, but the other part wants to go home. I pick up a brush.

"It's just as well you decided to help; otherwise you really will be here all holidays."

What?

"What?"

"Don't you know?" Your mum served my mum at Tesco yesterday. She told Mum you were loving working on *Shooting Star* and want to come here all the time."

"What?...I didn't....I don't!" My breath catches in my throat.

"That's what my mum told me. She said that it would be good for me to have company too; she even wanted you to come over the other day."

"What?!"

"It's okay. I told her you were an idiot." Dan smirks, then walks over to his bag.

What is my mum doing? It's bad enough having to work with Dan, let alone her becoming friends with his mum. They'll be having coffee together in each other's houses next, and then both his parents will come to dinner and they'll bring Dan. He'll be coming around at Christmas, getting invited to my nonexistent birthday parties. It's bad enough having a bully at school; now he's going to be in my house, in my sitting room, in my bedroom.

Dan puts on a pair of yellow gardening gloves that go right up to his elbows, then throws another pair at me. "Put them on," he says. "Don't want you ruining yours."

I ignore him because I know he doesn't mean it, but also because I've just seen the warning labels on the can.

Do not get on your skin.
Do not inhale.
Do not let creosote come in contact with plants.

Dan didn't need to drink poison: he's painting with it.

He dips his brush in the can and starts to paint. The smell of creosote burns my nose. I try not to breathe, but I'm too late; it's already gone up my nose, down my throat and into my lungs. Dan dips his brush again. "Come on! We'll never get her finished like this."

"But it's poisonous."

"It's okay. My dad said they banned the really bad stuff because it caused cancer."

"Cancer!"

"But he said this stuff is okay."

I sniff. The creosote hasn't just filled my lungs; it's filled the whole cave. All it needs is for a passerby to light a cigarette, and the cave will ignite and explode. The fire would be so fierce ten fire engines couldn't put it out. I'm not staying here. I need to get out.

I put my hand over my mouth and start walking out of the cave.

"You're such a wimp!" shouts Dan.

I walk out onto the seafront and take a deep breath. The sea air rushes through me and cleans me like detergent.

I turn and look back at Dan. He's painting away without any worries. No worries about the creosote. No worries about seagulls. No worries about what he did to me. He doesn't worry about me at all, but all the time I'm thinking this I'm worried about what the creosote might do to him.

34

Dan: It's not a holiday camp, but who cares!

Shark Face has already gone home and I'm clearing up the mess. I've got creosote everywhere: on my hands, in my hair, all over my clothes. Shark Face didn't get any on him. He didn't get close enough to. He just stood at the cave mouth, looking at the sea. It meant he didn't do any work, but it also meant I didn't have to look at him. Which was good because I still felt a bit bad about flushing his head. While I was painting, out of the corner of my eye I saw him looking at me. It was like he was waiting for me to say sorry. I am a little bit, but I can't say it, because Sophie would go nuts if she found out.

I put the lid back on the creosote can and throw the brushes into the pile of trash at the back of the cave. My stomach rumbles. I look at my watch. It's four thirty and time to go home. I text Mum, like she asked me to do.

I'm leaving now. What's for dinner?

She replies straightaway. Be careful. Wait and see. xxx

I put my phone in my pocket. She'll think I'm being good by

texting, but I only did it to warn them that I'm leaving so she can stop arguing with Dad by the time I'm home.

But sending the text doesn't work, because when I get back they're sitting in the dining room, ready to ambush me.

"Dan, come and sit down."

"I'm just getting a drink."

"Dan, just do as your mum says for once," says Dad.

I grab a drink and walk into the dining room. It doesn't seem like they've been arguing, but they are sitting side by side, looking serious.

I pull out a chair and sit down. Dad looks at Mum; Mum looks at me.

"Dan," Mum says with a straight face. "Me and your dad have been talking."

You mean arguing.

"Your mum's been talking," says Dad. Mum gives him a dark look.

"It's about the chat I had with Mr. Francis," says Mum.

"Yeah."

"Well..."

"Mum, you don't fancy him, do you?"

My mum laughs. "No, of course not.... W—"

"Because you said he looks like George Clooney."

"Did you?" asks Dad.

Mum shakes her head. "No...no...of course I didn't.... Anyway, it's not about that."

"What, then? I'm not changing schools."

"Dan, for God's sake." Dad puts his hand down on the table. "For once...JUST...BE...QUIET!"

"What is it, then?"

"We...I was just thinking." Mum pauses like she's going to say something really bad. "That it might be a good idea for you to go and see Ben."

My heart does a big thud in my chest. "Really? Are you serious?"

Mum nods. "We all think it might help you settle down at school."

Suddenly I can't sit still any longer. My legs are twitching like I could run a hundred miles. I jump out of my seat. "That's great! When can we go?"

"See," says Dad. "This is just what we didn't want. Getting him all worked up."

"I'm not worked up. I just want to see Ben."

"Just sit down, love," says Mum, holding my arm. "I know you're excited."

"Excited? This is the best thing ever. When? When?"

"Thursday," she says.

I pull my arm away. "I'll pack now—there's loads of stuff I need to get for Ben. I'll take our Xbox games and stuff." I turn to go into the hall.

"Dan!" Dad shouts.

I keep walking. I just want to get upstairs and start packing.

"Dan!" He shouts so loud I know he'll get angry if I don't stop. I turn and look through the door.

"Yeah?"

"Look, I know you're excited, but this isn't all fun."

"I *know*," I say, pretending to pull a serious face.

"No, you don't know." Dad stands up. "Dan, you've got to understand: Ben's not living in a holiday camp."

"Yada, yada, yada." I start to run up the stairs.

"Dan!...See, what did I tell you?"

I glance through the banister and see him glaring at Mum.

"I'm just trying to make two people happy," she says.

Dad says something, but I'm already in my bedroom, thinking of what I can take for Ben. I go into his room, pick up two comics, then take the *FIFA* disc out of the Xbox and put it in its case. Then I do the same with the film about the raft. What else? What else? I run into my bedroom, think of ejecting *Call of Duty*, but I need to play that before I go. I look along my shelf and grab the box set of *Game of Thrones*.

I can't believe I'm going to see him after all this time. My heart is beating like Rex's, and my hands are shaking like leaves. I sit down on my bed. I'll write him a letter. If he gets it, I hope he'll have time to reply to tell me what he needs.

Saturday

Dear Ben,

I've got some great news. You might know already, but Mum just said I can come and visit you. It's not for a few days but I can't wait.

I'm just getting some stuff ready for you. Do you want me to bring FIFA and Call of Duty with me so we can play it with Five X? I can bring the Game of Thrones box set with me so we can watch that after if you like. Did you want me to bring your football boots too, because you left them behind? Tell me if there's anything else.

It's a long way to Milton Keynes so I'll have to get up early. It'll be like it was when we went to Cornwall on holiday. Dad says you don't live in a holiday camp but I don't care. I just can't wait to see you again.

I painted Shooting Star with creosote today. I haven't drawn a picture because she doesn't look any different but she's waterproof now.

Mr. Kendall says hello and Mum does too and sends a kiss. Mum, not Mr. Kendall. That would be a bit weird!

Dad is busy at work, but I know he can't wait for you to come back and watch the Gulls.

Love, Dan

I read what I've written, then fold the piece of paper in half. I'll get an envelope from Mum and mail it on the way to the cave in the morning. I smile because this is the happiest I've felt in ages.

I'm going to see him.

I'm going to see my brother.

Alex: I had a dream

Last night I dreamed again that *Shooting Star* was mine. I had no worries and the sun was shining brightly, so I took her out on the sea and paddled toward the old pier. Lizzie was with me too. When we reached the old pier, we dropped anchor, then leaned over the side of *Shooting Star* and dropped our crab lines into the water. The water was calm, with nothing moving beneath the surface. Me and Lizzie left our lines in the water, waiting for a crab to bite, but they never did. All we caught was an old tire and a can of creosote.

Then it started to get dark and we started to get cold, so we wrapped ourselves up warm with the tarpaulin. There was no one else near us; there were no cars or buses on the seafront, and the pier was closed. The only noise we could hear was the water lapping against the wood and the only lights we could see were the stars.

Lizzie fell asleep and I started to feel tired too, but just as my eyelids began to droop I felt a tug on the line. I knelt up on *Shooting Star* and started to pull the line in. But the line went on for ages and it started to cut through my gloves. I kept pulling but it was like the line had no end. Lizzie woke up just as I heard something thrashing in the water. My arms were aching and I was running out of breath. Lizzie leaned over the side.

"What have we caught? A mermaid?" she shouted.

I peered down into the water. A dark shadow moved toward me, then turned toward the pier. My line went taut and the shadow tugged *Shooting Star* through the water like a speedboat.

"Let go, Alex!" shouted Lizzie. "Let go!"

I tried to drop the line, but it was glued to my fingers. The shadow kept tugging us. I could hardly breathe as we bumped over the waves with water spraying in our faces.

"Alex!" Lizzie screamed. "We're going to drown!"

Shooting Star dipped down under a wave. The water went over my feet, then up to my waist. Lizzie grabbed my arm.

I'm not ready to die, I thought. *I'm not ready to die.* I yanked on the line and suddenly—

Snap!

I looked at my hands. The line was slack, with a broken end dragging in the water. I put my arm around Lizzie.

"We're okay," I said. "We're going to be all right."

Lizzie mumbled something, but all I heard was her shivering.

I peered into the water again. Everything was still and quiet, but then the lights flickered on the pier, and the roller coaster climbed the track, but there was nobody on it. Lizzie started to cry.

"It's okay," I said. "We'll be all right."

And we sat on *Shooting Star* all night while a dark shadow circled underneath us like a whale....

*　　*　　*

"That's great," says Mum.

I've just told her about the dream as she drops me off at the seafront.

"Why's it great?" I ask. "It was scary."

"Because it's a good thing you're dreaming about being outside, for once."

Mum's right. I hardly ever dream about being outside. Even if it was scary, at least something exciting happened outside my room. That never happened before I started working on *Shooting Star*. It's like—

"Alex...Alex!" Mum nudges me.

"Yes?"

"Can you get out now, love? I need to get to work."

"Oh, sorry." I climb out of the car. "Drive safe."

"Drive safe."

I close the door and Mum pulls away.

When I reach the cave, I can't see Dan. All I can see is *Shooting Star*. Her base planks are now painted dark like a proper fishing boat.

"All right, Shark Face?"

Dan stands up at the back of the cave with a garbage bag full of bottles in each hand.

"Just thought I'd move these out here so we can see what we're doing," he says cheerfully as he walks toward me.

That's weird. For a moment, I thought he smiled at me, but he can't have. It must have been the sun in his eyes.

I walk into the cave and hang my bag on the hook. The light

flickers as a truck rumbles overhead. I glance quickly around the cave, checking for any new cracks that might have appeared during the night.

"They won't come through," says Dan. "These caves have been here for ages." He goes back for more bottles.

"I know," I say. "But the cement trucks haven't." I look up as another rumbles above. The Observation Tower must be nearly finished, because it's like all the trucks are moving out at once.

"Come on," says Dan. "The creosote has dried, so we can fix the bottles on now."

He sounds like he's in a hurry to get it done. Or maybe he's just in a hurry to get rid of me. Once we've fitted the bottles and buoys, he won't need me anymore.

He puts the bottles on the ground, then walks over to the diagram of *Shooting Star*. I stand next to him.

"We've got to put the bottles into groups of ten and then tie string around them, like that." He points at a drawing of bottles grouped together. They look like the cells you see under a microscope. "Then we have to tie the bundles under the base planks."

I look at the diagram. It all makes sense, apart from only fixing the buoys underneath and not at the sides, but he'll get angry if I mention that.

We go to the front of the cave and sit down on our buckets. I sit a bit behind Dan so the seagulls can't swoop down and get me.

"I know why you did that."

"Why I did what?"

"Sat there. It's so the seagulls can't get you. I've seen you running away from them."

I shrug. I can't tell him he's right. If he knows, then that's one more thing he can bully me about.

Dan picks up a garbage bag and empties the bottles onto the ground. Then he reaches down and starts to stand them up.

"You hold them," he says, "and I'll tie the string around them."

I lean forward. The bottles have been at the back of the cave, with all the damp and clumps of moss and other bits of dirt on the floor. All sorts of germs could be on them. I lift up my hand. I don't want to touch them, but if I don't, we'll never finish *Shooting Star*.

"Come on, Shark Face. We haven't got all day."

I grit my teeth and hold my hand over the bottles like the claw that grabs the Minions in the machine on the pier.

You can do it. You can do it. They're filthy.

You can. Last week you picked up planks and nets—you can do this.

I drop my hand down onto the bottles. It didn't hurt. I'm still alive.

I trap a group of bottles between my feet and hands. Dan wraps the string around them and ties a knot. Then he groups more bottles and we do the same. In half an hour, we do 4, but that's only 40 bottles and we've got to do another 260 before *Shooting Star* will be able to float. Dan empties another bag, then another. There are so many bottles that they start to blur. I block out the germs and start grouping them again. After we've tied twenty bundles, we pick them up and tie them under the base planks.

"She's looking great, Shark Face." Dan smiles and looks at what we've done. For a moment, I think he's going to pat me on the back, so I step away, but he's just putting his hands on his head.

Why is he so happy? He can be like this at school, making the class laugh, but the next minute he snaps like an elastic band, so I don't trust him. *Shooting Star* does look great, but we've only got one side fixed with bottles. We need loads more. If she went on the water like this, one half of her would be underwater and the other would be sticking up in the air.

Dan walks over to the diagram on the blackboard. "It must say five hundred." He scratches his head.

"What must be five hundred?"

"That."

I stand next to Dan as he points at a blurry number on the diagram.

"I asked him what it said when I wrote to him last week. But he hasn't replied."

"Who?"

"Ben."

"Why do you write him letters? Can't you just talk to him?" The words jump out of my mouth. I wish they hadn't. It's like lighting the fuse on a bomb. I should crouch down with my hands over my ears. But Dan doesn't explode. He's smiling.

"I can now," he says. "I'm going to see him this week."

"Where is he?"

Dan doesn't answer. I look at the diagram and pretend I'm reading the instructions by the side.

"He's in an STC," Dan says suddenly. I turn and look at him. "Ben...He's in an STC."

I don't know what an STC is, but I decide to look it up tonight on the laptop.

"It's a secure training center," says Dan. "It's where teenagers get sent instead of prison when they've done something wrong."

He sees the surprised look on my face.

"But it wasn't his fault. He was just unlucky."

"How...how long has he been in there?" I say cautiously. I shouldn't ask, but this is the most Dan's ever spoken to me about it.

"Three months, but it seems like ages."

Dan looks back at the drawing. Suddenly he looks upset, like when a teacher shouts at him.

"Do you miss—"

"I need to get more bottles!" he says quickly. He pushes his way between me and *Shooting Star*.

The bomb's gone off.

"Are you coming, Shark Face?"

I open my mouth, but no words come out. Last week he left me here on my own; now he wants me to go with him. It must be a trick. He's going to walk out with me, and Sophie and the Georges will be waiting by the pier and they'll throw me into the sea.

"Are you coming or not?"

"I'll stay here," I say.

"Suit yourself. But it'll be quicker with two of us."

The light flickers. I check the ceiling for cracks again.

Another truck, more cement. Enough to fill a black hole. Seagulls outside. Go with Dan. Get covered in cement. Go with Dan. Get covered in cement.

"Wait."

"You just said no."

"I changed my mind."

Dan: Shark Face turns into a robot

Shark Face walks over to his bag and searches through it. I look along the seafront. The clouds are moving quickly and the wind is so strong it's blowing the flags straight on the pier. I take a deep breath. Ever since Mum told me I was going to see Ben, I feel like someone has taken their foot off my chest, but it still upsets me when I talk about him. I was so excited that I couldn't sleep last night. I made a giant list of all the things I need to take and planned the car journey in my head. But all the time I kept fast-forwarding to the moment when I actually get to see Ben and we play *Call of Duty* and *FIFA* with Five X.

Shark Face jams a packet of disinfectant wipes into his pocket, then comes out of the cave. He ducks as a seagull flies toward us, then looks around nervously, like he's expecting someone else to be here.

He's so weird.

"What's wrong?"

"Nothing. I was—"

"Here, take one of these." I hand him a black garbage bag.

He looks at me like he thinks the bag is full of germs or even radioactive.

"Where are we getting the bottles from?"

"Bins, course."

"What?! No!"

"You're such a wimp. They're only full of chip wrappers and stuff. Come on. We'll see if Mr. Kendall's got any first."

Shark Face takes the garbage bag and follows me along the seafront. He looks even weirder wearing gloves when everyone else is walking around wearing T-shirts or lying in the sun. I only let him come with me today because there's no chance the Georges and Sophie will see us, because the Georges are at the pavilion and she's miles away at Thorpe Park.

I keep walking. Out of the corner of my eye I can see Shark Face taking little strides, then big ones like he's jumping over his shadow. "Why do you walk like that?"

Shark Face shrugs. "Just do."

"But it's weird."

Shark Face doesn't answer.

I walk to the front of a line of people waiting for ice cream at Mr. Kendall's stand. Mr. Kendall is leaning over, scooping ice cream out of a tub.

"Have you come to help?"

"No, just wondered if you had any empty bottles?"

"I have." He looks across the counter. "But I'm a bit busy. Come back later, with your mate." He nods at Shark Face.

He's not my mate! I turn around to see if Shark Face heard, but he's still looking at his bag like it's full of dog poop.

I walk toward the bins at the pier. Shark Face is beside me. I walk faster. I want his help, but what if people do think he's my friend? What if *anybody* from school saw me with him? It would be more embarrassing than when a teacher from my old school started talking to me in the fish-and-chip shop.

I reach the pier and stop by a bin. Shark Face takes another big stride and stops by the side. He doesn't want to touch the bins, but he nearly landed in it. I shake my head. Shark Face shrugs like he's used to people looking at him that way. I push open the flap of the bin.

It's full of candy wrappers and fish-and-chip papers, but I can see the tops of two bottles sticking out. I reach in and pull them out. Shark Face steps back.

"Dan! Dan!"

I spin around. It's Sophie! But it can't be! She's—

"Dan!"

Where is she? She can't see me with Shark Face. I scan the pier, looking for her.

"Over here!" a boy shouts, over by the doughnut stand, then waves.

My heart slows down. *Phew, it's not her.* Shark Face doesn't seem to have noticed. I don't know if it's just the wind making him grimace, but he doesn't look so worried as he did in the cave.

I go back to the bin, grab the two bottles. Shark Face opens his bag and I drop them in. I start to walk to the next bin. He follows me like a dog. I find three more bottles and put them in his bag. After five more bins, Shark Face's bag is full and mine is nearly halfway there. This is the quickest I've ever collected them, and we haven't even been to the big recycling bin outside the Grand Hotel. I smile

211

to myself. We'll get two hundred bottles easy today if we keep going like this. We'll have them fixed on in no time and I'll be able to show Ben a picture on my phone.

I walk to the next bin. It's different from the rest. It's like a silver dome with the litter flap on the side.

"It crushes the bottles," I say. "So it's no good for us."

Shark Face nods. "But it does look like R2-D2."

"It does."

Shark Face smiles, then looks at the bin. " 'You'll be malfunctioning within a day, you nearsighted scrap pile,' " he says in a voice just like—

"You can do C-3PO!" I say.

"Yep." Shark Face nods like he's pleased with himself. " 'Don't blame me. I'm an interpreter. I'm not supposed to know a power socket from a computer terminal.' "

I laugh. "That's brilliant! Who else can you do?"

I think Shark Face ducks as a seagull swoops overhead, but now he's bent over like an old lady resting on a walking stick.

" 'Judge me by my size, do you?' "

I laugh out loud. "Yoda! You can do Yoda!"

" 'Hmph. Adventure. Heh. Excitement. Heh. A Jedi craves not these things.' "

"Can you do them all?"

Shark Face nods. "Yep, pretty much. Can you do any?"

"No, not really, but Mum says I sound like Chewbacca when I'm grumpy. Do C-3PO again."

Shark Face stands up straight. " 'Sir, it's quite possible this asteroid is not entirely stable.' "

I laugh again. "How did you learn to do that?"

"Easy," he says. "I've got figures of them at home, and when I press a button they make the voices."

"Bring one tomorrow," I say.

"I can't. I'm going to my nan's." Then Shark Face makes a whistling noise like R2-D2. He looks really weird when he does it.

He *is* weird. What am I doing? Why am I laughing? This is Shark Face. I'm supposed to hate him, not laugh at the things he does. Sophie would go crazy if she saw me doing this.

My phone buzzes in my pocket. Shark Face stops whistling. I look at it. It's a message from Sophie. It's like she's watching me now.

Hey, Dan. George C. got the tickets.

"Great," I say out loud. "Sophie's got me a ticket for the Observation Tower."

I text her back right away. Thanks.

My phone buzzes again.

What are you doing?

I look at Shark Face. Just stuff.

I put my phone in my pocket.

Shark Face is looking at me like he's seen a ghost.

"You're going to the Observation Tower too?"

"Yeah," I say. "VIP!"

"Argh! No!" Shark Face scrunches his face like he's got a headache.

I think of asking him what's wrong, but from the shocked look on his face I think I know what it is. We're both going to the Observation Tower. If Sophie sees him, she'll be bound to pick on him, and I'll have to go along with it. I still think he's a weirdo, but somehow it doesn't seem fair to do that anymore. Something has changed, but I don't know what or why.

I press the button on the crossing and try to figure out what to do. We can't go at different times, because everyone wants to be on the first ride. And even if there's a different line for VIPs, we could still bump into each other on the Observation Deck. There aren't loads of separate pods, like the Brighton Wheel.

We cross the road and walk around the back of the Grand Hotel. I open up a giant bin and look inside.

"We're going to have to come back, Shark Face!" I shout. "There's loads in here." I reach in. Shark Face holds the bag and I throw the bottles in until the bag is full. I close the bin lid and we start to walk back to the cave. We pass the bin where Shark Face did C-3PO. I glance at him to see if he'll do it again. He walks by without looking. It's like someone has come along and taken his battery out.

37

Alex: No, Nan, I'm not cold

"Another red one."

"That doesn't count."

"Why not?"

"Because it's a fire engine, not a car."

"That's not fair. Mum! Alex keeps changing the rules."

"Alex." Mum glances in the car mirror at me. "Give Lizzie a chance. Let the fire engine count."

Lizzie grins. "Okay," she says. "So that's twenty-one red for me and fifteen blue for you." She does that annoying thing where she pokes her tongue out at me and wobbles her head at the same time. I shrug like I don't care, then look out the car window at the sea.

I'm in the car going to visit Nan and Granddad in Worthing. I can usually do the journey because it's only half an hour to drive along the coast.

I'm worrying about what will happen at the Observation Tower tomorrow. Everyone in Brighton is going to be there. I thought I had another five days without seeing Sophie and the Georges.

Last night I tried to contact Elliott to cancel it, but he'd gone to stay with his auntie for two days. We'll be in trouble if they see us together, but I shouldn't have to cancel it. I've been looking forward to going up the tower for weeks. My chest went tight when Sophie messaged Dan. It ruined the afternoon because he was being okay for once. Especially when he was telling me about his brother. I still don't know what Ben did, but Dan mentions him lots and, from the look on his face yesterday, I think he misses him loads.

"Another red one, Alex. I've got twenty-two!"

I nod just to keep Lizzie happy.

By the time we arrive at Nan's, Lizzie has won, forty-two to thirty-four. She tells Nan straightaway, but Nan is more concerned that I'm cold.

"Did you want the fire on, Alex?"

"No, Nan. I'm fine."

"Poor love, he looks cold!" Nan looks at Mum, then back at me. "I know." She pushes herself out of her chair. "I'll get you one of your granddad's sweaters."

"Mum, I told you. Alex isn't cold. He just likes to wear gloves."

"Oh well, at least let him sit next to the radiator, Francesca."

Mum rolls her eyes at me. I don't know if it's to make me move or because she hates it when Nan calls her Francesca, but I move closer to the radiator just in case. Nan thinks I'm cold every time I visit. She makes big pots of tea and then gets one of granddad's sweaters or puts a blanket on the arm of the chair, ready for me, like I'm an old man.

Mum's told her loads of times about my OCD, but she doesn't take any notice, which is better than Granddad, who thinks I should face my fears like he had to in the army. Sometimes when I visit he gets a bucket and sponge and tries to get me to help him clean his car in the hope that it will cure me. He used to make me go in the garden to feed the birds with him too, but I get out of that because Lizzie goes instead. I can see her out there now, opening the bird feeder and filling it with seeds. I hope she doesn't hug Granddad until she washes her hands; otherwise he'll be covered in bird germs and I won't be able to hug him when I leave.

Nan hands me a glass of orange juice. "So how's school, Alex?" she asks. "We've not seen you since Christmas."

"We *have* been busy," says Mum.

"Too busy to get Alex's hair cut?" Nan nods at me.

"He likes it longer, Mum."

"I know, I was only saying.... So how is school, Alex?"

Oh, it's great.

"It's okay."

"You're enjoying it, aren't you, Alex?" says Mum. "And tell Nan about the raft you're building."

Nan's eyes open wide. "Ooh, you're building a *raft*?" She says it slowly like she's spelling it out. "That must be really nice for you to get out. Tell Granddad when he comes in." She waves out the window and beckons to Granddad. He smiles and walks with Lizzie across the grass toward the back door.

Don't touch him. Don't hold his hand.

The back door opens. I listen for the sound of the taps running and the squeeze of the soap bottle, but I can't hear, because Nan has started telling Mum that there's a lady on *House Hunters* who looks just like a woman down the road.

217

Lizzy bounces into the room, munching a chocolate cookie. That was too quick; there's no way she had time to wash her hands. She puts them on the arm of the sofa, on Nan's shoulder.

"Can I change the TV channel?"

"Of course you can."

Now I can't hug Nan *or* touch the TV remote. Granddad walks in with a towel in his hand.

"You all right, Alex? You looked worried again." He smiles at me. *Please don't ask me to clean the car.*

"I'm okay."

He sits down next to me. "Lizzie says your guitar lessons are going well…and your singing. She says you've learned a new song.…Was it Dustin Beaver you said, Lizzie?"

"It's Justin Bieber, Dad." Mum laughs.

I glower at Lizzie. She's pretending to watch TV, but I can see her grinning. Granddad will want me to sing now.

"Oh, I don't know any of these new ones," says Granddad. "But let's hear what you've learned."

There!

I shake my head.

"It's okay, Granddad," I say. "I need my guitar."

"Go on, Alex," says Lizzie. "Sing 'Sorry,' like you did last night."

She shoves the rest of her cookie into her mouth and then jumps up. No way has she brought my guitar with us. We all came out of the house together.

"Okay, I'll do a show instead. Me and Gemma are doing it at school."

"But I was going to tell Granddad about the raft."

"What's that about a raft?"

"I'm—"

It's too late. Lizzie has started singing and is spinning around with her arms out wide, pretending she's wearing a ballerina dress.

I sit back on the sofa. For once, I've been outside and had something to tell Granddad, but now we've got to sit and watch one of Lizzie's shows and they go on for ages, and by the time she's finished, everyone will have forgotten I was supposed to tell them about *Shooting Star*. Suddenly Granddad gets up. I think that he's going to the bathroom, but then he beckons to me from the kitchen doorway.

Oh no, here comes the bucket and sponge.

He beckons me again. I dodge past Lizzie. Granddad sits down at the kitchen table and nods to me to sit down at the other side.

Oh no. It's not washing the car, but it's another idea to help me overcome my fears.

In the sitting room Lizzie has turned the TV up and is now dancing to music. Granddad leans over the table.

"Come on, then," he says quietly. "I know you want to tell me."

Can he see my worries?

"Tell you what, Granddad?"

"This raft. Where are you building it?"

"In a cave, on the seafront."

"With Dad?"

"No," I say. "With a boy from school."

"That's wonderful," he says, opening his eyes wide. "It's lovely you've got a friend and you're building it together."

219

"Well," I say, "it's not really my raft. It's his and his brother's."

"That's okay. I'm sure he'll let you go on it if you help."

I try to smile, but I'm shaking my head at the same time. If he knew Dan, he'd know there was zero chance of that happening. Granddad asks me what we've used to make *Shooting Star*, so I tell him how me and Dan nailed the base planks and tied them down tighter with string and how Dan painted her in creosote. He asks me what else we have to do. So I tell him that we need to get some oars and a mascot. My chest feels a bit less tight. This is the most I've talked to Granddad in ages. Usually I don't have much to say after I've spent all day in my room, but now that I've been outside I can talk to him properly.

"Sorry to break you two up, but it's time to go." Mum stands in the doorway, twiddling her car keys.

Granddad pulls a sad face. "Ah, that's a shame. Happiest I've seen this little guy in ages." Granddad's face turns to wrinkles. He pushes his chair back.

"I'm sorry," says Mum. "But this one's got yet another birthday party to go to." She puts her hand on Lizzie's head.

"That's okay," says Granddad. Then he looks at me. "And you just make sure you remember everything you do so you can tell me all about *Shooting Star* next time."

I nod and tell him I will.

They looked a bit sad when we left. I didn't hug Granddad and I couldn't hug Nan either, and now I'm huddled up against the car door, sitting as far away from Lizzie and her germy hands as I can. As we drive along the top road back to Brighton, I look down across the fields again. All of them are bright green and the sun has come out and turned the sea silver. We drive down past the racecourse and I can see the Observation Tower sticking up like a giant nail. My heart thuds hard and I can feel my hands sweating in my gloves. I want to go to the opening, but suddenly all I can think about is the crowds of people, and even if I can put up with them, I've still got Dan, Sophie, and the Georges to contend with.

I look at my watch. It's only three o'clock. Dan will still be down there somewhere, working on *Shooting Star*. I could tell Mum to drop me off and do two hours before it gets dark. I'm crazy for thinking that when I'm so worried about bumping into him at the tower. But Granddad is right. I've not been this happy in ages. It's got nothing to do with Dan, but everything to do with *Shooting Star*. She keeps me busy and pushes my worries away. I look down at the pier and suddenly I can't stop myself smiling.

"Forty-one red, twenty-four blue!"

Lizzie's won again, but I'm looking forward to working on *Shooting Star* so much that I don't really care.

Dan: Observation Tower day

Shark Face hasn't spoken much all morning and neither have I. All I've been thinking about is what will happen if me, Sophie, and the Georges bump into him at the Observation Tower. There's only an hour left until it opens. But I don't need to look at my watch, because my chest feels like I've got a big clock inside it, ticking the minutes away.

I walk over to the bottles and pick up a bundle. I squeeze them between the base planks and hand them to Shark Face, who's crouched underneath *Shooting Star*.

"Have you got them?" I say for the tenth time today.

"Yes." He grimaces as he holds the bottles against the plank. I wrap string around them and tie a knot. I see Shark Face peering up at me between the planks. He doesn't say anything; he just waits for me to get the next bundle. But from the worried look on his face, I know he's thinking the same thing as me: *What happens if Sophie sees him at the tower?*

I imagine what she'll do. She'll probably tell him to go for a swim with his sharky friends, like I did. And if he doesn't, she'll get us to drag him across the beach and throw him in the sea. But I don't want to do things like that to him anymore.

I walk over and get another bundle of bottles. Shark Face takes them from me, holds them against the wood, and I tie them on. He's still working like a robot, but every minute that passes, his face seems to look more worried, and every second the clock beats in my chest.

Shark Face is weird, but he has been funny, and if it wasn't for him, *Shooting Star* wouldn't be as good as she is. I can't think of a way out of it, though. Sophie will know something's going on if I leave him alone.

If Ben was here, he'd tell me to be a big fish and do want I want.

"Dan ... Dan!"

"What?"

"Get another bundle."

I look down at my hands.

"Oh, yeah." I've been thinking for so long that I've stopped working. I pick up more bottles. There has to be something I can do. It's going to be horrible seeing Shark Face back here after we've thrown him in the sea. I hand the bottles between the planks, then glance at my watch. It's only half an hour until we should leave. "We should stop," I say. "I need to eat my sandwiches before I go...."

"Okay."

Shark Face crawls out from under *Shooting Star*. We get sandwiches out of our bags and sit down on our buckets. I couldn't even say the words *Observation Tower* to him. I take a bite of my tuna sandwich, but it feels like if I swallow, it will get stuck in my throat. I

223

glance across at Shark Face. He looks even more worried than I am. I swallow and swig some Coke. I can't do anything to him. I can't, but what—"Let's avoid each other," I blurt out.

"What?" A bit of sausage roll drops from Shark Face's mouth.

"When we go to the Observation Tower. We'll avoid each other. I know that's what you're worried about."

Shark Face shakes his head like he's trying to catch up with my thoughts. "I don't think—"

"Yeah, it'll be easy." I stand up.

"How?"

"All me and you have got to do is make sure we don't get seen together."

Shark Face takes a drink like he needs time to think about it. "So, we don't walk along together?" he asks. "We leave here at different times so we don't get seen walking along the seafront."

"Yeah, that's right. See, easy!" I blow out my cheeks. I've been worrying about it so much it's like I forgot to breathe. But Shark Face doesn't look so relieved.

"But what if you do see me?"

"I'll pretend I didn't."

"Okay, that works, but what if Sophie sees me first?"

"Oh, yeah." I hold my breath again. It's easy to pretend not to see Shark Face, but it's harder to get Sophie to do the same.

"I'll tell her to ignore you." I say.

"It won't work. She does what she wants."

"It will, trust me. I'll just tell her to leave you alone."

Shark Face smiles wearily. "She won't listen, and why would you do that anyway?"

"Because..."

"Because what?"

I shrug. "I don't know, just because. Deal?" I hold out my hand.

Shark Face looks at me suspiciously. "What do you get out of it?"

"You help me finish *Shooting Star.*"

Shark Face smiles nervously. "Okay, deal."

I pull my hand away and check the time again.

"I'll leave first," I say. "Give me five minutes' start and we'll come back here after and do some more work."

"Of course." Shark Face takes his bag off the hook.

I walk out of the cave and take a deep breath. It's not the best plan, but it's the only one I have.

I just hope it works.

39

Alex: What am I?

I'm walking along the seafront toward the Observation Tower. I'm not going to be able to find Elliott because there are crowds of people everywhere. What makes it even worse is that I've got to dodge everyone so they don't touch me. Dan left five minutes before, so he's ahead of me somewhere, but there are so many heads and bodies they've all merged into a colorful blur.

I pass the pier and keep walking. The sun is shining bright on the water. There are people on the beach, looking through binoculars in the direction of the tower, and some children are running around with balloons. Ahead I can see crowds of people, so many that the colors of their clothes start to blur.

I wrap my arms around my body. It's warm, but I'm so anxious I can't stop shaking, and I want to pee too.

It's okay, you've been going outside all week and you've been working on Shooting Star. *It's only people. It's only people.*

But it's more people than at a football match.

It's only people.

But lots of them!

I glance at my watch. It's 1:35. My heart is racing and my jaw is clenched tight. The crowd is getting wider and deeper. The seafront has been closed to traffic, and there are so many people, I can't see where the pavement ends and the road begins.

"Alex! Alex!"

My heart misses a beat. I spin around. "Alex!" Lizzie runs through the crowd. "Did you get one of these?" She points at her blue hat with a picture of a hot dog and a bottle of ketchup on the peak. "There's a man handing them out over there. They're free!"

She points through the crowds, but all I can see are people buzzing around like bees. I don't want a hat with a hot dog on it, and I definitely wouldn't go through a swarm of bees to get it.

"You made it!" shouts Mum. "Well done. Well done!" She puts her arm around my shoulders and shakes me like I've won an Olympic medal. Yes, I'm here, but it's not over yet.

I pull away from her.

"I've got to find Elliott!" I shout.

"Can I go with you?" Lizzie jumps up and down.

"No."

"Why not? *Pleeeease*, Alex, *pleeease*." She continues to jump up and down. There's no way she's coming with me. It's bad enough trying to avoid Dan and Sophie. It'd be even worse if they saw me out with my little sister.

"Alex!"

"No." I turn away from Lizzie. "I'll see you later," I say to Mum.

"Okay, love. Come on, Lizzie, let's go and find the clowns."

They leave me on my own. I stand on tiptoe and look around for a marker to see where I am. I told Elliott I'd meet him by the railings at the bottom of Preston Street, but it's so crowded now that all I can see are the rooftops of buildings and the tower. It's like people are lining up to be the first to go on a ride to another planet. What if that's what it really was—a one-way space trip to Mars! I'd be pushing Sophie and the Georges on it if it was. But not Dan. We'd never finish *Shooting Star* if he went.

I try to go higher on my toes. I can't see Elliott anywhere. If I'm finding it this hard to see him, maybe it'll be hard for Sophie and Dan to see me. Through a gap I get a glimpse of the sea and the railings. I turn away from the tower.

The crowd starts to thin. Some girls run past me, screaming and laughing. I make myself small so they don't touch me. Then ahead of me, through the crowds, I see Elliott with some of the boys and girls from my class, leaning against the railings, swapping cards. I smile. I've come for the tower, but I brought my cards just in case. I pat my back pocket and check that they're still there. I've got two Wayne Rooneys, and I know Elliott's got Zlatan Ibrahimović, and I only need him and then I'll have the whole Swedish team.

I start to walk toward Elliott. There's no sign of Dan or Sophie and I can't see the Georges either. Knowing them, they'll have pushed their way to the front of the line for the tower.

"Alex!" Elliott shouts and waves to me. Then he looks to my right and slowly lowers his arm. I turn and see Dan walking in my direction. Sophie and the Georges are with him. My chest goes tight like someone is squeezing me. Dan said he'd tell them to leave me alone, that he'd ignore me, but now he's headed right for me, looking like the bully he is at school.

They'll walk past me.

I glance back toward the tower. Maybe they're on their way to join the VIP line. I turn my back and head in the opposite direction.

"Hey, Shark Face, who let you out?" Sophie shouts. Her voice makes me jump and I suddenly feel hot.

I keep walking.

"Hey, Shark Face, the sea's that way," she shouts again.

She's seen me before Dan has. Or maybe he just hasn't told her to leave me alone. I've tried to avoid them, but he hasn't kept his side of the deal.

I wait for the sound of their footsteps to come running behind me.

I should have known he wouldn't do it.

I wait for the shove in my back and for my bag to get pulled off my shoulder. They're taking ages. They should be here by now.

I turn around slowly. Dan is talking to Sophie. The Georges are standing beside them, scuffing their feet on the ground. They all turn in my direction. Is Dan telling them to ignore me, or are they going to come over and get me like they usually do? Sophie looks at me like she's trying to make up her mind, then turns and starts walking toward the seawall. The Georges follow. Dan gives me a thumbs-up when Sophie isn't looking. Then he turns away and follows her too.

A smile creeps across my face. I can't believe it. I let go of my breath. This can't really have happened, can it? He's really told them to leave me alone.

I hitch my bag up my shoulder and slowly walk toward Elliott, still thinking that Sophie and the Georges will come running after me any second.

Argh! No! I stop still.

Dan and Sophie have pushed their way into Elliott's group and are standing in the middle. I'm too far away to hear what they're saying, but I see Sophie push Elliott, and then Dan snatches Elliott's cards out of his hands. I slowly move closer.

"I'll have that one and that one," Dan says. "And does anyone want Buffon?" He shows the card to Elliott's group. None of them answer; they just step away like they think he'll pick on them too.

No, that's not what's supposed to happen. Dan, what are you doing? They can't stop picking on me so they can pick on Elliott again.

Sophie pushes Elliott in the chest. "What are you doing here, Piggy? You should be in your sty."

The Georges laugh.

George C. pushes Elliott until he falls back against the railings. He's surrounded by wolves and there's no escape. I can't leave him there. I know what it feels like.

I try to start walking toward him, but every time I go to lift my feet, it's like they've been superglued to the tarmac. I look around for help. There are thousands of people here, but none of them can see what's going on. Dan drops Elliott's cards and scuffs them under his heel. My heart stops and I feel sick. Elliott's staring at the ground like he's trying not to cry.

"Hold him," Sophie says, giggling.

Dan and the Georges grab hold of him. Sophie reaches into her bag and pulls out a marker pen. Elliott wriggles and moves his head from side to side.

Stop!

I try to move my feet again. It's not superglue, but it might as well be because I can't move an inch. I want them to stop picking on Elliott, but I don't want them to pick on me. Why do they have to pick on anyone?

I remember what Dr. Patrick told me.

I'm as big as an elephant, and all my problems are the size of ants.

Sophie draws a mustache on Elliott's face that's twice the size of his mouth.

Stop! Stop!

I'm an elephant. I'm an elephant. Dan's an ant.

Sophie's an ant.

The Georges are ants.

I'm an elephant. I'm an elephant.

Sophie shoves Elliott again.

"Let's leave him," I hear her say over the crowds. "The tower is opening soon." She walks off and the Georges follow. Elliott wipes his eyes on his sleeve. Dan turns around to me, but he doesn't say anything. He doesn't even look me in the eye.

That wasn't your plan. That's not what we agreed!

I try to tell him, but my tongue is stuck as fast as my feet.

I'm an elephant. I'm an elephant.

I grit my teeth and clench my fists. I'm so mad I could scream.

"Alex, I got you one." Lizzie's standing beside me, waving a blue hat. I shake my head.

"Don't you want it?"

I look at Dan.

No, that's not what I meant.

I'm an elephant. I'm an elephant.

Dan walks away. Elliott is kneeling down, picking his cards up off the ground, and I didn't do anything to help him.

I'm so mad at Dan that I feel like I could hit him. But I'm even madder at myself. Elliott is my friend and I just stood and let it happen. I'm not an elephant at all. I'm a mouse.

Dan: I'm an idiot!

I stand up and walk to the front of the cave with my phone. I'm going to see Ben tomorrow. I don't need to draw *Shooting Star*; I just need to take a picture. But she's gotten so big I can't fit all of her in. She looks like a real raft now that all the bottles are fixed on. All I've got to do is wrap a fishing net around her to keep the bottles on, get some wood for paddles and the rudder, and then find a mascot. I'll ask Ben what we're going to use for an anchor when I see him.

I hold my phone above my head and take a picture, then a selfie with *Shooting Star* behind me. I can't wait to show Ben what me and Shark Face have done.

I look at my watch. It's 10:35 and Shark Face hasn't arrived. I wonder if he might be ill, but I think his mum would have texted mine if he was. He was supposed to come back here after the Observatoration Tower opening, but I saw him walking toward the town with his mum and sister. I don't know if he got to go up the tower. I did. Me, Sophie, and the Georges were on the first ride. The deck rose really slowly, but when it reached the top you could look through telescopes and see for miles. I saw boats on the horizon and the Isle of Wight, and when I spun around, I saw the town center like a bird does, and I spotted the Albion football ground. I took a picture of that for Ben too.

I check the time again. It's 10:45. I text Mum.

Has Shark Face's mum texted?

I press Send, then realize what I've done.

Mum replies straightaway.

Who?

Sorry, meant for Sophie, I lie.

Dan, are you okay?

Yes ☺

I walk to the back of the cave and drag one of the fishing nets out to the seafront. I can't attach it to *Shooting Star* on my own, but at least I can flatten it out and check that none of the links are broken while I'm waiting for Shark Face to arrive. I find two broken links immediately and I fix them with bits from the other nets. All the time I'm thinking of going to see Ben tomorrow and all the things I need to take.

After I've mended another link, I look up and see Shark Face walking along the seafront. I'm so used to seeing him now that his gloves don't look as silly as they used to. But his funny walk does.

"All right, Shark Face? Thought you'd given up."

He walks straight past me into the cave. He never says much, but he hasn't ignored me like this.

I stand up.

"I was just checking the nets."

"Okay," he says quietly. Then he puts his bag on the hook and looks

234

at *Shooting Star*. There's something wrong. He's ignoring me like mum does when I've upset her at home. But I've not done anything. Maybe he's just had an argument with his mum. Or perhaps his sister. I don't know what it is, but he doesn't look like he wants to tell me.

I point at the corners of the net.

"You pick up that side, and then we'll drag it under *Shooting Star*."

Shark Face nods and takes a deep breath. We both crouch down and pick up our sides.

Shark Face pauses and looks across at me.

"What's wrong?" I ask. "Is it because I started without you? I only did it because I'm going to see Ben tomorrow, and we'll lose time."

"It's not that," he says quietly.

"So what is it, then?"

"Why did you do it?"

"Do what?"

"Yesterday."

I give him a confused look and stand up.

"I saw you," he says. "I saw you pick on Elliott."

"I know, but we still didn't pick on you."

"Argh!" Shark Face puts his hands on his head. "I didn't mean pick on him if you didn't pick on me."

"I thought—"

"No, that's not what was supposed to happen. Not to Elliott. It can't. It can't." He's never looked this upset when I've picked on him. It's like he cares about his friend more than he does about himself. "And what's going to happen when we go back to school? Will you pick on me or him?"

I shrug. I don't know what to do or where to look. I didn't realize he'd be this upset. I thought he'd be pleased we didn't get him. How could I get it so wrong? I try to think of something to say, but my mind is so jumbled I can't think of anything. I started the day feeling so happy about going to see Ben, but now I feel bad. I couldn't even fix it for one afternoon, so how can I fix it at school? I won't be able to stop them picking on him. I can't stop them picking on Elliott either.

We drag the net inside and put it under *Shooting Star*. Now we've got to wrap it around her so any stray bottles won't escape. I grab some nails from a jar and pick up the hammer. Shark Face pulls the net up over the bottles and base planks, and I carefully hammer the nails in. All the time I'm trying to think what I can do to help Shark Face, but I'm back to the same place as I was before. I can't do anything.

Shark Face lifts another part of the net.

I hammer in another nail, this time harder and faster. I can't work out what to do at school, and it's making bubbles of anger rise up inside me. I can't stand up to Sophie, but I can't let Alex get picked on like before.

I have to think of something.

41

Alex: Hammer and nails

Dan hammers another nail in. Each time he seems to hit it harder and faster, like he wants to get the net fixed before he goes and sees Ben tomorrow. I pull another piece of net onto the wood and he bangs the nail in and we move along the plank like we're parts of a giant sewing machine. He seems upset that he got things so wrong with Elliott, but he can't be as upset as I was last night. I couldn't sleep because my mind was going wild, but it wasn't my OCD; it was because I kept seeing Elliott's face every time I closed my eyes. It's all my fault. If I hadn't agreed to Dan's plan in the first place, they would have just picked on me instead of Elliott. Mum kept asking me what was wrong, but I couldn't tell her. I made her so worried that she made an emergency telephone appointment with Dr. Patrick this morning. He helped me for a while, but as soon as I put the phone down all my thoughts about what had happened to Elliott flooded back into my mind.

We reach the end of a plank. Dan wraps the net over the corner like Nan when she makes the bed, and he starts hitting the nails in again. His face is turning red and he's got a serious expression as he concentrates. Ten minutes ago I felt angry with him, but now I feel a bit sorry for him. He really thought he was doing the right thing. It was the wrong thing, but at least he tried.

We reach another corner. My hands are aching. Dan puts the hammer down and wipes sweat off his forehead with his arm.

"What time are you going tomorrow?" I ask.

Dan takes a deep breath. "I don't know," he says, "but Mum says I've got to get up early because it's a long way and we've got to go around London. I can't wait. I've taken two pictures of *Shooting Star* for Ben. I'll show you."

I stand next to him as he shows me a picture of *Shooting Star* on his phone. Then he grins at me when he shows a selfie of him with his eyes and mouth open wide. I smile.

"It's a shame she's not ready or you could have sailed her up the Thames."

Dan laughs. "I already thought of doing that." He nods at the blackboard, where he's stuck a diagram of the coastline from Brighton with a wriggly red line going toward Dover.

"What?"

"It's okay. I decided it was too dangerous."

"Definitely!"

Dan laughs as he picks up another nail. "But we could take her for a trial on Sunday if she's ready."

"I thought you were going to wait for Ben."

"We could just put her on the water, and I could get on just to see if she floats okay."

I look at *Shooting Star*. I'm not sure taking her out is a good idea.

The floats still aren't on and I know Dan wouldn't just stay in the shallows. He'd be so excited that he'd only be on it for two minutes and he'd be paddling toward France.

"I think you should wait for Ben," I say.

"It'll be okay. I just want to make sure *Shooting Star* will be ready for him." He picks up another nail. All he ever talks about is Ben, and from the serious look on his face, I think his brother is on his mind now.

"I hope he's okay tomorrow," I say.

"He will be, especially when he sees all the stuff I'm taking for him."

"What things?"

Dan lifts up the hammer. But he's too busy thinking about Ben to hear my question. I brace myself for the noise of him banging the nail in, but then he stops and looks at me like he's realized what I just said.

"I'll fix it, Shark Face," he says.

"Fix what?"

"Everything at school."

"But we were talking about your brother."

"Yeah, I know. But I'm just saying I'll fix it. After I've seen Ben. I don't know how, but I will."

He looks at me like he means it. I don't know what he'll come up with, but I hope it works better than his last plan did.

Dan: I visit BIG FISH

Call of Duty. Yes.

FIFA 2016. Yes.

Grand Theft Auto. Yes.

Game of Thrones DVDs. Yes. *All-Star Batman* comic. Yes. *Blue Beetle* comic. Yes.

Two packs of Rolos. Yes.

"Dan, how many more times are you going to go through that bag?"

"I'm just checking I've got everything."

"Well, it's too late now even if you haven't."

I put all of Ben's things back. I'm in the car with my mum and we're driving to St. Albans. I've been awake all night, and now that we're getting closer, I'm so excited that I can't stop yawning. I wish Dad was driving because he'd get us there faster. I asked Mum earlier why he wasn't coming, but she said she didn't want to talk about it then. At least I'm still going to see Ben, and that's all that counts.

I glance at the clock. We're going to be late. It's 1:45. We're supposed to be there by two, and we've still got six miles to go. I used to be able to just walk into Ben's room and talk to him; now we have to make an appointment, like we're going to see the dentist.

"Don't worry," says my mum. "We'll get there in time."

"I'm just excited." And nervous. I rest my head against the window and think of all the things I want to tell Ben. I want to tell him I've disabled auto brake and traction control on my Honda NSX-R, and I don't follow the suggested line on *Forza* anymore. And I want to talk to him about *Game of Thrones*, but I can't tell him what happens in Season 6, because he hasn't got cable. I'm going to tell him I've recorded them all so I can watch them all again with him. But most of all I can't wait to tell him about *Shooting Star*, and that me and Shark Face are working so fast that she'll be ready to sail by the time he comes out.

"Ah! *Forza Motorsport*!"

"What?"

"I forgot it."

"Stop it, Dan. You made me jump. My nerves are bad enough as it is."

"Sorry."

Mum puts on the turn signal and we turn off the main road and go down a smaller road into a village. We drive past a pub and a stone monument by a church, and then I see a sign at the side of the road— OAKHILL STC. We're nearly there.

I reach down by my feet and drag my bag onto my lap as my mum turns into a parking lot. She stops the car. I just want to jump out and run inside.

We walk across the parking lot toward a massive building with steps leading up to glass doors. It looks more like the new library in town than a place where they keep kids who have done bad things.

Mum pushes the doors open. Inside, the ceiling is really high and made of glass. Mum's shoes echo on the floor as she walks toward the reception desk. The room is so big it makes me feel small. There are big glass doors leading off it, and through them I can see corridors that go on forever until they disappear. It isn't anything like Ben described it. He made it sound like a big house, not a maze. I went in a maze once with my dad at the fair. It was full of mirrors and fake doorways and I got scared when we couldn't find our way out. I wonder if Ben feels like that here.

Mum walks over to a reception desk, where a woman is typing on a computer. I look around the room. There are big red buttons by the sides of the doors, and posters stuck on the walls. One of them says:

VISITING RULES: NO SMOKING. NO TELEPHONES.
NO SHARP OBJECTS.
ALL BAGS WILL BE CHECKED.
YOU MAY BE BODY-SEARCHED.

Beside it there's a poster with a picture of a boy and a police officer and the headline CRIME DOESN'T PAY.

A door swings open and startles me. A boy is walking between two men in blue uniforms like they're going to show him around the maze. He looks the same age as Ben, and when he catches my eye I wonder if he might be Five X and he's recognized me from the photo

Ben took with him, of me and him on the go-karts. I smile, but he just stares at me as he walks by.

I go and stand next to my mum.

"Yes, madam," says one of the men. "How can I help you?"

"Ummm, we're here to see..." My mum's voice sounds as shaky as I feel. "Ben...Ben Curtis."

The man glances up at a clock.

"Yes, they should be bringing him down now. Just take a seat for a moment and someone will be with you."

I follow my mum across the reception area and we sit down on seats that look like dice by the window.

"Okay?" she whispers.

"Yeah..." I look up at the ceiling. "...It's huge!"

"It is." My mum tries to smile.

We haven't waited long before a door swings open and another man walks over and stops in front of us. I look at his name tag— MIKE ASHTON. PASTORAL CARE OFFICER. He points to the doors.

"It's just this way," he says.

We reach another set of doors and he holds a card against a box on the wall and looks up at a camera. It's like we're in a film and about to rob a bank. The doors swing open and me and my mum follow him into a corridor where another man is sitting behind a desk— ANDREW MACMANUS. SECURITY OFFICER. I don't know whether he's here to keep people out or keep them in. He asks my mum to empty her bag. She puts her car keys, her purse, her phone, and a pack of tissues on the desk. Now I know why she was emptying her bag in the kitchen before we left.

"Okay, we'll let you have the keys and your phone when you come back out." Andrew MacManus then turns to me. "...And what about you, young man?"

I slide my bag off my shoulder. Andrew MacManus opens it up, pulls out the *All-Star Batman* and *Blue Beetle* comics, the computer games, and two packs of Rolos.

He flicks through the comics and rubs his hand over each page like he's flattening them out. I don't know what he thinks I could be hiding in a comic. "Okay," he says, handing them back. "They're fine, but these can't go in." He puts my Rolos and the games into a gray tray like they have at airports. "And do you have music or a phone?"

"Yes, but I wanted to show my brother a picture."

"Sorry, but it's the rules." He takes my iPod and my phone." Pick them up with your bag on your way out," he says.

I look at my mum.

"It's just a precaution," says Mike Ashton. "Don't worry, we won't eat the sweets." He chuckles. But I don't think it's funny. I feel like picking them up and throwing them at him, but I think I'd get into big trouble if I did that here. "Right. This way." He leads us to a door with VISITORS' ROOM written on it. "Just go on inside," he says. "We'll bring Ben in to you in a minute...and we'll have a catch-up after."

"Okay," says my mum. "But he's all right?"

"Yes, he's fine."

My mum's hand hangs down by her side. I haven't held it for ages, but I want to now. Sophie and the Georges would say I was a wimp, but I don't think they would like it here either. My mum takes my hand and squeezes it tight, and we walk into a room that's cold, with walls that are white and empty. There are five tables, one in each corner and one in the middle. A man and a lady are behind one, and another lady is jigging a baby on her lap behind another. The lady smiles, but the other two just stare into space like me and my mum aren't here. Mum walks toward the middle table and pulls out the chairs.

Okay? she mouths.

I nod, but I'm not really. I'm dying to see Ben, but this place is so scary it's making me want to go home. The man coughs and it echoes around the room. Then I hear footsteps clicking down the corridor; they stop, there's a scuffling sound at the door and then it opens. Mike Ashton walks in followed by two boys wearing identical blue T-shirts and jeans.

Andrew MacManus is behind them. The first boy walks to the table in one corner; the second boy glances around the room like he's looking for someone, then he sees me. I don't know that it's Ben until he suddenly smiles.

"Ben!" I leap up.

"Shush." Mike Ashton holds his finger up to his lips. I feel like I've been told off at school. Ben walks toward me. I want to hug him, but I don't know if I'm allowed to. No one else has hugged. The other boy just walked to his table and sat down without saying anything.

I sit back down. Ben sits opposite me. I smile at him. He smiles back, but he doesn't look like he did at home. His hair is cut really short and the skin under his eyes is dark like he's smeared it with camouflage paint. He doesn't look like my brother. He looks like a soldier. As he gets closer, I see it's not paint; it's because he's tired.

I go to speak, but after waiting so long to see him, my mind has gone blank. I can't stop staring at him. Mum ruffles my hair.

"Thought you might like to see him," she whispers, like we're in a hospital.

Ben smiles at her, then rubs his hand over his head. "You get used to it, Danny," he says quietly. "But it's a bit cold."

I try to smile. He doesn't look like Ben and he doesn't sound like him either. He's usually shouting and messing around. I can't tell if he's quiet because he's in here or if he's feeling bad about what he's done.

Someone coughs and makes me jump. I glance around the room. Everyone is leaning over the tables and whispering. I look back at Ben. I want him to jump up and grab my neck and wrestle. I want him to tell a rude joke. I want him to do a fly kick like Kazuya on *Tekken*. But he doesn't look like he's going to do any of those things, and I don't think I would if I had to stay in a place like this.

Mum leans forward. "Dad sends his love. And he says he'll come next week."

Ben tries to smile again. Then Mum clears her throat.

"Dan's brought you a few things....Haven't you, Dan?" She nudges me, but I'm not really listening. I'm still staring at my brother. "Dan?"

I slide the comics across the table. "I got you these," I say. "Dad gave me the money."

"Thanks, Danny." Ben flicks through the pages. I still can't think

246

of anything to say to him. I wish I'd made a list like Mum said, but I thought it'd be easy to talk. I thought it would be just like at home.

Mum nudges me again. "Tell Ben about *Twinkling Star.*"

Ben looks up and laughs. "Yeah," he says. "What have you been doing?"

I smile. That's the first time he's sounded like my brother. I pull my chair closer to the table.

"She's brilliant," I say. "I had a picture of her, but they took my phone. But she's great. We've got all the bottles on, and all we've to do is get wood for the oars and the rudder, and a mascot."

"Get it from the same warehouse where we got the base planks. They've got loads, and you can get the mascot there too."

Mum puts her hand over her ears. "Umm, I don't think I should be listening to this," she says.

Ben laughs. "What else have you done? Have you got a sail?"

"No, not yet, but me and Shark Face are working on her again tomorrow."

"Shark Face? Is that the weird one who wears gloves all the time?"

"Dan!" Mum jumps in. "That's not very nice. His name's Alex."

"Yes, that's him. But he's not weird. Well, he is weird, but he's okay now."

"Sounds like it." Ben smiles.

"He's helped lots, but I told him *Shooting Star* is ours."

"It's okay. I don't mind if he's helping. Means I don't have to do so much when I—" Ben jumps as the door opens. A guard walks in with a boy who must be a head taller than Ben. The room goes quiet as everybody stops talking. The guard points to the back of the room.

"Go on, Booth, you've not got long."

Booth glares at Ben as he walks past us, like he's daring him to speak. Ben looks down at the table. My heart is thudding in my chest. This place is full of boys who look like men.

Ben's still looking at the table. Mum always says he can talk for England, but he's hardly said a word today. It's like nothing happens in here for him to talk about.

I take a deep breath. I only just got used to whispering; now I've got to start all over again. I think of the list that I should have written down.

I tell him little bits about *Game of Thrones*, but not enough to spoil it. Then I tell him about the Albion, that I don't go to the games because it's really quiet without him, but our dad still goes. When Ben looks down at the table again, I know I've said the wrong thing. I ask him what his lessons are like. He just shrugs and says they're okay. Then I ask him about some of the teachers he wrote about in one of his letters, and he just shrugs again. It's like he's told me all the exciting bits in his letters and now he's got nothing to say.

I've been talking nonstop, but all my stuff about football and *Shooting Star* can't be very important compared to the things that happen here. Now that I've stopped talking, all I can hear is whispering at the other tables.

It's nothing like when me and Ben used to talk at home. I would sit on his bed and he'd tell me about how he'd got into trouble at school, but that I couldn't say anything to Mum. Then he'd talk about the things he was going to do when he left home, like saving lots of money and getting a motorbike, and I could go on the back and he'd

248

take me to the Albion games when Dad couldn't go. One time he said we could get on a ferry and drive through France and Germany. He didn't know where we would go, only that we'd never stop. I used to love listening to him because he made me feel like the most important person in the world. But in here it's as if the guards have stolen his tongue.

The woman in the corner gets a bottle out of a bag and starts to feed the baby. Ben nods at the boy she's visiting.

I lean forward. "Is that Five X?" I whisper.

Ben looks down at the table like he hasn't heard me. I lean closer. "Ben, is that Five X?"

Ben looks up. "Who?"

"Five X."

"Five X?"

"Yeah... you talk to him loads and he beats you at *FIFA*."

"Oh... oh yeah. Yeah, that's him." He glances across at Five X. Five X stares back at us. He doesn't look very friendly. Ben looks down at the table. Five X doesn't look like the sort of boy who plays *FIFA*—he looks like he should be in WWE. If he did play *FIFA*, I think I'd let him win.

"Dad says Albion are doing well," says Mum, like she's trying to cheer Ben up. "He says to tell you Murray is scoring loads and... and Sam Baldock." She says it like she's reading it.

Ben smiles. "It's all right, Mum. You don't have pretend you like football."

Mum shrugs. "Well, I was only trying."

Ben flinches as a door opens. Another guard walks in and talks to

Mike Ashton. Ben looks down at the comics like a strict teacher has just walked in. Mike Ashton checks his watch.

"Five more minutes," he says.

"What?" I jump and Ben flinches again as the voice of the boy who stared at Ben echoes around the room.

"I've only had ten minutes."

"And whose fault was that?" asks the officer. He stares at Booth like he doesn't want him to answer.

Booth stands up, storms past our table. The guard opens the door and they go out into the corridor. When Sophie loses it at school, it's not half as scary as this.

I look at Ben. His eyes have gone darker and his face has turned white.

"Dad'll come soon," says Mum. She puts her hand on top of Ben's. He slides it away in case someone is looking. Ben swallows hard and his eyes start to water.

We can't be going. Coming here is worse than going to the doctor's, going to the dentist, and being sent to the headmaster all on the same day. But I don't want to leave yet.

Five minutes. We've only got five minutes, but I can't think of anything to say. And neither can Ben because his face is frozen like he's seen a ghost.

Are you okay? Mum mouths.

Ben nods, but his eyes are so shiny I know he isn't.

I wish he could walk out of here with us, get in the car, and go home. But the guards would stop him; they'd recognize his clothes. I wish we could swap places. But my sweater would be up to his elbows, and my trousers would be up to his knees. It's a stupid plan anyway, because it means I'd be stuck in here instead of him.

"Okay," says Mike Ashton. "Let's call it there."

Chairs scrape across the floor. Ben gets up slowly. I want to give him a hug and cling to him. Mum wraps her arms around him. Ben closes his eyes.

"I'm sorry, Mum," he whispers.

"I know, love. I know." Mum rubs her hand across his back. "Just keep going and we'll see you soon." Her voice is shaky like she's talking underwater.

Ben lets go of her. I walk around the side of the table and he wraps his arms around my head.

"Don't forget to look after Horace until I come back." He sounds like he's underwater too.

"I won't."

Then he squeezes me tighter and whispers, "Keep working on *Shooting Star*, Danny. It won't be long."

"I will." I try to tell him I'm working on it again tomorrow, but he's already walking toward the door. My chest is aching and I can hardly swallow. Mum holds my hand so tight that I can feel the blood pumping through my fingers.

We follow Mike Ashton back out into the corridor. All I can hear is the distant sound of someone shouting and our footsteps. Mike Ashton stops when we reach reception and says he wants to talk to Mum. I walk outside into the parking lot. The sky is dark and cloudy and it's starting to rain. I turn and look at the building. It looks bigger and colder now that I've seen what it's like inside. I imagine Ben

251

walking back through the corridors, past all the other kids who look like adults. I think of him sitting all alone in his room, staring at the wall.

Ben isn't having fun; he's scared. He doesn't play on Xbox. I don't think Five X is his friend. Dad's right. This isn't a holiday camp. It's a horrible place. I don't care about being a big fish anymore. I just want my brother to come home.

43

Alex: I want pavement, I want concrete, I want tarmac

"Alex, just this once."

"No, I can't."

"But I haven't seen a cat go on the grass for ages."

What about the squirrels, the badgers, and the foxes?

"I can't."

"But you've been working on that stupid raft all week."

"It's not a stupid raft."

"Is."

"It's not!"

"*Pleeeeeease.* It's boring on my own."

"I can't. I'm sorry."

"Pig! I hope your hands drop off." Lizzie scowls at me and runs out of the sitting room. Five seconds later I see her outside, bouncing up and down on the trampoline. Even if I could make it across the grass, I wouldn't be able to bounce on it. It's got little white marks all over it, and the edges have turned green. I can't remember the last time I went on it, but it was about the same time I stopped going on my bike.

Lizzie keeps bouncing, then pokes her tongue out at me.

I wish I was down at the cave working on *Shooting Star* today. Last night I designed a name plaque for her. I added five more *O*s to *Shooting* and then drew a star rocketing across the sky. I thought of taking it down to the cave to show Dan, but he's probably designed a plaque with Ben. They might even be doing it at the STC right now. They'll be sitting side by side and Dan will be drawing *Shooting Star* and telling Ben about all the work we've done. Then they'll sketch out a design for a plaque that will be way better than mine. It's their raft, after all.

I hope Ben suddenly realizes that he's put the buoys in the wrong place, so I don't have to tell Dan. I don't want to bring it up again in case I upset him like I did last time. Maybe they've already chatted about *Shooting Star* and now they're playing *Call of Duty* or *FIFA*, like Dan said they would. I bet they're having a great time even if the STC seems like a scary place. I looked it up last night. I don't know what Ben did or why he was sent there, but from the wire fences and walls I saw around the buildings, *STC* sounds like another word for a *prison*.

Lizzie stops bouncing, then holds her finger up to get my attention.

Watch this! she mouths. She does four more bounces, then a forward flip. I smile. She brushes her hair out of her eyes. *And this!*

She starts to bounce again, but I'm not really watching. All I can think about today is *Shooting Star*.

Lizzie stops bouncing.

Come out! Pleeeease! She put her hands together.

I feel sorry for her. Why can't I just go out and bounce like a normal brother? I walk into the kitchen.

Mum's by the sink, putting the laundry in the machine.

"Oh, Alex." She points at my T-shirt and hoodie on the worktop. "You can't keep putting stuff in the wash after only wearing it once. It wears them out quicker, and it wears me out too."

"But it's dirty."

"It's not." She picks up my hoodie. "It's not. I can't see a mark on it."

I stare at my hoodie. Mum can't see a mark, but I can see hundreds. Where I sat in Dad's car, where my elbow knocked a lamppost on the seafront, where my cuff brushed against the wall.

Mum puts the hoodie back down on the worktop. "Where are you going?" she asks.

"Outside," I say, "to play with Lizzie."

Mum smiles. "I'm glad," she says. "Working on the raft has done you a world of good. Did I tell you that me and Dad are proud?"

"Yep."

"Ah well, doesn't hurt to say some things twice." She reaches out to touch me but then realizes she's got a pair of Lizzie's underwear in her hand.

I pull a weird face. Mum laughs.

I step outside and follow the path around the side of the house.

"Yes!" Lizzie shouts. "I knew you would."

I stop at the edge of the grass. I've been going out all week; maybe I can do this.

"Come on," says Lizzie. "You can help me flip."

I look at the grass.

Rats, squirrels, birds, cats. Rats, squirrels, birds, cats.

Nope.

I stay at the edge of the patio and watch Lizzie bounce.

44

Dan: Nightmare!

I'm back at the STC. I'm running through a corridor, pushing open doors, looking for Ben. He wasn't in the Visitors' Room and he wasn't in the bathroom. I push open a door marked INTERVIEW ROOM. He's not in there either. I run back out into the corridor, through two doors, into another corridor that looks exactly the same as the one I just came from. Visitors' Room, bathrooms, Interview Room. I check them all again. Still I can't find Ben. He must be in his room, but where is his room?

More doors, another corridor, Visitors' Room, bathrooms, Interview Room. All of them empty. I'm running around in circles. I stop and lean my back against the wall. *Ben, where are you? Just shout so I can hear.* Guards' voices echo down the corridor.

"Keep looking!"

"He can't have got far."

"In here! In here!"

I see Mike Ashton's face through the window in the door. He pushes the door open and runs down the corridor, followed by two guards.

257

"I don't know where he is!" I shout. "And I wouldn't tell you if I did!"

"Got him!" shouts Mike Ashton. "Quick, grab his arm."

"No!" I shout, and try to wriggle free. "What are you doing? I'm just visiting my brother. What have you done with him?"

Mike Ashton puts his face up close to mine.

"You said you wanted to swap with him."

"I didn't. I didn't say it out loud."

"Too bad," says Mike Ashton. "You're stuck in here now."

"No!"

I sit up on my bed. It's soaked with sweat and so am I. I look around me. All the corridors and rooms have gone, and so have the guards. I put my hand on my chest and catch my breath. All I can hear is my heart and the squeak of Rex as he runs around on his wheel.

I don't want to swap places with Ben. I just wish we were both here.

45

Alex: Waiting for Dan

"Drive safe."

"Okay, drive safe, now off you go."

I wave to Dad, then walk toward the cave. I wonder if Dan has thought of a way to stop Sophie and the Georges from picking on me. I've been thinking of ways too, but all the things I've thought of end up the same way: Sophie and the Georges picking on me, and Dan joining in again.

I walk past the pier, then the aquarium and the big wheel. The sky is gray and the sea is grayer and it's so early that no one is on the beach yet and the shutters are up on Mr. Kendall's stand and his ice-cream boards have been blown over by the wind. I look along the seafront. I can see the cave, but I can't see any sign of Dan's bike. I look at my watch. It's nine thirty. It's the earliest I've been here, but Dan said he's always here by nine.

I keep walking. Dan said he's never been late. Maybe he had such a great time with his brother that him and his mum have stayed in Milton Keynes so they could see Ben again today. Dan's probably been so busy that he hasn't even thought about what to do at school on Monday. But we've only got two days left if he really meant it about taking *Shooting Star* out for a trial. There's no way he would want to be late for that.

I look back toward the Observation Tower to see if he's cycling along the seafront, but the only people I see are two joggers and a man out walking his dog.

An ambulance light flashes along the seafront.

He's had an accident. A bus has knocked him off his bike. He's in the back of the ambulance going to hospital now.

He hasn't had an accident. He—

My heart slows down as I see Dan swerve out from behind the two runners and head toward me. I never thought I'd feel so pleased to see him.

Dan gets off his bike and half smiles at me.

"Sorry I'm late," he says quietly. "My tire was flat. I had to wait for Dad to fit a new tube."

"No worries," I lie.

He half smiles at me again as he lays his bike on the ground. I want to ask him about Ben and about the trial run and what we're going to do on Monday, but I don't know which to ask first. He unlocks the cave door and turns on the light, and then we pull the tarpaulin off *Shooting Star*. Two weeks ago she was just four planks of wood; now all the planks are joined and the bottles are fixed on. All we have to do is fit the buoys and she's ready to go.

"She looks great," I say.

"Yeah." Dan rolls the tarpaulin up and throws it in the corner. He doesn't look like he's thinking about *Shooting Star*; he didn't even look at her. He sits down on his bucket and starts scrubbing the buoy again. If he scrubs it any more, we're going to shine out like a beacon. I hate it when it's this quiet. We've been talking a lot more the past few days, but now it's as if all the air has gone out of him, like it did from his tire. It's like he's mad at me for doing something wrong, but I haven't done anything. I've not even seen him. Something must have happened when he went to see Ben.

"Did you have a good day yesterday?" I ask cautiously.

"Yeah." Dan keeps scrubbing.

"How was Ben? Did you get to play *Call of Duty* with him?"

"Yeah." Dan looks up. "We played it all morning. Then we went to the cafeteria and then we played football all afternoon."

"Brilliant," I say. "Did you get to see Five X too?"

"Yeah, he's really funny. But he stinks at *FIFA*."

I smile. "I'm glad you had a good time."

"I did. . . . I did." He looks down at the buoy. I'm not sure he did.

Dan: I didn't lie—I just didn't tell the truth

I look down at the buoy for so long that my eyes go blurry. I don't want to blink, because if I do, my tears will fall. I can't cry. Not in front of Shark Face.

"Are you thinking about Ben?"

"Yeah." I look up and see a concerned frown on Shark Face's face.

I take a deep breath. I'm used to people talking at me, not being interested in me. Every time Mum and Dad ask questions it always turns into an argument, so I don't bother talking, and Mr. Francis is a teacher, which makes it hard to talk. I swallow a lump in my throat.

"I think about him all the time," I say. "When we're here. When I look out the window at school."

"I thought that was because you were bored."

"That too." I laugh, and a tear escapes down my cheek. Shark Face looks at *Shooting Star* like he's pretending he didn't see. Ever since I went to see Ben, my chest feels like it's going to burst open. It was like that as soon as I sat in the car with Mum to go home. I didn't tell her, but I looked out the window so she couldn't see how upset I was. Mum didn't talk much either, and when we got home I don't know what she said to Dad, because I went straight upstairs to my room. I kept thinking that if Ben was that scared when we were there, how scared must he be when he's on his own?

I turn and look at Shark Face. He's waiting for me to say something, but I've not told anyone about how I feel since Ben went. I've not even told anyone what he did. I want to tell someone now, but my throat is aching so much that the words won't come out. All I can think of are the blue lights flashing outside our house when the police came for Ben that night. And the neighbors looking out their windows. I thought everything was going to be okay, that the police were just telling Ben off in the sitting room. But then I heard the door click open, and then the front door opened too. I looked out my bedroom window and watched Ben walk up the path between the two policemen. I wanted him to turn around and tell me everything was okay, a joke, but he just kept walking, head turned to the ground. Then they put him in the back of one of the cars and it drove away. That's when Mum came in, crying, and gave me a hug.

"You don't have to tell me," says Shark Face.

"He was in a car," I blurt out. "He stole a car with some friends late one night and they crashed it into a liquor store. Then he jumped out and went into the shop and stole loads of beer and cigarettes." I stop talking because the blue lights are flashing in my head again now. But I have to keep going. I have to get the words out. "Ben says he's really sorry, but it wasn't his fault. He wasn't the one driving. It wasn't him that ran the girl over."

Shark Face is so quiet I can't tell if he's still here.

"Is she...is she dead?" he asks softly, like he's scared to hear the answer.

I shake my head. "No. Broken legs and an arm. The others ran off, but Ben stayed with her and called an ambulance."

I stop talking and puff out my cheeks. I've replayed it in my head so many times it's almost like I was there in the car.

I look up at Shark Face. I feel tired and empty inside. I've told him everything except how much I miss my brother, but I think he knows that. If he wanted to, he could go back to school on Monday and tell Sophie and the Georges what happened, that he saw me cry. But he just smiles at me.

"I'd miss my brother if I had one," he says.

"You've got a sister."

"Yes, but *who* would miss her?"

We both laugh. I wipe my tears on my sleeve.

"Why are you being so kind?" I say. "After all I've done to you?"

Shark Face shrugs. "Don't know, just am."

"If I was you, I'd want to hit me."

"I'd lose."

"Wait!" I stand up. "That's it!"

"That's what?"

"When we go back to school. You've got to hit me."

"What?"

"We've got to have a fight."

"How will that work?"

"It'll be easy." A minute ago I was crying, and now I can't stop

264

myself smiling and I've got goose bumps. It's an amazing idea. I walk over to Shark Face. "We have to have a fight in front of Sophie and the Georges. You just have to smack me right here." I point to my right cheek. "Go on, practice."

"What, now?"

"Yeah."

"But you'll hit me back if I do it at school!"

"I won't," I say. "...Well, not hard."

"See, you will."

I laugh. "Well, I can't let you win. The idea is that it's a draw. That way Sophie and the Georges will think you're cool for standing up to me."

"But what if I hit you and you fall down and crack your head open on the floor?"

"What?"

"And the ambulance comes and it goes so fast to save your life that it crashes on the way to the hospital?"

"Shark Face, you worry too much!"

"I know."

I shake my head slowly and smile. "Okay," I say suddenly. "Now put your hands up."

"I can't now."

"Why not?"

"Because."

"But you'll do it on Monday?"

"I'll think about it," says Shark Face.

I throw two punches and pretend he's hit me back. "Pow! Ow, that was really hard, Shark Face," I say.

"You're crazy," he says.

"Is that a yes?"

Shark Face holds his arms out by his sides.

"I give up!"

We both laugh.

47

Alex: Noah's ark

It's Saturday morning and me and Dan are walking along the sea-front on our way to get some wood for the paddles and a mascot. Dan's dancing around in front of me, pretending to throw punches—"Pow, pow. Pow, pow!"—but I'm too busy watching the pavement and sky to throw any back. He says he was practicing in his bedroom last night and that I should be too. But there's no point practicing anyway, because his plan will never work. Sophie and the Georges would never believe that I'd have the courage to hit Dan. And I'm not sure I'm brave enough either. Dan doesn't seem to be worried about it. He just keeps bobbing and weaving in front of me, and I do find it funny, but I wish he'd stop calling me Shark Face now. Shark Face. It only takes a second for him to say, but it hurts me for ages. I want to tell him to stop, but I don't know how.

Dan stops and presses the button on the crossing. I don't know where we're headed, only that we're going to get the paddles and the mascot and I have to follow him. When the lights turn red, we run across the road. I follow Dan past the chip shop, through a parking lot, then down a narrow street.

At the end of the street Dan stops and puts his finger to his lips. "We need to be quiet." He checks behind us, and then we walk down the side of a fence. Through the gaps in the posts I can see a big gray warehouse.

"This is where I came with Ben to get the base planks," he whispers.

This doesn't feel right.

"We can't go down there," I say.

"Why not?"

Dog poop. Mud. Weeds growing along the fence where people go to the bathroom.

"It stinks."

"Come on!"

I tuck my arms in so my elbows don't touch the fence, and I put one foot directly in front of the other so my feet don't touch the weeds or anything else.

"You look like you're walking a tightrope at the circus." Dan laughs at me. I can't tell if he's teasing me or not, but that's what I feel like. Any minute now I'm going to wobble and fall off into the saw-dust, and the clowns will come into the ring and carry me away. I try to take a deep breath and concentrate. Dan stops at a gap in the fence.

"Look," he whispers. "Through there."

I look through the gap. On the other side there's a yard full of yellow skips, and the skips are full of wood.

Dan puts his head close to mine and points at two men in blue overalls who are standing by the warehouse doors and talking. "They make cabinets and things," he whispers. "And they store all the stuff for the carnival too. Wooden pirates and animals."

"I'm not going in there."

"You've got to."

"Why?"

"Because I don't want to do it on my own."

"That's not a reason," I say.

"It's the only one I can think of." Dan smiles. "Come on, it'll be fun."

I know we're about to do a bad thing, but I like that Dan wants me to go with him and I don't want him to be upset, like he was yesterday.

I look through the fence again. The men are still talking, and inside the warehouse there are three pirates leaning against a wall, and beside them are two elephants and two giraffes, and farther back in the warehouse I can make out a cutout of Noah's ark.

"When they're not looking, we'll take the wood and then grab a pirate. Okay?"

I nod, even though I shouldn't.

A truck drives into the yard and stops. The two men walk over to it and start talking to the driver.

"Come on. . . ."

I can't do it. It might be exciting, but stealing is wrong. I've never stolen anything. Apart from when me and Elliott picked up two Batman comics by mistake from WHSmith.

"No."

Dan opens his eyes wide. "You want to go on *Shooting Star*, don't you?"

"Am I going on her?"

"Course you are. I told you ages ago."

"You didn't."

Dan shrugs. "Well, I just did. Now, are you coming or not?"

He turns sideways and squeezes through the gap. There's no way he told me. I'd have remembered something as exciting as that. I want to celebrate that I'm going on *Shooting Star*, but all I can think is:

Fence-dirt-germs. Stealing-theft-crime.

I'm going on Shooting Star*! I'm going on* Shooting Star*!*

Dan holds the fence open for me. I know I shouldn't be doing this, but I'm smiling so much after what he just said that I don't care. I feel like shouting out "THANKS!" as I watch him scamper across the yard. He stops behind a yellow skip, then beckons for me to follow. My grin must be as wide as my head.

Dan beckons again. I check that the men are still talking. I'm so excited I feel like I'm going to be sick.

Now! Dan mouths.

The men aren't looking. I have to go.

I can't.

I clench my fist, then run across the yard.

Dan grins at me. I smile nervously back, then he peers over the top of the skip.

"Change of plan," he says.

"What? What are you going to do now?"

"I've just seen two oars by the ark."

270

"But we want paddles, not oars."

"Same thing. Anyway, if they're too big, we'll just cut them in half. Now come on, let's do it!" Dan flips his hood up over his head, checks that the men aren't looking, then scurries like a rat across the yard.

I hesitate. Dan reaches the warehouse and beckons to me. *Come on!* he mouths.

I pull my hood over my head, then run as fast as I can toward him. My heart is racing. I feel like I'm escaping from a prison camp in the war, and any second my back is going to get peppered with bullets from the guards.

"Ha-ha, this is brilliant," Dan says excitedly when I reach him.

I get my breath back and glance over at the truck. The two men are still talking to the driver.

"Come on," whispers Dan. "We'll take one each and I'll come back for the pirate."

I feel bad for taking them, but *Shooting Star* won't go far without oars. Dan hands me one. It's as tall as my dad, but not so heavy. We look back out into the yard.

"It's clear," says Dan. "Let's go!"

We run across the yard to the fence. I feed my oar between the gap, then take Dan's and do the same. Dan turns away. I grab his arm and pull him back.

"It's too risky; we don't need the pirate."

"I know we don't." Dan pulls his arm away.

"So where are you going?"

"I want a giraffe!"

I open my mouth to tell him no, but he's already running toward the warehouse. The trucks engine revs. Dan grabs the giraffe, then races back across the yard with it under his arm.

"Hey, what do you think you're up to?!" The men in blue overalls run after Dan.

"Go!" Dan shouts. "Go!"

I slide through the gap in the fence and scramble around for the oars. Dan follows me with the giraffe.

"Come on!"

I pick up an oar in each hand and drag them as we run along the side of the fence. My heart is beating so fast that I don't look behind or even worry about where I'm going.

Dan's giggling behind me.

"It's okay," he says. "I don't think they're coming."

I start to laugh too. I can't help it. Dan looks really funny running with a giraffe under his arm.

We stop and get our breath back when we reach the parking lot.

"You did great," Dan puffs.

I gulp for air. I don't know if I did great, and stealing definitely isn't great, but I do know that the last ten minutes were so exciting and scary that all my bad thoughts disappeared.

A car turns into the lot. Me and Dan pick up the oars and the giraffe and start walking again, but the giraffe is so tall it keeps slipping from Dan's arms.

"Maybe we should leave it behind," I say.

"No, Jeff's my friend." Dan stops and puts his arm around the giraffe's neck.

"How do you know its name?"

"I didn't, but that's what he's called now."

"You're weird."

"*I'm* weird?!" Dan raises his eyebrows.

I laugh as we walk out of the parking lot and past the fish-and-chip shop. People stop and stare at us as we walk along the seafront. I'm used to people looking at me because they think I'm weird, but never because I'm walking with a giraffe.

48

Dan: Sunday. Launching the *Star*

"It's okay," I whisper. "He said we could borrow it."

"I don't know. It feels like stealing."

"We're not; we're borrowing."

"Then why are we whispering?"

"Umm...I don't know. Come on, just pick it up."

Me and Shark Face are in a cave six away from Mr. Kendall's, getting a dinghy trailer to move *Shooting Star*. Ben said the man who owns it said we could borrow it, but that was last year. I think he might be ill or has moved away, because I haven't seen him forever and the locks on his cave doors have been broken for ages.

I bend down and pick up the front of the trailer. Shark Face shakes his head like he's still not sure.

"It's okay," I say. "We'll bring it straight back."

"Okay." Shark Face picks up the other side and we pull the trailer out of the cave like two horses pulling a cart. I can't stop myself from smiling as we walk along the seafront. Apart from the pirate flag, *Shooting Star* is ready for her trial run. After we got back from the warehouse yesterday, me and Shark Face cut the oars in half and made them into paddles, and this morning we fixed the big buoys underneath *Shooting Star*. Shark Face kept asking me if I was sure that's where they should go. I said we'd followed Ben's instructions all the way through, so we shouldn't stop now.

We reach our cave entrance and reverse the trailer in. I go to one side of *Shooting Star*, and Shark Face goes to the other. I get ready to lift, but he's just standing there looking at me.

"It's okay," I say. "I said we'd take the trailer back."

"It's not that," he says. "I just think..."

"What?"

"I think we should wait for Ben."

I look at *Shooting Star*. "But we've got the trailer now."

"I know, but I've been wondering about it for ages."

"I thought you were as excited as me."

"I was. I am," says Shark Face. "But he drew the plan, and it was both your idea. He should be the first one on it with you."

Shark Face is right, and from the look on his face, he knows he is. I know I should wait, but I want her to be perfect for Ben. I want to be certain she floats. It would be horrible if after all this time we took her down to the water together and a wave smashed her to pieces before we even got on. But it *would* be more exciting with him.

"Okay," I say. "You're right." Shark Face looks relieved.

I walk out of the cave and look at the sea. I've waited three months. I can wait another one.

I look toward the pier. A man and a boy are carrying a raft down the slipway onto the beach. Its base blanks are so thin they bend in the middle.

"Hey, Shark Face," I say. "Come and watch this." He stands beside me and I point at the raft. "If a wave hits it, it'll snap in half."

Shark Face smiles. "It might be okay," he says.

The man and the boy put the raft on the sea and push it out through the waves.

"It's nowhere near as good as *Shooting Star*," I say. "Theirs hasn't got any seats."

"Or a giraffe," says Shark Face.

I laugh. "Jeff's way better than a pirate."

Shark Face laughs. "Yeah, he is!"

We walk along the seafront to get a closer look. The boy climbs onto the raft, then slides straight off the other side. We won't do that on *Shooting Star*. She's big enough and sturdy enough that when we put her in the water she'll sail above the waves. Ben will love her.

I turn around and look at Shark Face. "You were right," I say.

"Thanks." He grins. "I'm not just an interpreter."

I laugh and suddenly I remember that we've got to go back to school tomorrow and I won't be able to laugh at the things he does then. I put my fists up and dance around in front of Shark Face.

"Pow, pow!" I bob and weave. "Come on," I say. "Have you been practicing?"

"No."

"Why not, Shark Face?"

Shark Face sighs.

"What's wrong? We agreed."

"It's not that."

"What is it, then, Shark Face?"

Shark Face scrunches his face like I've already hit him. "Do you have to keep calling me that?"

"What?"

"Shark Face."

"But it's your name."

"It's not. My name's Alex." He looks at me like he means it. I lower my hands. I hadn't even thought about it. I just say it. I think of saying sorry, but I'd have to say it a thousand times to take all the Shark Faces back.

I hold up my fist. "So...have you been practicing, A-L-E-X?"

Alex shakes his head and laughs.

"What?"

"Nothing. It just sounds weird when you say it."

"Oh, shall I go back to Shark Face, then?"

"No!"

I laugh as he holds up his skinny arms. He throws a punch. I dodge it.

"You have to keep still," he says.

"What? No, Sophie will smell a rat right away."

I dance in front of him again. Shark Face tries to do the same, but he looks like more like C-3PO without even trying. I dodge one punch, then another, and he dodges mine.

"You're getting better, Sh—Alex. No one will come near you after this!" He draws his fist back, ready to hit me, then suddenly looks up at the sky.

I hear a splatting sound.

"Arghhhhhhhhhhhh! No!!!!!!"

There's bird poop splatted on the pavement all around us. Alex's face is frozen and his body is stiff, like he's just been struck by lightning.

"Did it get me?" he asks. "Did it get me?" His jaw is clenched tight. "Did it? Did it?" He looks over his shoulder and spins around like a dog chasing its tail. I start to laugh, but Alex looks so worried I immediately stop. "Tell me!" His voice is squeaky with panic. "Did it get my back?"

"Stand still," I say, "and I'll look." His hoodie has got white bird poop on the shoulder, and there's a line of it trailing down his back. "It's not much," I say.

"How much?"

"This much." I stretch my thumb and index finger as far as they'll go, even though it's really three times as much as that. "It's only bird poop," I say. "My nan says it brings good luck."

"Good luck? No! It's bad. Really bad. Aaaargh!" Alex scrunches his face up like he can smell it. I don't know why he's so upset. It's just bird poop.

"It's okay," I say. "We'll get some tissues and water from Mr. Kendall and wash it off."

Alex arches his back. "No, we can't touch it. Oh no! I knew it! I knew it. I should have stayed in the cave." His voice cracks like he's going to cry.

I look at the stain. It's only a bit of bird poop, but Alex is freaking out.

"Stop panicking," I say. "Are you allergic to bird poop or something? Like some people are allergic to nuts?"

278

"No! That's not funny!" he snaps in a panic. "Just help me take it off." He holds on to the cuffs of his hoodie and pulls his arms inward so that he looks like he's got no arms.

"What do you want me to do?"

Alex shuffles a bit closer. "Just pull the sleeves and I'll put my arms up and push the collar over my head."

I rest Jeff against the railings. Then Alex leans forward and we pull the hoodie off over his head. "Is that better?"

He brushes his hair out of his eyes. I go to hand him his hoodie, but he jerks away quickly, like I'm holding a bomb.

"I don't want it," he says. "I just want to go back to the cave."

"But what shall I do with it?"

"Throw it in the garbage."

"What?"

"Just throw it in the garbage and *don't* touch the bird poop. . . . You haven't, have you?"

"No . . . but what will your mum say? Mine would go crazy."

"I'll tell her I lost it. You didn't touch it, did you?"

"No."

"Promise?"

"Yes, I only touched the sleeves." I go to tell him he can't just leave it here, but he's already headed back to the cave, taking his giant strides. He looks even weirder when he's going twice the speed.

I run after him. He's got a worried look on his face like he gets at school. I try to talk and keep up at the same time.

"Alex," I say, "slow down. What's wrong? It's just bird poop. I haven't touched it." He doesn't answer.

He's weird about cleaning his hands all the time, but just a little bit of bird poop has turned him crazy. I hold his hoodie in front of me. There's a white line across the back, but it's not wet and doesn't have any yellow or green bits in it, like bird poop does. It's not bird poop...it's chalk! He must have got it on him when we climbed over the wall.

"Alex!" I shout. "It's not bird poop!" I get ready to shout again, but he's walking away faster than I can run.

49

Alex: Something's burning

I feel a tingle in the middle of my back. The bird poop has gone through my hoodie onto my T-shirt. I want to pull it away to stop it seeping through to my skin, but I can't touch it, not even with my gloves on.

The cave is cool when I get there, but sweat is pouring down my neck. I try to take deep breaths and calm down, but my thoughts are crashing around and around in my head like waves. I need to write them down. I have to write them down.

My worries.

I need a pen and paper. I look around the cave, but all I can find is a pencil and Ben's drawing of *Shooting Star*. I walk over to the blackboard where the drawing is pinned.

The bird poop is on my skin, burning, spreading over my ribs and spine and into my bloodstream.

I pick up a piece of chalk and start writing as fast as I can on the board.

My Worry List

1. Everyone is going to die.
2. I'm going to die. The bird poop has burned through my hoodie onto my skin and it's in my blood and spreading through my body. I need to wash if off. I need to get it out of my body. I could run in the sea.
3. The sea is full of germs. I've seen them washed up on the beach, brown froth and seaweed and old plastic bags. I have to stay in the cave.
4. The cave is going to collapse and trucks will fall in on top of me.
5. I'll suffocate and die under the cement and no one will find me. But Dan knows where I am.
6. Dan's going to die too. He touched my hoodie, he touched the bird poop. I know he did. It's burning through his skin too.

I pause to catch my breath. My heartbeat begins to slow. *It'll be okay. It'll be okay.* I look at the chalk.

This chalk is filthy. It's been on the floor with rats.

I've got to throw the chalk away, but I need to finish my list. Aaaaaargh!!!! I start writing again.

Dan: All the things in Alex's head

"What are you doing? Alex!"

Alex jumps. A piece of chalk falls onto the floor. He looks at me, then back at the board.

"You're not supposed...nobody is supposed to—argh! No!" He puts his hands up to his head and turns away.

I try to read what he's written, but it's so scrawly. I can only make out a few words.

My Worry List. Everybody is going to die. I'm going to die... something, something. The cave is going to...something, something...trucks, cement. Dan's going to die too...burning through his skin...The pier is going to...I'm...at school.

I don't understand. What is this?

"Alex," I say quietly. "What does it mean?"

"I can't...you shouldn't..." He turns around. His eyes are shining like he's going to cry. "Please don't tell anyone."

"I won't." I read the board again. *Everybody is going to die. I'm going to die.* It's like he's written a horror movie. I shake my head. How can I tell anyone about it when I don't even know what it is?

My Worry List. I read it again. *My Worry List.*

Alex walks past me and takes his bag off the hook.

"Wait," I say. "Are those things in your head?"

"Yes," he says quietly.

I blow out my cheeks. "That's a lot of things."

"I've got a lot of worries."

"Wow! That's crazy. No wonder you're good at writing stories."

Alex sits down on a bucket. It's like writing down all his worries has worn him out. I don't know what to say to him now because it must be horrible worrying about things like that all the time. When he screws his face up at school, I just thought it was because he didn't like things touching him, but this list is way worse than that.

Alex looks over his shoulder at his back.

"There's nothing there," I say. "I'm not sure it's even bird poop." Alex scrunches his face when I say "bird poop."

"I want to go home," he says. "Can you text your mum?"

"But there's nothing there."

"I just want to go home now. Can you just text your mum so she'll tell mine?"

There's no use in talking to him. It's like even if I swore on the Bible he'd still think there was some on his back. I wish I could help him.

I look back at his list and read all the things he's written again. I can't stop people dying or the trucks crashing into the cave. And I can't stop Alex from thinking the bird poop is burning through both our skins. But I can do something about the last thing on his list.

"Alex."

"Yeah."

"Why are you still worried about school tomorrow? I told you it'll be okay."

"Please, just text your mum?"

"Okay, but do you believe me?"

Alex shrugs. "I don't know. That thought's not just in my head. It's real."

51

Alex: Don't blame me... I'm just weird!

Dan takes his phone out of his pocket and texts his mum. I don't know what he texts, but two minutes later his phone buzzes and he tells me that my mum is on her way down. Then he sits on his bucket and starts talking to me about the Albion, *The Force Awakens*, how we can take *Shooting Star* out the first day that Ben comes home. I know what he's trying to do. He's trying to take my mind off the thing that's burning through my clothes onto my skin.

I felt horrible when he saw my list. It's like someone had taken the lid off my head and found out all my secrets inside. I thought he'd laugh and spread it all around the school on Monday, but I don't think he's going to do that, because he really looked like he cared. He's still talking now, even though I'm not really listening. I just want Mum to hurry up and get here.

Dan stands up in front of me. "Tell me what you think. I've been practicing."

"Practicing what?"

He makes his body go stiff and puts on a funny voice.

" 'Don't blame me. I'm an interpreter. I'm not supposed to know a power socket from a computer terminal.' "

I laugh. "That's terrible," I say. "That just sounds like you're talking into a tin can."

Dan smiles. "I thought it was good."

I stand up. "It's like this: 'Don't blame me. I'm an interpreter. I'm not supposed to know a power socket from a computer terminal.' "

Dan laughs. "Do Yoda again."

I put my hands out like an old lady resting on a walking stick. " 'Judge me by my size, do you? ' "

Dan shakes his head. "It's great. You've got to do that at school."

"I don't think so."

"Maybe not tomorrow," he says. "But after—"

Dan's phone buzzes. He reads out the message. "Your mum is with mine. They're waiting by the pier."

I walk over and pick my bag off the hook.

"Wait," he says. "We can't leave *Shooting Star* out there on the trailer."

Argh! I forgot about that. He's right—we can't leave her out there. Anybody could come along and take her out onto the sea, and we've done too much work to let that happen. But it means I have to go back out there.

Dan walks out onto the seafront and looks up at the sky.

"It's okay," he shouts back. "They've all gone." He holds his hands out by his sides.

The birds might have gone, but it will only take a few flaps of their wings for them to come swooping back. I edge toward the mouth of the cave and look out. There are no seagulls here, but there's a flock circling by the pier.

"Come on," Dan says. "They're too busy looking for fish and chips to worry about you. And I'll keep lookout anyway."

I check the sky again, then dart out onto the seafront. Dan picks up the front of the trailer and I push from the other end. Slowly we wheel *Shooting Star* back along the pavement. All the time we're both looking up at the sky like we're expecting the seagulls to return and bomb me at any second.

"Made it!" Dan puffs as he puts his end of the trailer down.

We might have made it, but my heart is beating fast, like a mouse's.

Dan's phone buzzes again.

"We'd better go," he says.

I nod. I don't want to go, but I have to. I edge to the cave mouth and look back at *Shooting Star*. Dan picks up his bag and puts it over his shoulder.

"We could come down next weekend," he says. "We don't have to do anything—we can just sit and look at her."

I smile, but I don't think I'll be coming back, not after what just happened. I can wash the poop off my clothes and my skin, but the thought will stay in my head for weeks.

Dan: Something's wrong

I'm on my bed. Rex is crawling around under my hoodie. Mum and Dad have been arguing, and this time it was so bad I'm too scared to go downstairs. When I got back, Dad was shouting full blast, saying he knew this was going to happen, that's why he wanted nothing to do with taking me to the STC. Then his phone rang and everything went quiet. He took the phone outside.

I went into Ben's room and looked out the window. Dad was talking while walking around in a circle in the garden. He was out there for ages; he didn't even come in when it rained. When he did, he went straight into the sitting room with Mum. They must be talking in whispers, because even if I go halfway down the stairs I can't hear a thing. I'm worried it's something bad, but I'm also worried about school tomorrow.

It was horrible what happened to Alex today. It must be horrid to have thoughts like that in his head. And it must be even worse when he gets picked on at school. I told him we'll be okay tomorrow, but

I'm not sure we will. What if the pretend fight doesn't work? I hope he's practicing his boxing moves now. I should be, but the house is so quiet I feel like I can't move. The only time it's been this quiet was the day after Ben went away. It was like he was dead then, and this feels just as bad.

The door clicks open and I listen to Dad's footsteps on the stairs. I get up and put Rex in his cage. Dad comes into my room. His face is blotchy, and the veins are sticking out on his neck.

"Dan," he says. "I need to talk to you."

"Is it about Ben? He's not dead, is he?"

"No, he's not dead."

Phew.

"What, then?"

"There's been a bit of trouble at the STC; he got in a fight."

"Did he win?"

"Dan, don't be silly. This is serious. It doesn't matter who won; the fact is, he's not coming home when we thought."

"But it'll only be a week. That's how long Josh Hardy got suspended for at school."

"Dan, listen. It's going to be a lot longer than that." Dad looks at me and takes a deep breath, like it's going to be much more than a week.

"What, a month?" I say.

"I really don't know, Dan, but it's likely to be longer than that."

"Two?!"

"I said I don't know. We'll find out more when me and Mum go up there tomorrow."

290

My heart is bursting in my chest and my throat is aching. I stand up. "But it can't be, it can't. I've been waiting for ages."

"I know, Dan, but we all have to be brave. Ben especially has to be brave."

I try to breathe, but the shock has taken away my breath. Dad holds out his arms, but I don't want a hug. I just want to see Ben. I can't wait another three months. I want him here now. I sit down on my bed. Dad sits down next to me.

This isn't fair. Ben can't stay in the STC any longer. He looked so scared when me and Mum saw him. I bet it's Booth. It's his fault, not Ben's. Ben can't stay in there. He can't. He can't. My chest tightens and my throat feels like it's going to explode.

"Are you okay, Dan?" Dad puts his arm around my shoulders.

I don't care about me; I care about Ben. He's stuck in the STC, with its corridors and echoey rooms and boys that look like men. I shrug Dad's arm away.

"Get off me!" I jump up off the bed.

"Dan, calm down." Dad stands up.

"NO!" I shout. "GO AWAY!"

"Dan..."

"I said NO! Leave me alone!"

"But—"

"LEAVE—ME—ALONE!" I shout so loud that my voice hurts my throat.

"Leave him, Dave." Mum's standing in the doorway. Her eyes are red and she's got black lines running down her face. She steps toward me and opens her arms.

"No!" I shout. "You leave me alone too!" I slam the door closed.

This can't be true. It can't be.

I could smash the windows. I could throw my Xbox against the wall. This isn't happening.

I put my hands up to my face and fall onto my bed.

53

Alex: The fight. Round 1

The sun is turning all the white buildings whiter, and the seagulls are hovering in the sky. My hands are sweating, and the worms are back eating my stomach. Every step I take toward school, I want to turn back. I have to do it—I have to hit Dan. Otherwise everything will go on the same. But I've never hit anyone. Until now I've never even thought of hitting anyone, not even Dan when he was bullying me, but it's impossible to think of hitting him now that he's my friend. I clench my fist into a ball and punch into my palm. Maybe my punches won't hurt him so much if I'm wearing gloves.

I practiced my punches in my bedroom last night, but Lizzie kept coming in and asking what I was doing. I told her I was trying to catch a fly.

My stomach is doing somersaults as I walk through the school gates.

There are groups of boys and girls talking in the playground while others walk past them toward the main door. Dan said we're going to do it at first break. I put my head down and walk through the door. I'm more nervous than I was on the first day I came here.

I walk down the blue corridor toward my classroom. Boys and girls are swarming everywhere, shouting and laughing, but I'm so nervous that all I see are blurry colors and all I can hear is a buzz. I turn into my classroom.

"Michael?"

"Yes, miss."

"Sarah?"

"Yes, miss."

"Elliott?"

"Yes, miss."

"Alex?... Alex?" Miss Harris looks up.

"Yes, miss." She looks at me like she's surprised I'm here on time. But it's easy to get here when I've been up since six o'clock.

I glance over to the window where Sophie and Dan sit. Sophie's smirking right at me; Dan is staring out the window. Miss Harris tells us to check over the history homework we did during the holidays while she continues with attendance.

Emma smiles as I sit down next to her. She whispers something about the holidays, but I'm too nervous to answer. I get my book out and start to read about Alex Rider. I hear a giggle, and then someone kicks my chair. I keep my head down and pretend it didn't happen. My chair squeaks on the floor as someone kicks it again.

"Hey, Shark Face!" I glance over my shoulder. "Still know your name?" Sophie's grinning right at me with a ruler in her hand. She lets go of it. A piece of rubber pings against the side of my head. Sophie laughs and nudges Dan. I wait for him to help me. Sophie nudges him again. He turns and stares at me like I'm not here. He's broken his promise already. Nothing has changed. I was stupid to think it would.

I look back at my homework. I feel another kick on my chair. Then someone kicks Emma's. Out the corner of my eye I see her turn around.

"Take it!" says Sophie. "Or we'll get you too."

I know what's coming next. Emma turns back around and slides a note onto my desk.

> Hey Shark Face. Welcome back.
> We're going to get you at break.

The worms in my stomach start to squirm. I want to crumple up the piece of paper up and throw it at Dan. The class starts to babble.

Miss Harris clicks on her computer, then tells the kids by the windows to pull down the blinds. The room goes dark, and a video about the First World War starts to play on the screen. I try to watch and listen, but I'm so confused and hurt that all I see is grainy pictures, and the narrator's words are so jumbled up he could be talking Japanese. I glance over my shoulder again, but all I can see are eyes looking at me like wolves in the dark.

Dan: Breaking point

I'm in the Rainbow Room with Sophie and the Georges. I'm catching up with the history homework I didn't do over the holidays. Mr. Francis is on the computer, helping the Georges research how the war started. I'm supposed to be drawing a picture of a howitzer firing shells across a trench, and it's Sophie's job to write about what's happening underneath. But I'm just doodling, not paying attention, and Sophie's too busy talking about Thorpe Park to notice. It's impossible to concentrate on anything since I found out that Ben's not coming home.

Mum and Dad left to go to the STC at the same time as I left home this morning. They asked me if I needed a lift, but I wanted to be on my own.

I was so busy thinking about Ben that I don't remember crossing any of the roads on the way to school. I've been waiting for him to come home for ages, and now he's got to stay in that scary place for even longer.

"Hey! I'm talking to you." Sophie nudges me. "I said it was a great day out. I was too small last time I went, but this time I got to go on Stealth, Swarm, *and* Colossus."

I shade in the tread on the tracks. She already told me all this at the Observation Tower. I wasn't interested then and I'm not now.

I can't stop thinking about what's happening with Ben. I keep imagining Mum and Dad in the car. They must be nearly there by now. I'm glad they're going. At least Ben won't be on his own. But it'll only be for a few hours. Then Mum and Dad will leave and he will be. And all I can think of is how small and scared he looked when we left him last time.

"Hey! Swat!" Sophie shoves my arm and makes me jump.

"Get off!"

"What, did I mess up your guns?"

"No!"

"Well, *so–rry.*" She pulls an annoying face.

"Dan, Sophie." Mr. Francis looks up from the computer. "More work. Less talking."

Sophie leans close to me. "What's wrong with you?" she sneers.

"Nothing."

"There is. You were really quiet at the Observation Tower, and now you've been acting weird all morning."

"Sophie!" Mr. Francis is starting to look cross.

Sophie picks up her pen and starts writing, but only a few seconds go by before she begins talking again.

"You're just jealous because I went to Thorpe Park. . . . I bet you've only ever been to Legoland."

"I have been," I say. "My mum and dad took us last year."

"Bet you never went on Nemesis."

"I did," I lie. Ben did, but I was too short.

"Sophie! Dan. For the last time!" Mr. Francis walks over to our table and rests his hands on our desk. "Come on.... Dan, you've barely started. Don't make me have to split you up." He stares at us for a long time and then walks back to the Georges.

"Dumbass!" Sophie whispers.

I pick up my pencil and try to draw, but all I can think about is Ben shouting on the ride at Thorpe Park. Ben drawing *Shooting Star*. Ben looking scared and lonely at the STC. A lump builds in my throat. If I think about him any more, I'm going to cry.

"So what *did* you do?" Sophie whispers.

"What?" I gulp.

"During the rest of half-term?"

I went down the seafront *with Alex* and worked on *Shooting Star*. *Alex* did *Star Wars* characters voices when we were collecting bottles. Then I broke into a warehouse *with Alex* and stole planks of wood and a giraffe. Then I took *Shooting Star* out of the cave *with Alex* and a seagull pooped on him and *Alex* freaked out—

"Just stayed in...played *Call of Duty* and *FIFA*."

"*Boooor*-ing!" she says. "But it won't be boring later."

"Why not?"

She grins as she gets a black marker pen out of her bag.

"For Shark Face," she says. "We'll get him like we did Elliott, write all over him and then give him a mustache."

My heart sinks into my stomach. I've been so worried about Ben that I didn't even notice Alex in homeroom and history. He'll think I'm going to forget our pact. He'll think I'm going to bully him again.

I imagine Alex wriggling on the bathroom floor with me and the

Georges holding him down while Sophie stands behind us with the pen in her hand. I can't do it to him now that I know all the things he worries about. I don't want to do it to him. I don't even want to be in this school. Sophie reaches over me and scribbles across my drawing.

"What did you do that for?!"

"Checking it works!"

"But you've ruined my picture!"

"Aww, poor Danny!"

"Don't call me that!"

"You two!" Mr. Francis is standing in front of us again, looking annoyed. "I warned you both." He looks at my piece of paper. "Dan, come with me."

"But I wasn't doing anything."

"I'm not saying who it was. Just move over here by the window."

"But—"

"Here."

"Bye, *Danny.*"

"I said, don't call me that." I turn and see Sophie grinning at me. Only Ben gets to call me that. I take a deep breath, but I can't stop the anger building inside me. Building and building until my blood feels like it's going to burst out of my veins. I have to get out of here. I don't want to pick on Alex. I want to see Ben. *I can't take it anymore.* I thump the desk with my hands as I stand up, and suddenly my legs kick over a chair. It's like they're a separate part of my body. The chair clatters onto the floor.

"Dan!"

"It's not fair!" I shout. The bubbles rise further, like steam pouring from a kettle. "It's not fair!" I shove another chair and it skids across the floor. I think I hear Sophie say something and Mr. Francis too and then Sophie laughs. I want to scream, but I feel like I've fallen down a well and nobody can hear me. The rest of the class is looking at me, but all the faces and the noises are so jumbled that nothing makes sense.

"Dan." Mr. Francis is standing in front of me. He doesn't look angry anymore. He looks worried. "You need to calm down."

"You don't understand!" I yell. "No one understands."

Mr. Francis is staring at me. Mr. Francis is going blurry. I'm going to cry. I need to get out. I need to escape.

I make a dash toward the door. Mr. Francis reaches out and grabs my arm.

"Get off me! Don't you get it? My brother's not coming home!"

I wrestle my arm free, run past two tables and out into the corridor. My chest is aching. The lump in my throat is so big I can barely breathe. *He's not coming home. He's not coming home.* I run down the corridor. I don't know where I'm going, only that I have to run.

"Dan!" Mr. Francis's voice echoes down the corridor. My head feels like it's spinning. The corridor seems to go on forever as I run past one blurry door, then another, until I get into the entrance hall I run past people whose faces I can't see, whose shouts I can't hear. I pass them all. I'm out the main doors. I'm nearly at the gates. It's raining and misty. I stop and put my hands on my knees as my head spins even faster. I can usually run fast and forever, but my heart is beating so hard it hurts.

"Dan!" Mr. Francis rushes out the main doors and stops when he sees me. "Come back in. Let's talk about it."

I look at the traffic rushing by, then back at Mr. Francis.

"Come on." He beckons me in.

I shake my head. I don't want to go back in. I don't want to talk about it. He won't understand. Nobody does except Ben. Even I don't understand why I feel the way I do. It's like all my problems are jumbled up in my head and my heart at the same time, but every time I think of opening my mouth and telling someone, it's like someone else takes over and shouts.

I just want everyone to go away and leave me alone.

I just want to see Ben.

I take a big breath. Mr. Francis steps toward me.

In one quick movement, I turn toward the gates and run.

55

Alex: Breakout

It's morning break and I'm walking around the edge of the playground, like me and Dan agreed. Some Year Eights are playing football, and some of the kids from my class are running around playing tag. The sky is dark and it's drizzling. I'd hoped it would be a wet break so I could stay inside.

"Hide me, Alex. Hide me!" Emma runs behind me as she tries to avoid getting tagged by Harry. They dodge to either side of me, and then Emma runs toward the "safe zone" wall by the science block.

I dip my head and walk over to the corner of the basketball court. I wish I had a safe zone, because nothing has changed.

"Alex! Alex!" I jump and look around. It's not Elliott or Dan. It's a boy shouting at Alex Preddy from Year Eight to pass the ball to him. Alex dribbles between three players, scores a goal, and waves his hands above his head. I wish I was like him. He's not as good as Cristiano Ronaldo, but he plays on the school football team and scores a hat trick every week. I can do it on my PlayStation, but that doesn't really count.

"Here he is!" My heart jumps a beat. I spin around and see Sophie standing with the Georges by her side.

"Thought you could hide from us, did you, Shark Face?"

I look around for help, but the only teacher here is Mr. Anderton and he's busy talking to Mr. Jevons.

I search for Dan, but I can't see him anywhere.

Sophie puts her face up close to mine. "I've got something for you." She reaches into her bag and gets out a marker pen. "Thought you might like a mustache," she sniggers.

The Georges stand on either side of me, getting ready to grab my arms.

Dan, where are you? We're supposed to be pretending to fight.

He's nowhere. He isn't going to sort this out; he's just left them to pick on me on their own.

Sophie takes the top off the pen.

"Hold him still."

The Georges grab my arms and I smell the chemicals from the pen as Sophie waves it under my nose. *Where is he? Where's Dan?* I pull my head away from the pen. I was stupid to think Dan would be here to stick up for me. I knew I'd watched too many happy films. Nothing ever happens like it does in films.

Sophie holds the pen right under my nose. I manage to wriggle one arm free.

"I can't hold him still," says George C. "Let's wait for Dan."

"Dan's not here," says Sophie. "And he won't be coming back today. They might even expel the crybaby for running off."

What? Crybaby? What does she mean, Dan's run off?

George C. grabs my arm again. I rip it free.

"Where's Dan?" I ask. "What's he done?"

"Oooh! *Where's Dan? Where's Dan?*" Sophie says in a whiny voice that's supposed to be me.

"I mean it! Where is he?"

"He ran out of class blubbering," says Sophie. "He was saying something about his brother not coming home. He lost it big-time." She laughs.

"What?"

She pushes me roughly. "Why are you so interested? What's it got to do with you, Shark Face?"

The bell rings for the end of break.

"Okay!" shouts Mr. Anderton. "Everybody back to lessons."

The Georges step away from me reluctantly as Sophie puts the pen back in her bag.

"I guess the mustache can wait. But we'll get you later," she snarls. They turn and walk away.

What's she talking about? Dan's been crying? His brother's not coming home?

All the time I've been worrying about my own problems so much I've forgotten about his. He ran out of school because Ben's not coming home. Dan must have been really upset if he cried in school; no one ever does that. *Where did he run off to? Why didn't Mr. Francis stop him? If Dan's that upset, he won't take any notice of the traffic and he could get knocked over on his way home, and even if he gets*

there, his mum and dad might not be in. If there's something wrong
with Ben, they're bound to be going to the STC.

"Hey, you!" Mr. Anderton shouts at me. "Yes, you. Get a move on."

I start walking across the playground.

But what if he hasn't even gone home? What if he's gone to the
cave? He'll be sitting there on his own. I need to go down and help
him, but I'll get in just as much trouble as him if I leave school.

I reach the science-block doors and stop.

But what if he's not sitting there crying? Sophie made it sound
like he'd gone crazy. What if he's—

Oh no! He's gone to the cave to take Shooting Star *to see Ben, like*
he drew on the board.

Don't be silly—you're overreacting. He can't be.

No, he has. He's upset, and Mum says people do silly things when
they're upset. He's going to take Shooting Star *out. She's not fin-*
ished. We've not moved the buoys. If Dan takes her out, she'll flip
upside down and he'll drown.

He won't. It won't. He won't. Go away. He will.

I've got to stop him. I've got to get to the seafront.

I can't. I can't run out of school. I can't risk the seagulls.

She's not ready. The buoys will flip him up. He'll drown. He'll
drown.

"Argh! I'm an elephant. I'm an elephant. I've got to stop him," I
say out loud.

I turn away from the doors and run as fast as I can across the
teachers' parking lot.

"Hey, you!" Mr. Anderton shouts. "I said get to lessons."

Dan's gone to the cave. Dan's going on Shooting Star.

I've never deliberately missed a lesson. I've never broken the school rules. I step up onto the wall and jump down to the path.

"Hey!"

I look for a gap in the traffic and run across the road.

56

Dan: My great escape

I run along the seafront. The rain is pouring onto my head, down my neck, and sticking my clothes to my skin. I run past the Observation Tower, then the clock tower. I wish I had my bike, but I'm running as fast as I can. I put my head down and try to sprint, but the wind is blowing in my face, almost pushing me backward. I feel like Rex stuck in one place in his wheel. My legs are aching and I'm running out of breath. But I'm not going to stop. If I stop, I'll cry.

I push on past the boarded-up doughnut shop, Al's Pizza, the big wheel, and Mr. Kendall's ice-cream stand. I stop outside the cave, put my hands on my knees to catch my breath, but I want to see Ben so badly it's like I'm breathing through straws. I look up at the cave. At the padlock. The key! I haven't got the key! I turn and run back to Mr. Kendall's stand. He's got a spare that he used to leave in case Ben forgot his. I run around the back, check along the seafront, so no one sees what I'm doing.

But the mist is coming in off the sea so quickly that I can't see anyone and I don't think anyone can see me. I reach under the wooden hut and feel sand and tiny stones under my fingers, then the cold metal of the key. I rush back to the cave and undo the padlock. The door flies open and I turn on the light.

The first trip on *Shooting Star* wasn't supposed to happen like this. It was supposed to be a sunny day, not rainy, and me and Ben would have sandwiches and drinks, and Alex was supposed to be here too. But neither of them are here and I've got no sandwiches or drinks because I left my bag at school. But I can't go back for them now.

I drag the tarpaulin off *Shooting Star*, then look around for what else I need, but suddenly my mind is blank.

I bend down and pick up the trailer. It's heavier on my own. I grit my teeth and pull harder. The wheels begin to turn, and then *Shooting Star* starts to roll out of the cave.

If they won't let Ben out, then I'll break him out.

57

Alex: What am I doing?

Push the button. Push the button.

It's germy. It's germy.

It's raining. That'll clean it.

It won't—it just spreads the germs. It—

I can't—

I step off the curb and sprint, dodging between the traffic, and make it to the other side without touching the button.

The buoys are in the wrong place. Shooting Star's going to flip over. Dan's going to—argh! Dog poop!

I jump over it. My heart is thudding in my chest. I don't have time to check my shoes, so I keep running away from the thought in my head until I reach the seafront.

I stop and catch my breath. The seafront is wet and empty. I look down onto the beach. The sea is gray and choppy, like a giant toothed monster that's about to swallow up any boats that dare to sail. *Shooting Star* would flip if it was calm. She'll fly ten feet in the air if it's as rough as this.

I look along the beach to see if I can spot Dan, but there are just lots of pebbles and lots of gray before everything disappears into the mist. Even the top of the Observation Tower has been swallowed by the clouds.

I start to run—

A seagull squawks above my head.

Ah! No!

There are six of them hovering above me on the wind. It's my nightmare. It's dive-bomb alley. They're circling and squawking, getting ready to attack me now.

Dive-bomb alley. Dan's going to drown. I take a deep breath.

I am an elephant. I am an elephant.

I look up. The seagulls haven't shrunk. They're getting bigger. They're big gray fighter bombers in the sky.

I am an elephant. I am—

Run. Run. If you don't go now, Dan will drown.

I drag my feet off the ground, one in front of the other; then I start to run, fast, then faster. The seagulls are still above me.

It's harder to hit a moving target.

I swerve around the benches, dodge the bins. I don't even look at the pavement. I can't look at the pavement. And I don't dare look at the sky.

I make it past some workmen by the Observation Tower, then the pier, Al's Pizza, the big wheel, and then Mr. Kendall's ice-cream stand.

I stop outside the cave door and try to gulp in as much air as I can, like a fish. I peer into the cave.

You're too late!

Shooting Star has gone. All that's left are the tires we used to prop her up and the tarpaulin strewn across the floor.

And the life jackets are in the corner!

I grab them and run out onto the seafront. I need to get help, but there's no one around.

There's a pay phone near the cinema. *It's full of germs. People breathe in them. People cough in them. People pee in them.*

It's too far anyway. I could run back to the workmen, but that's even farther, and by then it might be too late.

Dan can't have gotten far. If he ran out just before the end of the lesson, he can only be fifteen minutes ahead of me.

With the life jackets tucked under my arm, I run down onto the pebbles. There's no sign of Dan, just a sea mist all around me. I've never known it this thick. I couldn't even make out a ferry if it was thirty feet in front of me. I look up and down the beach. If the beach was sand, I could search for Dan's footprints, but the pebbles are so jumbled that they don't give me a clue. I stumble across them to the water's edge. There's something moving around in the waves, too dark to make out, like a big black eel. I need to find out what it is.

I take a deep breath and put one foot into the sea, then the other.

The sea's filthy and full of sewage.

I've got my gloves.

The black thing swims around me. I bend down and fish it out. My heart sinks into the pit of my stomach.

In my left hand is a shoe, and in my right is a sock. They have to be Dan's. This is where he took them off. This is where he went into the water.

This is where he drowned.

He didn't.

He did.

I look all around me.

"Dan." I try to get the words out, but it's like they're stuck in my throat. I wait for a reply, but all I can hear is the rush of the waves.

Which way would he go? Right is Bognor Regis. Left is Eastbourne. Straight ahead is France. I think of the sketch he drew on the board. He had to have sailed left, away from the pier. I drop the shoe and sock and try to run, but the pebbles are turning my ankles, and my legs are burning. I stop and look out, but all I can see is a mass of gray and the white tips of the waves. Then I spot some empty bottles and pieces of string washed up on the beach.

No! This can't be happening!

My stomach starts to ache and I feel sick.

I should have gone for help. I should have told Mr. Francis that I knew where Dan was going.

You're a bad person. Your friend has drowned. You could have saved him, but you didn't. It's your fault!

"Dan!" I shout. "Dan!"

The beach starts to tumble and turn like a washing machine.

"Dan!" I shout again. Then I feel my heart stop as a voice cuts through the mist.

"What?"

58

Dan: Lost and found

Alex stumbles toward me through the mist. His trousers are soaking wet, and water drips from his gloves.

"I thought...I thought...I thought you'd drowned." Alex shivers. His eyes are so wide they look like they're going to pop out of his face.

"No. I'm okay." I pat *Shooting Star*. I'm sitting on her base planks, and her buoys are lying beside her on the pebbles. "I didn't even get on her before she started to sink."

Alex looks at *Shooting Star* and gasps as he tries to get his breath back.

"Did you really...Did you...I was really worried." His face is scrunched up like he's in pain.

"I'm sorry," I say. "I just had to get away, but then—"

"Then you remembered you'd forgotten these?" He lifts up the life jackets.

"Sort of."

"Sort of?"

"I remembered I can't swim."

"You idiot!" Alex gulps, then drops the life jackets on the ground.

"I'm joking."

"I hope so."

"I am."

Alex looks relieved. I feel bad for making him worry.

"I'm sorry," I say. "How did you know I'd be here?"

Alex shrugs. "Just did. Sophie said you shouted out that Ben wasn't coming home."

"I did. She was winding me up. She's so spiteful and annoying."

"Yeah, I know." Alex goes quiet. Then he nods at *Shooting Star*. "I told you she wasn't ready."

"I know."

"You were really lucky."

"I know that too." I look at him. He's still mad at me, but it looks like he really was worried. I should thank him for running to the seafront. But I can't think of the right words.

"What?" he asks.

"Nothing."

"Then why are you looking at me like that?"

He blinks. "I'm not looking like anything. I'm just cold."

"Me too."

He walks around *Shooting Star*, checks the ropes and the bottles.

"We've lost a few bundles here," Alex says. "And the buoys have broken away."

"I know."

I wait for him to say something else, but he just keeps looking at *Shooting Star*. I pick up a handful of pebbles and let them fall through my fingers.

"Did you really think you could get there?" he asks.

I take a deep breath. "No. But I wanted to. When I ran out of school, I really thought I was going to do it, but by the time I'd dragged *Shooting Star* into the water I knew it was a bad idea."

"Because you forgot the life jackets."

"Yeah...and Jeff!" I laugh and hope Alex will too, but he just shakes his head. I feel silly about what I've done. But I couldn't stop myself.

Alex wraps his arms around his body. He's shaking like crazy, but he hasn't been right in the water like me. I can't believe what he's done, though. He's run out of school, all the way here. He would've had to cross roads, press the button on the crossings, run along the pavements with dog poop and with seagulls all around him. Sophie and the Georges don't have any of those worries, and they wouldn't have ever done anything like that. No one has done anything like that for me, not even Ben. I want to say thank you, but he's staring at the waves and biting down on his lip like he does when he's thinking in class. I throw pebbles into the water.

Alex turns around. "What's happened with Ben?"

"He got in a fight. Dad said he might not be home for at least a month, maybe two, or even longer. I don't know."

"Maybe it'll only be another week, like when the headmaster suspended that boy in Year Eight for stealing."

"Maybe." I nod. Alex is trying to cheer me up, but I think it will be longer than a week. Ben isn't at school. He's in an STC. The guards are in charge, not a headmaster. I think of Ben waiting in the Visitors' Room. Mum and Dad must have gotten there by now. They'll be

315

talking to Mike Ashton, and he'll be telling them what Ben did that means he can't come home yet. I hope it's not really bad.

I take a deep breath, then another. I don't want to get angry anymore. I don't want to cry. I just want Ben to come home.

Alex wipes a plank with his glove and then sits down beside me.

"It's okay." He taps *Shooting Star.* "We'll rebuild her."

"Do you think so?"

"Yeah...maybe we needed more time anyway. We'll get more bottles and new wood, and we'll tie them tighter, and this time we'll make sure we fix buoys on the corners. And then we won't go on it until Ben comes home."

I chuckle. "Yeah, and we'll get another life jacket for Jeff in case he falls off."

Alex smiles. "And we need another seat."

"Yeah. We do."

He smiles, then looks at the sea. "I hope Ben won't be in there much longer."

"Yeah," I say. "Me too."

59

Alex: Endgame

I'm in the cafeteria, eating my sandwiches. Elliott is sitting three chairs away from me.

"Everyone knows," he says. "Did you really run to the seafront and save him? Harry said you stole one of the hire boats and went crashing through the waves like James Bond."

I shake my head. "No, that's not what happened."

"But you did save him?"

"Not really."

"Harry said it'd be just like Dan to get rescued but still keep picking on you."

"I don't know. I don't think he will."

"Hope not.... Did you see *Police Interceptors* last night?"

"No." I shake my head. I'm too busy thinking about Dan to talk about *Police Interceptors*.

"You should've. They chased a Range Rover at a hundred and twenty miles an hour for ages. Then it hit a roundabout and flipped over ten times. It was brilliant. Watch it On Demand."

I take a bite of my sandwich and look around the cafeteria for Dan.

I can't spot him, but I can spot everyone staring at me. Elliott's right. Everybody in school seems to know what happened. It's like they're all waiting for me to give them the details. Elliott leans toward me.

"Hey, Alex," he says. "Maybe a television crew is coming and you'll be on the six o'clock news tonight. Superhero Alex saves the school bully!"

I force a smile. I don't think it's funny. I just want to know what's happened to Dan.

I haven't spoken to him today. He was in homeroom but then Mr. Francis came into class and asked Dan to go with him, and I've not seen him since. I thought maybe he'd been sent to detention or told to go home, but halfway through science I saw his mum walking through the main gates.

Elliott nudges me and slides a card across the table.

"Take it," he says. "It's Zlatan. I got him for you."

"Who'd you want for him?"

"Bale."

I reach into my pocket and then stop. Sophie and the Georges have just walked in and joined the lunch line. The Georges are talking to each other, but Sophie's staring at me like I'm the only person in the room. I find Gareth Bale and give the card to Elliott. Elliott looks over his shoulder, then back at me.

"I'm sorry." He sees the worried look on my face. "Even if he stops picking on you, I don't think he'll be able to stop them."

I jam my cards in my pocket and try to eat my sandwiches. I don't know if Dan has spoken to them or not, but I do know Sophie's looking at me like she wants to dunk my head down the toilet again.

"Keep the line moving," barks Mr. Anderton. "And don't forget to clear your tables when you leave."

Sophie and the Georges jostle each other and burst out laughing.

Nothing's going to happen. Nothing's going to change.

I look out the window and wish I could leave now. My stomach tightens when I see Dan walking across the playground with his bag on his back. He's smiling like nothing has happened. I watch him go along the path beside the cafeteria. He's looking in through the window, but he doesn't see me.

"Let's sit here." I look up and see Sophie smirking at me.

"You don't mind, do you, Shark Face? Move over!"

Elliott slides along the bench toward me so it's him and me at one end and Sophie and the Georges at the other. I don't need to look up to know that they're staring at me now.

I glance out the window and see Dan disappearing through the blue corridor doors. He can't be getting sent home yet, because the blue corridor only leads to the math block, then back around to the cafeteria.

"Hey, Shark Face, heard you tried to go and swim with your friends in the sea."

"And Dan told you to get lost," says George W.

"He didn't," I mumble.

"He did," says Sophie. "He said you were such a wimp that he had to save you from drowning."

"That's not what happened."

"Tell us what did, then. What were you doing down there anyway?"

Elliott gives me a look as if to say *I told you so.*

319

I put my sandwiches in my lunch box and close the lid. Nothing is going to change. It's going to be exactly the same. Every day, every week, every term. There's no point in talking to them. Dan obviously already has, and he's told a load of lies. It's like he's two different people. Nice when he's with me, but horrible when he's with them.

I put my lunch box in my bag.

"Dan! Where do you think you're going?" asks Mr. Anderton.

I look toward the door. Dan has ignored Mr. Anderton and walked straight past the lunch line. He looks across all the tables. Sophie waves her hand in the air.

"Over here, Dan!"

He nods when he sees her, then starts to walk toward us. His face is straight, and one of his hands is bunched in a fist. *Is this when we have the fight? Have I got to get up and throw a punch at him now?* I clench my fist. *I can't do it. I can't.* I feel Elliott tense as Dan glances at me. Does he think I've been talking about him, that I've told everyone about Ben? Sophie moves her plate over.

"Sit here, Dan," she says. "What did Francis want?"

Dan walks past her, past Elliott, and sits down beside me.

"Hey!" hisses Sophie. "What are you doing?"

Dan takes his lunch box out of his bag and looks at me.

"All right?"

I nod. I feel like there's a bite of sandwich stuck in my throat.

"Good." He grins at me. "That's all right, then."

I relax my fist. The snake loosens in my stomach. I nod again. I'm all right.

320

60

Three months later
Dan: This *Shooting Star* is ours

I'm floating on *Shooting Star*. The sea is blue and the pebbles are golden. There's a line of ten people waiting for ice cream and Mr. Kendall is wiping his forehead, trying to serve them all. Ben is walking up and down the beach, collecting money from people sitting in deck chairs. The big wheel is turning, and along the beach the Observation Tower is rising like a spaceship into the sky.

Alex dips his gloved hand in the water.

"This is great," he says. "I'm glad I came. I nearly didn't."

"Because of the seagulls?"

"Yep!" Alex shrugs. "But I think they might be too busy hovering around to steal fish and chips." He nods toward the chip shop on the seafront.

My stomach lifts, then falls as a wave passes underneath us.

Ben collects money from another person, then turns and waves at me. I wave back. He's been home three weeks now. He had to stay in the STC three months longer. Booth had thrown a chair against a window, and Ben tried to stop him and got in a fight.

Two days after I ran out of school, Mr. Francis called me into his office. I thought he was going to suspend me, but he just wanted to talk to me about Ben. I told him that my house felt empty without Ben and that I was missing him like crazy. Then I went quiet and he asked me if there was anything else bothering me.

That's when I told him what I'd been doing to Alex.

That's when Mum and Dad were called down to the school. That's when I got suspended for a week.

61

Alex: The last round

Dan paddles us over a wave. I drag my hand backward and forward through the water. It bubbles and circles like there are fish darting around for food underneath.

It could be a piranha.

It's not.

It is. They're under there now, nibbling at your gloves.

They're not. We don't get piranhas in England.

It's a shark, then.

It's not. A shark wouldn't waste time eating fingers. It would eat your whole arm.

I'm glad Ben came back. It was weird at first. Dan was talking to Ben all the time and I felt like I was at a party that I hadn't been invited to, but as soon as we all started working on *Shooting Star*, that worry went away. Ben agreed that the buoys should go on the corners, and he drew the picture of the pirate on the flag. We couldn't find a proper anchor, so he filled a sack with pebbles and tied a rope to it instead. *Shooting Star* looks brilliant now. I told Granddad that she's the best thing I've ever made. And then he made me wash his car!

The week after I went to the seafront to save Dan, I was told to go to Mr. Francis's office. I thought I was in trouble or that something bad had happened to Mum, like a stack of baked beans had tumbled over and trapped her underneath, or that Dad's work had been burgled and the burglars had tied him up and locked him in a cupboard. But when I got to Mr. Francis's room, he was sitting at his desk, looking really calm. Dan was there too. I hadn't seen him all week because he'd been suspended and so had Sophie and the Georges. He tried to smile at me, but he looked embarrassed and then looked at the ground.

Mr. Francis told me that Dan had told him he'd been bullying me and that he felt really bad about it. I didn't know what to do or say. Then Dan looked up and handed me a letter.

This is what he'd written.

Dear Alex,

I am sorry I bullied you. I am sorry I made things hard for you when you were at school. Bullying is a horrible thing to do and I wish I'd never done it. I'm sorry that I made you miserable and that things got so bad you had to stay at home. I'm sorry if I upset your mum and dad and your sister.

Bullying is for cowards and I won't do it again. I know I was upset about Ben but that didn't mean that I should pick on you or Elliott.

> I hope we can be friends, but I wouldn't
> blame you if you don't want to. But if you do,
> we can go on Shooting Star all summer.
>   Dan

I didn't know what to do after I read the letter. Dan was still looking at the ground, and Mr. Francis was looking right at me like he
was waiting for me to say something back. I told him that Dan was
all right. Then he asked if I wanted to meet with Sophie and the
Georges. I said I didn't want to see any of them. The Georges have
left me alone since they came back, and Sophie hangs around with
some girls in Year Eight. He said they'd write a letter too and then
asked me if I wanted to say anything else. I looked at Dan. I knew
he was sorry for all the horrible things he'd done. But I couldn't see
the point in telling Mr. Francis how bad things had been, because I
couldn't change what had happened and it was all over now.

A wave lifts *Shooting Star* and we sink behind it. I watch as it moves
away from us and then crashes on the shore. I look along the seafront. The Observation Deck is sliding down the tower, ready for
people to get off and new people to get on. It goes up and down all
day, every day.

Shooting Star rises over another wave. The flag flaps in the wind.
I look up, see the pirate and his eye patch, and Jeff the giraffe standing next to him on lookout.

I pick up a paddle and dip it in the water. Dan's already got one in
his hand.

"Where do you want to go?"

I shrug.

Dan starts paddling. "Come on," he says.

"Where are we going?"

"Jeff's never seen a bumper car."

"You're weird."

"You think *I'm* weird?!"

We laugh, then dig our paddles in the water and head for the pier.

Acknowledgments

It seems a long time since the idea for this novel came to me, as I walked the corridors of Saffron Walden High, trying to figure out if I had what was needed to be a teacher. When I stopped and read the school noticeboard, my decision was made. So I'd like to extend a big thanks to Pete Wilson, then my mentor, for being so understanding that week, but also for a brilliant discussion on bullying that we had with his Year Seven, "Can we have empathy for the bully?" From that question and subsequent discussion, *All the Things That Could Go Wrong* was spawned.

Big thanks also to: Sam Drew, for listening when I'm stuck then sending me away unglued. Jade Craddock, who worked on my early drafts. Rachel Mann, who listened to and supported the idea, then edited the first hundred pages, before she left me in the wonderful hands of Lucy Rogers, my editor. We got there in the end, Lucy, even if the late nights left our eyelids half-closed. I'd also like to give a massive thanks to everyone at Little, Brown Books for Young Readers for loving this story so much and bringing it to the USA. Big love to my daughters: Lois, who was also brilliant at helping me with ongoing edits and Alex's worry lists; and Tallulah, who did nothing to help, but we did have great chats in Nando's. Also big thanks to my mum and dad, who must have wondered what was going through my head as we watched Monday night football.

And absolutely not least, I am hugely grateful to Jonathan Bentley-Smith for *I want pavement, I want concrete, I want tarmac*, but most of all for his friendship and his manuscript *The Palladium Cafe*, which gave me invaluable insight into the inner life of someone with obsessive-compulsive disorder. Thanks, Jon, for trusting me.